Angel in Flight

Other books by HelioTerra Media, LLC

by Shelly Pulse

Match Mail

The postmistress of a small Wisconsin town shoots Cupid's arrows by mixing up the mail. Sometimes they are a bit poisonous. See what happens when one hits her.

Priscilla

Three martyred fourth-century Spanish Bishops reincarnate in modern-day Central Oregon to avenge their deaths at the hand of the evil judge Evodius.

Angel in Flight

Shelly Pulse

Canby, Oregon

Copyright © 2022 by HelioTerra Media, LLC

All Rights Reserved.

This book is a work of fiction. Any reference to historical events, or real places are used fictitiously. Names, characters, businesses, places, events, and incidents are either the products of the author's imagination or used in a fictitious manner. Any resemblance to actual persons, living or dead, or actual events is purely coincidental.

No part of this book may be reproduced or used in any manner without the express written permission of the publisher except for the use of brief quotations in a book review.

Published by HelioTerra Media, LLC,
1109 SW 1st Avenue Ste F 705, Canby, Oregon 97013
https://helioterra.com/
shelly@helioterra.com

ISBN: 978-1-7364827-1-1

For Sean.

Table of Contents

Acknowledgments	vi
1 Tumbling in the Wind	1
2 Angry Wounds	11
3 Bell Bottoms and Skates	19
4 Cloud of Sorrow	29
5 Maiden Flight	37
6 First Kiss	45
7 Turbulence	49
8 The Hero	53
9 Tree Angels	55
10 Storyteller	57
11 The Cemetery	59
12 Integrity, Honor, and Respect	65
13 The Inner Self	71
14 Angel Michael	79
15 Angels in White	85
16 Spinster Margaret	93
17 Cracked Heart of Glass	99
18 Double Root Beer Float	105
19 Playing House	111
20 Love, Jeremy	119
21 Two Brushes	127
22 *Friend* is Good	131
23 Perry!	139
24 Climbing the Mountain	147
25 Patch of Ice	159
26 Still Life	165
27 Margaret in Waiting	177
28 Diamond Christmas	181
29 Adoption	189
30 The Bus	195
31 Winter Conference	207

32 Bunny Hill	217
33 The Healed Angel	223
About the Author	231
Author's Notes	232

Acknowledgments

The dedicated labor of the members of the Gresham Writing Group made the completion of this book possible. The encouragement and kind critique of each member at our biweekly meetings kept the story moving.

Thank you, Marshall Welch, David Schneider, Jennifer Helgerson, and Dave Baker, for pointing out ways to improve the technical and grammatical components of the story.

Tiffany Martin, Suzi Wiser, and Nannette Taylor went beyond what was expected and gave a full final read and thorough analysis. They each discovered several plot holes and inconsistencies.

As always, I would like to acknowledge Doug 'Diego' Hartley. These projects would never happen without his constant attention, hours of work editing, formatting, and input. Thank you, love!

As noted later in the author's notes, Sean Delgatto contributed greatly to the chapters dealing with aviation. Being a screenwriter, helicopter mechanic, and private pilot, he brought detail to those scenes and lent his storytelling gift. He is sorely missed. Colon cancer took him from us way too soon at the age of forty. Happy angel flight, Sean.

ANGEL IN FLIGHT

1 — Tumbling in the Wind

Summer 1976

Watercolor pencils, an eraser, acrylic paint tubes, and paintbrushes scattered on the grass like a plane crash debris field. Robin juggled the black portfolio tucked under her arm. Too late. Drawings of angels floated in the early summer breeze like cottonwood fluff.

"Hey! Watch where you are going!" Robin yelled at the boy who bumped into her.

The boy's feet spun, trotting backward like a wide receiver about to catch a football. He kept running, jeering at Robin discourteously.

Shuffling her twisted feet at the end of severely bowed legs, Robin trembled with repressed anger as she watched the collection of artwork descend to the wet turf. How in the world was she going to gather them all up?

Kneeling caused her immense pain. One knee on the ground, she extended her other leg since it did not bend. She plucked at her art supplies and dropped them back in the case.

Another boy raced past, chasing after the first. Two of his footprints embossed the drawings with green grass clippings. Robin crab-crawled toward the scattered paper tumbling in the wind. Fire shot up her shin, thigh, and into her lower back, forcing her to sit awhile until full consciousness returned.

Head cleared, Robin rolled over and pulled herself along with her elbows across the recently irrigated lawn, soaking her black corduroy pants. Holding her drawings close to her chest, she tried to dry them on her long-sleeved white cotton blouse, staining it a tint of muddy green. The once detailed renderings warped into a watercolor wash. Tears ran down her face the way the colors did on the paper. Gathering up as many as she could reach, she stacked them back inside her portfolio.

The shadow of a thin figure cast over her. "Looks like you could use some help," a young boy's voice suggested, startling her.

The sun blinded Robin from seeing from whom the voice came. The rays of light painted a brilliant halo about him. Squatting next to her, she got a closer look. The boy's long, curly blond hair bordered a tanned, youthful face and eyes as blue as the sky behind him. Kneeling, he gathered the drawings Robin could not reach.

"Thank you." Robin blotted away the tears with the back of her sleeve.

"Did you draw these?"

What a silly question. Of course!

"Uh-huh," she said through her snuffs.

"They are outstanding," he said, dangling one to admire it more closely.

"Thanks," she said blithely, being used to compliments more on the patronizing side of the scale.

"No. Really. They are." The boy cocked his head and tipped the drawing sideways.

Robin thanked him a little more heartily the second time.

"What are they?"

"Angels." Most of her sketches lacked wings, but did not make them any less angelic.

Leafing through the pages that lay wedged in her portfolio, he said, "That's what I thought. You must really like angels."

"They are all I like to draw." Robin grabbed at the stack. "Please give them back."

The boy retreated outside her reach, sifting through with surprise manifest at each page-turn. "How did you become so good?"

Fingers fluttering like a bird's wing, she insisted he return the pictures. "I've been drawing them since I was four."

"Why?"

Angels had attended to her while she lay dying and nearly frozen in the snow, saving her life. Now she would spend what time she had left drawing and painting angels to honor them. Kids always made fun of her when she told them *why*. The drawings told the story better than she ever could.

"Because."

The boy expected more and would not return them unless he got a better answer.

ANGEL IN FLIGHT

Exasperated, Robin replied, "I like angels. They are pretty."

The boy's red polyester shorts and light blue polo flexed as he rose, handing her the drawings. The rest of the colored pencils dropped into the box with a clatter. She snapped the lid shut, then sandwiched the artwork back into her portfolio. Gathering up the items from Robin, he waited for her to stand.

Embarrassed, she swiveled her hips and tried to push herself up on her bent knee. Collapsing face-first back into the grass, she felt mortified. This boy towering over her would surely ask, 'What happened to you? Why can't you stand?' Questions she had gotten her whole life.

Instead, he set down her things and placed a hand on her arm. "How is the best way to help you up?"

Most kids and even adults simply walk by without offering to assist. Accepting his help meant shattering her barrier to autonomy. Only lawn and cement sidewalks lay between her heap of once-shattered bones and the destination. At grass level, she saw no bench or lamppost to aid.

Robin's aunt, Margaret, who cared for her since the accident, had bought her crutches and a secondhand wheelchair—both of which she rejected. Accepting them meant succumbing to being perceived as *handicapped*. No, thank you! She preferred hours of excruciating therapy over the stabbing pain of peer opinion. Oh, how she wished she had brought those crutches now!

"Stand next to me like a tree trunk and hold out your arms like branches. Let me climb up you."

The boy planted his feet right next to her thigh. Robin rolled over. With him having no pants to grasp, she clutched his leg and inched herself up into a half-seated position. The pain once again shot through her body, forcing her to rest for a moment. Other students walked by, whispering to each other and pointing at her.

A girl with black hair and eyes to match set down her shoulder bag. Genuine compassion painted each of the girl's movements and words.

"Is everything okay?"

Shielding the sun, Robin admired her sleek, muscular legs with flesh the color of cinnamon.

"I'm fine," Robin said, rubbing her shoulder.

"What happened?"

The hand she placed on Robin's felt calloused. Usually, Robin avoided contact. Hundreds of hands had touched, poked, held, rubbed, and caressed her during her lifetime, frequently causing her pain. Robin had learned a lot about a person by the palm's texture, the manicure, and the gentleness of touch. This girl spent more time roping cows than doing dishes, that was certain.

"Those idiots about tackled her," the boy related accusingly toward the two adolescents frolicking as if they were goats.

The boy and girl each wrapped an arm around Robin and carefully lifted her to her feet. Crying out and gasping for breath, she steadied herself.

The boy handed Robin's box to the girl and tucked her portfolio under his arm. Together, the three made their way toward the whitewashed mechanic shop, now art classroom.

"Thank you, guys."

"I'm Jeremy," he said, holding out two fingers in a peace sign.

"I'm Tina." The girl with a broad nose and high cheekbones bowed, miming the tip of a cowgirl hat accompanied by a slight curtsy.

"Nice to meet you both. I'm Robin. Where are you from?"

Jeremy slapped his narrow, boyish chest, almost dropping her portfolio. "St. George. And you?"

"Bountiful," Robin replied.

Jeremy's arms were thin compared to others his age. At fifteen, boys typically developed a little muscle definition, but not him. 'Skinny as a rail,' her aunt would always say. Robin was definitely not skinny and not exactly sure what a *rail* even was. Exercise was out of the question for her broken body.

"Bountiful? Close to me," Tina said excitedly. "I live in Eden, just up from Ogden."

Jeremy held the spring-loaded door for the girls.

"Such a gentleman." Tina winked.

Stepping conscientiously over the deep threshold to the classroom, Robin sensed an uneasiness pervade her mind. She observed an arbitrary and disorderly arrangement of benches and easels. Illustrations and drawings also haphazardly covered the stark-white walls. The scene induced pure anxiety.

Other students already occupied most of the seats. A few were empty toward the front. She had hoped to arrive early enough to find an inconspicuous spot at the back. Not today.

A man, probably in his fifties, with frizzy gray hair, a white gauze shirt, and high-waisted slacks, directed their attention toward the empty benches in the front row. "Have a seat."

ANGEL IN FLIGHT

Another man, dressed in jeans and a long-sleeved plaid shirt with mother-of-pearl buttons, perched quietly on a counter toward the back of the room, legs dangling off the edge.

This chaotic and informal scenario failed to match Robin's vision of a college art class—orderliness and a teacher with a bow tie and apron, like in the movies.

"Class. Let's get started. We've got a lot of ground to cover. I'm Professor Anderson, and he's Professor Matthews." He nodded to the short, portly man at the back.

Matthews waved to everyone.

Pointing at the rude boy Robin had encountered earlier, Anderson ordered, "Greg. Take a seat."

Greg, a name Robin would not soon forget.

The boy defied the professor's request.

Drawing in a breath, she held it.

"You too, Tom."

Greg slapped his buddy on the shoulder. "Yeah, Tom. Do what Teach tells you to do."

Exhaling, Robin deduced this jerk was going to be trouble. Avoiding him would be her primary aim throughout the summer.

The simple benches appeared to have been designed and constructed in a high school wood shop class. Comprising three planks of wood fashioned after a hobbyhorse without rocking feet, one short piece stood upright at the back, attached to another taller one at the front by a horizontal bench. The students straddled the flat part and leaned their artwork against the larger section.

How was she going to cope with these? Why not ordinary desks and chairs? This contraption was like riding a carousel. The one time her aunt had set her on a giraffe at the amusement park ended poorly. It hurt her hips to straddle the animal, and she lost her grip when the merry-go-round lurched forward.

Assessing her dilemma, Jeremy angled her bench, so she could face forward.

Robin glared at him. "Please put it back."

Shrugging, he did as she requested. "Just thought it might help."

The less attention she drew to herself, the better. To avoid being treated differently, somehow, she was going to *ride* this horse like everyone else.

Leaning the portfolio against the front end, she attempted unsuccessfully to straddle it. Catching Jeremy gawking as she lifted her leg, she glowered at him.

This was not happening again! Jeremy was acting like Perry. A boy back home always stared at her and continuously offered to carry her books. Wherever Robin went, Perry was there to pull out a chair or open a door, annoying her to no end. More than once, she had to tell him to leave her alone.

Jeremy simpered when Robin resorted to sitting side-saddle, facing him. She wrinkled her nose at him, but restrained herself from sticking out her tongue.

Thank goodness the classroom's attention shifted from Robin to the tall, thin, late-comer with the poofy Farrah Fawcett hair. That poster-goddess won the lustful eye of every boy and the jealous appreciation of every girl in the room. The door closed behind her as she sashayed to the front of the class. Time stood still, like slow motion in a movie, as her hair unfurled behind her.

Robin's lip curled; she would *not* like this chick. This model of perfection reminded her of the cliquey coquettes back home, who made it impossible for Robin to be noticed by anyone but the nerds and stoners.

The girl smiled at Robin as she walked by. Wait? Was that a smile of pity? Or authentic gentleness? Blondie hadn't witnessed Robin's fall, so sympathy was out of the question. Some girls, as beautiful as she, may well be genuinely kind and not stuck up. Time would tell. She decided not to pass judgment—not yet, anyway.

"Sorry I'm late, Dr. Anderson," the goddess said breathlessly.

"It's okay, Julie. Put your homework up here and find a seat." He pointed at the chalkboard.

Julie? Robin expected a name like Faye, Bridgette, or Olivia. And why did she already know the professor? Maybe this was her second year in the program.

The brochure said the directors would invite the best of the first-year group back for two more summers. Perhaps Julie had returned more for her allure than her artistic ability. The piece she placed on the ledge at the front looked like something a child would have painted. Some artists never mastered the abstract. That discipline certainly held little appeal for Robin.

Greg and Tom each took a side and dragged an empty bench between them, making space in the middle for her. Instead, Julie sat in front, between Tina and a boy with a ripped t-shirt and cut-offs. Introducing himself as Adrian, he flashed her an actor-like smile and flexed his muscles.

ANGEL IN FLIGHT

Robin quietly squeed her bemusement. Funny—no one was eager to make room for her like that, except that creepy boy named Perry. In fact, Jeremy might have been his twin the way he kept staring at her. Why weren't his eyes ogling Julie like everyone else?

Professor Anderson called out, "Would the students from the back row please come forward and place your work on the chalkboard?"

The students pushed through the maze of benches. Greg elbowed Jeremy threateningly as he passed. Robin shifted to avoid another collision with him. Resisting the urge to stick out her foot to trip him as Greg went by, Robin held on to her trembling knee.

"We have selected you from high schools all over Utah to take part in a college-level commercial art course. May I remind you, this is *not* high school."

Groans and horseplay broke out again between the two boys toward the back. The impulse to yell at them and tell them to grow up jammed in Robin's mouth; she had already drawn enough attention to herself for one day.

"Sit down!" The professor waited for everyone to be seated. "Most of your parents paid for you to attend. A few made sizable donations to the School of Art to make this program possible. Some of you are here on scholarship because we think you have the greatest potential. Your friends are home lying out by the pool, camping, water skiing, and wasting their summer away. You all are here because you want to jump headlong into an art career."

The latter of those listed applied to Robin. The tenth-grade high school art teacher, Mr. Spaulding, had completed the application on her behalf. When the university accepted it and granted her the scholarship, he paid several visits to the house and finally convinced her aunt to allow her to attend.

Laughter erupted when Greg pushed a bench over, forcing a student to tumble to the ground. Professor Matthew slid down from his roost and stood between the boys.

Why didn't they kick Greg out? How sizable a *donation* did his parents need to make for the professor to babysit him all summer?

Professor Anderson continued his lecture with passion. Robin thrilled at his words. The high school teacher lacked this eloquence. This one inspired her to pursue her dream of becoming a professional artist, unlike everyone else who treated it as a hobby.

SHELLY PULSE

Home and hospitals were all she had known until the seventh grade. Aunt Margaret had coddled Robin after kindergarten, protecting her frail health, and insisted the school send a tutor a few times a week to the house.

For the first time, Robin felt equal to the other students in the room.

Suddenly, Professor Anderson's demeanor flipped. "I want you here. On-time!"

That shocked Robin.

He glared at Julie. "When you become a professional commercial illustrator, you will work under pressure. You will have deadlines. Mommy won't be your alarm clock." Derision dripped from his words.

What happened? Other students also showed their stunned reactions. The cloud Robin floated on evaporated, sending her plunging.

The professor's focus moved toward the boys in the back row. Greg's shoulders slumped. The room fell silent, waiting for a sarcastic response from Greg. None came.

In an instant, the professor had transformed from an articulate orator to a drill sergeant. His voice elevated a notch. "You will not have the luxury of telling the client that you are sorry that you couldn't make the deadline because your hair dryer broke!"

Twirling her golden locks with her long, painted fingernails, Julie smacked her bubble gum and glanced around the room at everyone who snickered at her.

"What did I do?" she asked with a whine, then a giggle.

Now he loomed menacingly over Tina. "The client will not care. They will fire you and find the next illustrator." Sweeping his hand across the assignments on display, he said, "This is not a course in fine art, people! You don't have three years to paint your masterpiece." The professor picked up one piece and held it up for the students to see. "Who belongs to this?"

Greg's hand shot up. "Me!"

The professor turned his back to the class. Setting it down, he stared at the work while stroking his chin. "Well done. You followed the instructions. You've got contrasting shapes. Asymmetry, yet balanced." His finger hovered over various areas of the painting. "Love the contrasting primary and secondary, visually intense, vibrating hues. Very well done." The professor searched the bottom corner for the artist's name. "And it's signed. Mr. Greg Malstrom. A-plus."

Tom gave Greg a 'high-five.'

'Malstrom,' Robin mouthed. The origin of words and breaking them into their components was her passion, second to art. Most of her vocabulary was self-taught from the countless books in her aunt's library. That fit. 'Mal,' on the front of any Latin word, usually meant 'bad.' No wonder.

"Thank you very much," Greg said, bowing to the class.

After evaluating a few more pieces, Professor Anderson invited the next row to bring their work forward. The process continued until the front row had presented its work.

Selecting one from the middle, he asked, "This one?"

Jeremy lifted his hand. "Me."

The professor picked up the piece. Facing the class, he held it high in the air. "What is wrong with this?"

One girl from the second row responded sheepishly, "It's symmetrical?"

"Yes. What else?" The professor chose another student whose hand crept up.

"Different hues?"

"Correct."

Wilted like a flower in a vase with no water, Jeremy hung his head and slumped. Robin was unsure how much more of this criticism he could tolerate since they had just met.

"Mr. Kess," Professor Anderson said, hovering directly over him. "You did not follow the assignment. Yes, you have contrasting primary and secondary colors of yellow and violet, but different hues, as pointed out by one of your fellow artists. Everything is round and symmetrical." The professor placed his hands on both sides of the top of Jeremy's piece and, with one swift movement, tore it in half. He dramatically pitched it into the trash bin next to the chalkboard.

Gasps of disbelief resonated off the walls.

Robin placed a comforting hand on Jeremy's shoulder and stared up at the professor. "Shouldn't we also point out the elements that were done correctly?" she asked meekly.

Jeremy smiled at Robin with his misty eyes, even though his lips displayed shame.

The professor wedged himself next to Jeremy and placed a hand on his other shoulder.

"Alright, class, something you've got to learn before we start this course. Get to know the word, *critique*. Learn it well. Look it up in the dictionary. Compare it to the word criticism. They are not the same. One means to tear down and destroy, the other, to teach, build, and edify. That, my friends," he said, gesturing at the garbage can, "was the highest form of critique any of you will ever receive from me. I know what Jeremy is feeling right now."

He looked down into Jeremy's tear-filled eyes. "I also know what he can achieve. I have seen his work. And if you are the best of the best, your work will go in the trash if I know you can do better."

Sitting a little straighter, Jeremy wiped his nose on the back of his arm.

If Robin could put it to a vote, she was positive all would classify that little object lesson as *criticism*. She hoped to see more of Dr. Anderson's gentler and inspirational persona, not this Mr. Hyde.

"All your work is excellent. That's why you are here."

Everyone sat at attention, mouths open, eyes wide. Even the two class clowns appeared stunned by the incident.

The professor patted Jeremy on the back. "Do the assignment over. Have Robin teach you asymmetry and hue values. Oh, and the difference between a circle and a square." He winked at Robin.

How did he know her name? Did he already maintain a file on her? Had her aunt talked to him about her condition? She hoped he would evaluate the work by her talent and not her disability.

Professor Anderson indicated the next piece on the board. "Which one of you is Tina?"

With one arm crossed over her short-sleeved blouse with the shirttails tied up in a bow, Tina raised her other arm, timidly at first. Then, with the ferocity of a dozen attacking wolves, she planted her huarache sandals firmly on the ground and sat up straight. The flaming eyes, framed by her cute pixie haircut, challenged the professor, daring him to criticize her piece.

"What's wrong with it?"

"Nothing. All the elements of the assignment are present. It's fine," Dr. Anderson said, retreating to the other end of the row.

Lowering her arm, Tina relaxed. Robin grinned, softening Tina's intensity into a smile. The two of them were going to get along great!

ANGEL IN FLIGHT

2 — Angry Wounds

On the second day, Robin stood in front of a full-length mirror in just her bra, panties, and satin shorts. The matching camisole hung from her dorm room chair. Her aunt had purchased the set, hoping they would make Robin feel pretty. Going off to college for the first time might mean having to undress in front of a roommate. Robin would make sure that never happened, even if it meant changing under the sheets.

The dorm mother had granted Amanda's request to be reassigned to another room. Robin was happy with that. She now had this one to herself. Just as well. She did not want anyone to know how bad her scars were, anyway. Robin's aunt, and the surgeons and nurses who put her back together, were the only ones who had seen them. Fortunately, her face had suffered no injury and needed little makeup—a touch of mascara and eye shadow. Today, she applied them generously.

Robin turned her arm over to reveal a long, deep scar running from her wrist to her elbow. She followed the line with a bead of lotion, then rubbed it in—a ritual she and her aunt had done for eleven years. The doctors said it would help make the redness fade. She was not sure it made any difference after all.

Angry wounds on her chest stared back in the mirror. Her fingertips traced the lines that looked like a bear had mauled her. Robin's aunt said it was where pieces of broken glass from the airplane's windshield had cut her. She put extra lotion there. Letting her hand rest for a moment, she closed her eyes and felt her heartbeat. It was strange to hear the blood surge in her ears at the same time.

Robin picked up a hand mirror and tried to peer at the back of her head. At home, she had a three-way folding mirror in the bathroom. That way, she could cover the big gash in the back of her head. She brushed her hair this way and that, then stood still. Carefully, she picked up a can of

Aqua Net hairspray. The room filled with a thick choking mist as she cemented her hair in place.

Picking up the hand mirror again, Robin inspected the work by lightly patting the back of her head. She hoped it would stay.

A hat would make her whole life simpler. Her aunt had packed several. The style was too floral and floppy for Robin's taste, and kids at school always made fun of them. After her first day in college, she lacked the confidence these students would be any different. For the time being, the hats would remain in the suitcase.

Robin gathered the camisole into a loop and threaded her head through. Next time, she would put it on first, then fix her hair. A towel on her shoulders would stop the hairspray from making it sticky. She inspected the back of her head in the mirror again to be sure the scar was invisible. Happy with the result, she smiled at her reflection.

Resting a moment on the corner of the bed, Robin strategized how she would put on her pants. She relied on her aunt to dress her. At home, she practiced standing, sitting, even laying down on the bed.

Her left leg twisted a little, so that side always went on first. A bent wire hanger made the perfect hook to pull the pant leg over her foot by the belt loop. Her right leg bowed at an awkward angle.

She inserted her right foot. From there, she could dispense with the hanger and pull the pants up to her thighs. She laid back and wriggled like an earthworm. Unbroken people knew little of the exhaustion others experienced doing what should be a simple daily routine.

Margaret always encouraged her to wear one of the twenty long dresses hanging in her bedroom closet at home. They hid the scars on her legs but were too lengthy to be in fashion. Her peers wore skirts hemmed up to their bottoms. She would rather endure the agony of putting on slacks than to be seen wearing one of those.

Standing, Robin buttoned her trousers. Zipping them up was the simple part. Next, she pulled a long-sleeved white blouse from the tiny closet, put it on, and buttoned it up to her neck.

Robin hoped the stains would wash out of the one she wore yesterday. It lay in a heap at the bottom of the closet. She held it up to the light. It looked rather pretty how the colors had transferred and left a tie-dyed splotch on the front. She decided she would wear it even if the stain didn't come out. Her aunt would be less than pleased. Robin would simply explain that she needed a new painting smock in class, like the one she wore in kindergarten.

ANGEL IN FLIGHT

Besides, her clothes and all her maintenance came from insurance money and other inherited assets. Aunty had once mentioned the words, 'set for life,' but Robin was not sure exactly how much that was. A ruined shirt was not the end of the world.

A line of students formed behind Robin outside the door to the classroom. She searched for Jeremy's blue eyes among all those staring back at her. A pair of dark brown ones brightened when they lighted on Robin. Tina jumped out of line and joined her at the front.

"Glad you made it back," Tina said, examining what Robin was wearing. "Little warm?"

The sun reflected off the white wall, making what was already a scorcher even hotter. Robin felt a bead of sweat dripping down the back of her neck, but could do nothing to stop it without ruining her hair.

"Hey, get back in line," one student protested.

"She's my best friend," Robin fired back. "I saved her place."

Tina chuckled. "You better wait until you get to know me."

"We got here first!"

Tina faced the student and stalked stealthily toward her, the wolf emerging again. Robin expected an attack. The student cowered back in line. The professor unlocking the door probably saved that girl.

First to enter, Robin chose the farthest bench in the back corner, wishing it to be her home for the rest of the eight weeks. She hoped Jeremy would arrive early enough to sit by her. To save one for him, Robin set her things on *his* empty seat.

Tina chose the same bench as the day before and waved at Robin to join her. She shook her head and motioned for Tina to come to the back. It was too late. Most of the seats filled quickly. Robin found the behavior of these creatures amusing. Given the freedom to sit where they like, they chose the same place as the first day.

Professor Matthews set up props on a stage at the back of the room while Professor Anderson listed art-related vocabulary words on the chalkboard.

Greg made his grand entrance known by bursting through the door, slamming it against the wall so hard Robin thought it might shatter the glass.

"Careful! You'll knock the door off its hinges," rebuked the professor.

Greg patted the door. "Sorry, door. I didn't mean to hurt you." He shut it with exaggerated care.

Professor Anderson returned to his office, shaking his head.

Greg spotted Robin sitting where he and his posse had staked claimed yesterday. His face turned red with rage.

"That's Tom's. Go sit in the front by your boyfriend," Greg breathed threateningly as he rushed to claim the back row his own. He shoved Robin's case onto the floor and knocked over her portfolio. Then he picked up the bench she had saved for Jeremy and set it closer to the others with one swift motion.

Robin guessed Greg was used to bullying the weaker species, and she was tired of being on the receiving end of that sort of behavior. She remained firmly planted, defiant. The bench provided support as she reached down to pick up her things.

"What's wrong with you? Are you deaf too? I said that is Tom's seat," he hissed. He shoved the box out of her reach with his toe, causing Robin to lose her balance. She tumbled onto the cement floor. That gave Greg the chance to grab her bench and place it closer to the others.

"No one said anything about assigned seats," Robin said softly, grasping another bench to pull herself up.

He held a hand to his ear. "Maybe I'm the deaf one. I didn't hear what you said."

Tom placed a hand on Greg's arm. "No big deal, man. I can take the one in front of you."

"This is yours, and you are going to take it." He shoved Tom, forcing him to sit down. "Even if we have to carry this lame little hen up and plop her back on her own perch, where she belongs."

"What? Are you going to chop my head off, pluck me, and have me for dinner, too?" Robin wondered where those words came from. She had never stood up for herself like that before.

Greg's fury returned as Professor Matthews, a few inches shorter but twice as muscular, tapped him on the shoulder and said, "Enough."

"She was in Tom's spot," Greg spat.

Professor Matthews scowled as he clutched Greg's arm, turned him around, and herded him toward an empty bench two spaces over. "This will do, and Tom will be just fine in that one." He pointed at the spot in front of him. Tom took that seat without hesitation. Greg was about to protest, but something Professor Matthews whispered in his ear immediately shut him up.

ANGEL IN FLIGHT

The professor returned with Robin's bench, placed it precisely where she first found it, and stood by while she pulled herself up. He picked up her box and propped up her portfolio.

"Thank you."

He nodded respectfully and returned to his work on the stage.

Robin's heartbeat throbbed in her head when Jeremy entered the class right at nine o'clock. It made her dizzy. He scanned the room while taking the last remaining bench in the front between Tina and Julie. Was he searching for her? Now she regretted her decision. Was his hair actually that blond, or did he bleach it on purpose? The curls hanging over his collar were a little too perfect and did not match the straighter hair on top. Perhaps it was a perm.

After Jeremy sat, he surveyed the room one more time. Oh, how Robin hoped he was looking for her. She sat up a little straighter and smiled at him.

Just then, Professor Anderson emerged from his office and announced the beginning of class, diverting Jeremy's attention.

Sadness and jealousy filled Robin. She had never felt this way before toward a boy. Especially not Perry. But then, if Perry were to stop doting on her, would she miss it and want more? That thought made her laugh out loud, capturing curious glances from some students and Professor Anderson. Perhaps she should not get her hopes up. As soon as Jeremy found out how severely scarred she was, he would probably run away.

Robin forced herself to pay attention to the lecture, but her eyes kept drifting back to Jeremy. He was shorter than most other boys, but he made up for his lack of height with his good looks and kindness. His gentle nature is what Robin found most attractive.

Man, it was hard to concentrate. She picked up only about half of what the professor said. She did not catch all the homework instructions—something about painting an object with a mirror behind it.

Robin raised her hand. "So, we put something in front of a mirror and then paint just what we see in the reflection?"

"No. You illustrate both." Professor Anderson demonstrated by holding up a student's box. "Let's pretend this is your subject. You would include the image of the box." He gestured behind the object. "In the mirror, you would see the opposite side and paint that. In this area here above, you would include an object that fits the subject but isn't there."

"Like a ghost?" asked a student without raising his hand.

"Perhaps." The professor put the box down and paced. "Questions?"

A few students talked among themselves.

Robin glanced over and caught Greg's sinister stare. Those dead eyes revealed to her a tortured soul. She wondered how such creativity could come from someone so unkind. It was possibly his coping mechanism. He was enduring pain for all she knew, perhaps not physical, but emotional. At that moment, she felt sorry for him and smiled tenderly. That made the veins in his neck pop out. Clearly, he misread her intended compassion.

Professor Matthews cleared his throat and meekly called out, "Turn your benches around. We are going to learn to paint some quick sketches from a live model. Is there anyone who doesn't have the supplies on the list?" He waited for a show of hands. None lifted. "Good. Fill your cups with water, then lay out your palette with the three primary colors, then black and white."

All the students stood while the room filled with the cacophony of screeching wood on cement. Robin plugged her ears until it ceased. She wondered why the noise did not bother others. Was her hearing damaged in the accident or merely sensitive to loud noises since the crash?

So much for being invisible. Now everyone would stare at the back of her head. Just her luck!

Greg did not look all too pleased by the switch-a-roo. "No one said we were painting a model today. The syllabus said artist lecture," he objected to Professor Matthews.

That was the first time Robin had seen Professor Matthews smile and shrug.

Tina walked by on her way to the sink and nudged Robin. "You should sit with us. There's plenty of room."

Here Robin had a front-row view of the subject; she'd be closer to Jeremy back there. She had to remind herself this program was about becoming a professional artist, not chasing boys, so she shook her head. "Thank you. But I'm fine," she said as she glanced longingly over at Jeremy, who was smiling at her from his place in line near the sink.

Tina laughed. "You like him, don't you?"

"No," Robin said defensively.

"Let me help you move closer." Tina picked up Robin's bench about as nimbly as Greg.

Part of Robin wanted to protest. Then, one more look at Jeremy and, "Okay," was all that came out.

"Let me help." Julie's hair floated, like an angel, as she stooped quickly to fetch Robin's things. Julie would make a superb model for one of her angel drawings someday. Robin hobbled behind her as they followed Tina.

ANGEL IN FLIGHT

Strategically placing Robin's bench next to Jeremy's, Tina gestured for her to sit. "Will this do?"

Robin nodded. "Wow! You are strong."

"We live on a ranch. I'm always bucking hay, riding horses, or pushing cattle up a chute." Tina flexed one of her biceps.

Robin poked it and nodded in agreement.

"Hello again," Jeremy said, startling Robin from behind.

Robin squeezed out a, "Hi."

"I tried coming over last night, but your dorm mother said visiting hours were over. I hadn't unpacked until then."

"Why?"

"Why what?"

"Why did you come over?"

Jeremy frowned. "Uh, the teacher said you are supposed to help me do my assignment over. You don't remember?"

"Oh." Robin had hoped it was because he wanted to spend time with her, not because he needed her help. "That's right." She counted on her fingers, "Asymmetry, hues, and—"

"Shapes." Jeremy finished the count for her.

"Maybe tonight?" she offered.

"I think everyone is going skating. Do you want to come?"

Skating? Robin could not skate. The last time she tried was at a friend's birthday party when she was twelve. That was a disaster. She fell twice in the first minute and paid the price for a month after.

"Sure. I'll come watch."

SHELLY PULSE

3 — Bell Bottoms and Skates

A cartoon map of the university campus and downtown Logan, Utah, was among the items in the packet Robin received when she first checked into the dorm. She had to ask someone for directions when she got to the main street in town. Soon she discovered the map wasn't to scale as she hobbled approximately a mile to the skating rink.

Exhausted and sweaty by the time she reached her destination, Robin heard the thump of a steady disco beat. She struggled to open the big glass front door and wedged herself in sideways. Several art students congregated by the back wall, including Greg and Tom.

But where was Jeremy? This was not her scene. If he was not there, Robin did not want to be there either. She ordered a root beer from the snack bar and sat near the door. A few youngsters skated around the edge, clinging to the rail as they waddled along like ducklings.

A man, Robin estimated to be in his thirties, whizzed around the floor like a professional ice skater. He made it look so easy and held out his arms like he was flying. The long sleeves of his sapphire silk shirt fluttered in the breeze like wings. She wished she had a camera. This image would make a wonderful angel painting. For now, she would rely on memory.

The loudspeaker boomed, "Mark, you're needed at the skate counter. Mark, skate counter."

The presumed 'Mark' flew off the rink floor and skidded to a stop in front of the skate stand where Jeremy and Tina stood. Perhaps she stood a little too close. Jeremy picked up two pairs of skates from the bench. They appeared to be 'his and hers,' from what Robin could tell. She knew Tina was strong enough to carry her own. In fact, she should hold them after the little demonstration of her strength. Julie walked close behind, lugging her pair.

Now would be a good time to slip out the door. Clearly, Jeremy was flirting with Tina.

As Robin made her move for the door, she heard a female voice call her name, followed by, "Come join us!"

Robin was not sure if it was Julie or Tina who hollered. Pretend you didn't hear them and leave!

Then Robin heard Jeremy's voice coming closer. "Robin. Where are you going?" He grabbed her arm and swiftly turned her around, making her almost drop the rest of her root beer. "Aren't you going to stay?"

"No. Like I said, I don't skate." Robin wanted to add that Jeremy didn't need her hanging around while Tina was all over him, but she let that go.

"We'll go as a group and hold on to each other. It'll be fun."

Robin shook his hand off her arm. She glanced over at the girls and back at the door. It was decision time.

Jeremy threw his thumb over his shoulder. "Please, we want you here."

"*We?*"

He hung his head, then looked up, moving closer. "I... I want you here."

Jeremy's blue eyes appeared green in the low light of the roller rink. Her head spun like the twirling giant disco ball hanging from the ceiling.

"Will you be careful with me?"

Now she was sure Jeremy's curiosity awoke. 'How badly were you hurt?' she could see him ask himself as his gaze wandered up and down her body.

"Of course."

He stuck out his arm like he was escorting a princess to the ball. And, for a moment, she was, until Greg came rolling up, with Tom right behind.

"I see you found your boyfriend," Greg taunted. "Don't fall down. You might not be able to get back up." He rolled off, laughing, with Tom trailing.

"Ignore them," Jeremy said. "Happens to me all the time."

That shocked Robin. Why would *he* be teased like that? He was perfect.

"You do?"

"Yes. I was a runt growing up. I'm the guy everyone liked to bully. After a while, you get used to it. There are three guys back home who love to torment me. They stick my head in the toilet and flush. One girl hangs my coat on a hook with me still in it."

ANGEL IN FLIGHT

That last image made Robin suppress a little chuckle. "I don't believe you." The pain in his eyes said he was telling the truth. She held him closer. "I'm sorry."

"Someday, they'll get theirs."

Robin shuddered a little. By his hand or someone else's? Admittedly, she hoped a few bullies who tormented her would *get theirs*.

Tina and Julie greeted Robin warmly while they were putting on their skates. "Where are yours?" Julie asked.

"I'm just going to watch," Robin said, sitting down next to Tina.

"No. You are skating with us," Jeremy insisted. "What size are you?"

Robin shook her head and scooted closer to the wall in defiance. Jeremy stooped in front of her, and before she knew it, he had unlaced and slipped off her sneaker.

"Hey, put that back on!" He did not know how long it took to tie her shoes. She kept the laces loose so that she could slip her feet in and out.

Jeremy peeked inside. "Size six. You have little feet," he announced. Just as quickly as he had removed her shoe, he expertly put it back on her foot again, lacing it tighter than she preferred.

"How did you do that?"

"What?"

"Put it on like that."

"My parents own a shoe store. I work there after school." Jeremy jumped up and headed for the counter. "Be right back."

Robin glanced up to find Tina and Julie staring at her, mouths gaping.

"Now that is what I call personal service," Julie remarked.

"No one's ever done that for me before. Of course, we shop at the farm co-op. You try on your own shoes there," Tina said.

Robin sensed a hint of jealousy in Tina's voice.

Jeremy returned with roller skates and kneeled in front of Robin again. He showed Robin the little number six with a line under it. "See. That's how you can tell a six from a nine. A nine has a dash under it this way," he said, demonstrating with his finger.

Robin knew that little tidbit of information was wrong, but was not about to correct him. Jeremy loosened the laces and held out the skate for Robin to stick in her foot. Slipping it in, he pressed on the toe. The few freckles on his nose wrinkled.

"I think it's too big."

Julie flipped her hair back. "The line means six and a half. Even I know that." All three girls laughed.

Jeremy grew gloomy. "I think these are mis-marked."

Robin winced when he quickly removed the skate from her foot and returned to the counter.

Tina hid Jeremy's skates under the bench while Julie covered them up with her oversized purse. That sent the three girls tittering with restrained delight.

"What's so funny?" Jeremy asked when he returned.

"Nothing," Tina said, trying to keep a straight face.

Robin hoped they did not keep up the joke too long. That kind of thing had happened to her all the time, and it grew tiresome.

Jeremy went to work putting on Robin's skates, wrapping the laces around her ankles twice. He pulled the bell-bottoms down. Only the toes were visible.

"Aren't you a little warm in those pants?" Julie asked.

Robin felt the blood drain from her face. Now for the lie. She'd gotten good at making them. "My legs are too white for shorts. I haven't laid out yet this summer."

Tina and Julie nodded approval as they both stared down at their bare legs.

Greg and Tom rolled up. "Hey, Jeremy. How d'you feel when the professor threw your picture in the garbage?" Greg's eyes lacked benevolence in his question.

"I deserved it," Jeremy said, searching around the floor for his skates.

Robin directed him with her eyes toward the area under Julie's seat.

He smiled and dove between the girl's legs.

"How's the air down there?" Julie joked as Jeremy wriggled out from under the bench, holding his nose.

Greg moved in circles and turned backward, making figure eights.

"Show off!" Tina shouted.

Julie slugged Tina in the shoulder. "Shh! Don't piss him off."

Greg slid up to the rail and glared at Tina, then smiled at Julie. Of course, every guy smiled at Julie. Next, he turned his attention to Jeremy, who was tying his skates. "I thought you was gonna cry." He rubbed his eyes with his fists.

Tina planted the rubber stoppers on her skates and pushed Greg back off the rail. "Oh, you're a tough guy! I bet you would have bawled like a baby with his diaper full of crap!"

Greg rolled back, then looped around the rail by the benches, hovering menacingly over Tina, "At least I know how to follow directions." He skated in a small loop in front of her. "I know the difference between a circle...," he stopped, glaring inches from her face, "... and a square." He and Tom laughed hysterically.

Tina viciously bared her wolf teeth. Robin grabbed the hem of Tina's shorts and pulled her back. "He's not worth it."

Julie flipped her hair back as she tried to pull herself up on the wheels, her legs widening into the splits. Greg caught her just before she tipped over.

Cradled in his arms and looking up into his eyes, Julie said, "I thought he was a complete jerk. Jeremy worked hard on that assignment. We all did. But yours was especially good."

Greg turned all shades of red, but this time not because of anger. Julie had masterfully diverted his attention away from Jeremy.

Not to be upstaged, Tom pulled Julie's hair. "I think Dr. Anderson was talking about you. Did your hairdryer break?"

Greg swatted Tom away. "Hey. Hands off!"

Julie showed Greg a grateful smile.

Robin gestured like she was sticking a finger down her throat. "Gag me."

"I know what you mean," Tina whispered back.

Julie broke away from Greg and steadied herself. "No. I was late because the paint was still wet."

Greg frowned. "Acrylics dry fast. Unless you did the assigned on your way here."

Tina teased, "She was probably busy with a guy the night before." She pointed at Adrian, who was skating leisurely around the rink, holding another girl's hand.

Robin admired Tina's attempt at deflecting Greg's lust away from Julie, but right now, he needed to focus on someone besides Jeremy.

"What? An all-night date with Mr. Muscles over there?" Tom waved at Adrian dismissively. He pulled up his t-shirt and flexed his chest. "I've got more than him." Robin had to admit, Tom's physique was a close contender.

"Not all night," Julie said dismissively. "After class, we were sitting outside the dorms, talking. He got a little too frisky with the hands, so I pushed him away. He got all mad. Next thing you know, a Frisbee falls at our feet. He threw it back to a bunch of local girls. Soon, he's playing with them and ignoring me. He ran off with the one who flashed him a smile."

Julie flipped her head back, making a strand of her hair stick in her mouth. She spat it out and licked her lips. "Watch this."

She entered the floor right in front of Adrian and skidded to a stop. Avoiding the collision, the girl's legs flew out, and she landed on her butt.

"Look where you're going!" Adrian shouted at Julie while everyone else laughed from the sideline.

Julie offered a helping hand to the girl, who was struggling to stand. "I'm so sorry. I'm really clumsy on these things."

Adrian pushed Julie away and helped his date to her feet.

"Are you hurt?" he asked, placing a hand on her backside.

The girl glared at him and pushed his hand away.

He sneered at Julie as he escorted his partner off the floor toward the snack bar.

Julie gave him back a seductive smile and flipped him the bird. "What? She isn't giving you any, either?"

He rolled his eyes and turned away.

Julie rejoined the gang. Everyone congratulated her for skillfully taking down the competition.

Jeremy swayed on his skates, trying to balance. He held out his hand to Robin to help her up.

She simply stared and shook her head. "I can't."

Tina pulled up behind Jeremy, scaring him. He grabbed onto her to steady himself.

"You can let go anytime," Tina said, peeling his hands off her, taking one of them in hers. She held her other hand out to Robin. "I got you."

With one swift movement, Robin went airborne as Tina lifted. She waited for the pain in her legs, but it never came.

The three entered the rink slowly. Robin pulled herself along the rail, still holding onto Tina.

"You're doing great!" she shouted over the loud music. After reaching halfway around, Tina joined Jeremy and Robin's hands together and let go. "You two go slow and have fun." She caught up with Julie in the center, and off the two girls glided like birds on the wing.

Tom trundled up behind Tina and grabbed her hand. Robin was sure she would reject him. Instead, she whipped him around and sent him flying across the floor. He recovered amazingly well and came back for more. That seemed to impress Tina, as she held out her hand and repeated the slingshot move at the next turn.

This made Robin happy. Now Tina had someone else to flirt with and would leave *her* Jeremy alone.

Greg spooked Jeremy as he slid up from behind. "Ooh. Jeremy has to hold on to his girlfriend, so he doesn't fall down and go boom."

ANGEL IN FLIGHT

That made Jeremy lose control. Robin felt terrible that she had to let Jeremy fall as she secured herself to the rail.

Greg doubled over with amusement as he rolled away.

Now that he lost his minion, Tom, to Tina's allure, Greg's next mission was to win him back. "Let's blow this joint and go find us some hot foxes!" Greg yelled loud enough for the whole place to hear.

"Nah, I'm fine here," Tom said.

Greg advanced like he was going to punch Tom. Tina pulled him around behind her.

"Then, fine. Julie and I will go skate together." Greg grabbed Julie's hand, and off they rushed.

Jeremy crawled off the floor and pulled himself up by clinging to the rail.

"Look out!" Robin shrieked as Greg brushed past Jeremy, knocking him down again.

Julie let go of Greg and circled back. "You alright?"

Jeremy nodded, grabbing his ankle, and rocking side to side. "I'll be fine."

"I'm sorry he's such a jerk. I'm trying to keep him off you," Julie assured him.

"Thank you. I appreciate it."

Julie offered a hand.

Jeremy shook his head. "Nah. I'm done," he said, untying a shoestring.

She shrugged and returned to the group of students assembled in the middle of the rink.

Jeremy crawled under the railing and pulled himself up to the bench next to Robin. "Can we go now?"

She nodded. Jeremy took off his skates, then helped Robin off with hers. They limped stocking-footed to the skate return bench.

Greg sailed by and shouted, "Pussy!"

That caught Mark's attention. He flew out from behind the bench after Greg and ordered him off the floor. The crowd cheered when Mark ejected him from the building and threw his shoes into the parking lot.

Robin, worried about retaliation, asked Mark when he returned, "Is there a back door out of here?"

He nodded toward an exit sign on the back wall. "Who was that guy?"

"A speeding train with a washed-out bridge around the bend," Robin offered.

Mark narrowed his gaze at Robin.

She shrugged. "Something my aunt would have said."

"Your aunt sounds pretty smart."

Jeremy sat on the floor in front of Robin. He winced with pain as he tied her shoes, then slipped on his sandals.

"What's wrong?"

"My butt hurts."

Robin, putting on her most sympathetic face, tugged on Jeremy and helped him up. Together, they peeked out the back door and looked both ways. There was no sign of Greg. They made a dash for a row of parked cars as fast as Robin's legs could carry her. They hid long enough to be sure Greg was not lurking.

She could feel Jeremy's body heat hovering over her as the cool evening breeze whiffled about. Robin wished he would at least put his arm around her.

As she was working up the nerve to grab his hand and sling it around her, Jeremy said, "I think the coast is clear." He inched along the parking stalls toward a side street.

Robin followed. "How's your butt?" she asked, slapping him on his behind.

He furrowed his brow. "My A-S-S is better," he said, spelling out the word and making her laugh. "Now, my feet are killing me. Next time I'm asking for a bigger size."

Robin grew concerned. Jeremy suddenly seemed distant as he limped as far on the opposite edge of the sidewalk as he could. She grabbed his hand just as he almost fell off the curb.

"You don't skate much, do you?"

"Nah. I try. There's a rink at the edge of town. I've never gotten the hang of it. Running and soccer are more my thing." He let go of her hand and pretended to kick an invisible ball. "How about you?"

Here we go. It was time to lay it all out there and test how he reacts. What did she have to lose?

"I have to be careful. I've had too many broken bones and surgeries. So I can't do sports."

Robin waited for a thousand questions, but none came. He stared ahead as they strolled along. She tried reading his face. His eyes darted back and forth as if sorting through all the possibilities in his head.

Why wasn't he saying anything? He stopped and glanced up and down a cross-street. She pulled out the map from her purse.

"Can you figure out where we are?"

ANGEL IN FLIGHT

Jeremy unfolded it and studied the signs. "We're way off." He glanced down another street. "We need to be going that way."

Robin didn't care if it took all night. In fact, she wished she had hidden the map now that he was marching off in the new direction.

"Wait up!" she called out to him.

He faced her while walking backward. That's when she noticed what he was wearing. It had been rather dark in the roller rink.

"What is that on your midriff?"

Displeased at her question, Jeremy screwed up his face. He held out the hem of the shirt that barely made it to his belly button. "This is not a midriff. It's a half-tee! Midriffs are for girls."

Kind of sensitive, isn't he? "Okay. Half-tee. But what is it?"

He pulled it taut and pointed. "A glass heart."

"I know that, but why?"

"You know the song, *Heart of Glass* by *Blondie*?"

She nodded. Robin had heard it once. Her aunt limited radio time. She kept a pocket transistor and a cassette tape player next to her bed. Aunt Margaret approved of singers like *Karen Carpenter* and *John Denver*. Occasionally, she would tune into a rock station when she guessed her aunt was asleep. Margaret once took away a *Beatles* cassette a girl from school had lent her. Robin had to beg for it back, so she could return it. *Blondie* was definitely not on the acceptable playlist.

"I'm not allowed. My aunt calls it, um, *hippie trash*."

Jeremy stopped. Robin stumbled into him, making him catch her. "Your aunt? Why doesn't your mom tell her to mind her own business?"

Robin lowered her gaze and focused on the glowing red heart on his shirt. "I wish she could." When the confusion formed on his face, she asked, "Where did you buy the shirt?"

"I painted it myself." He pounded his chest proudly.

"You did that?"

"Yep. With acrylics. I also did one of a chrome soccer ball. I can wear that one tomorrow if you like."

It was her turn to admire his work. "Wow. That's pretty good." She stooped and examined it a little closer. "See, it has a tiny crack in it." She playfully poked him in the chest. "Someone broke your heart?"

He gathered Robin into his arms. She laid her head on his shoulder. "More than once."

SHELLY PULSE

4 — Cloud of Sorrow

Tiny waves lapped at the Bear Lake shoreline. Most of the students frolicked in the water. Some laid out tanning on a grassy area next to the volleyball net.

Robin chose a spot under a tree in the shade. She laid down a blanket next to some low-hanging branches, testing them to be sure they were strong enough to hold when she got up.

It was Saturday—no class. A *required* field trip on a bus over winding roads to a lake an hour away was not on her list of favorite things to do. She would rather stay in her dorm and redraw the damaged angel pictures or complete her mirror homework assignment.

Professor Anderson had said, 'It is important to play as hard as it is to work.' Robin guessed it was a way for him to get girls to prance around in their bikinis.

Today, Robin had pulled her bangs back in a ponytail to cover her scar. Over that, she wore one of the broad-brimmed hats her aunt had packed. The hairspray would not hold with the humidity left from last night's rainstorm.

As she unpacked all her pencils and drawing pad, Jeremy, dressed in nothing but swim trunks, approached, juggling a Nerf football.

"How come you aren't out here with the rest of us?"

There was that halo glow, like the first time they had met. Robin wanted to ignore him, as he did since that night after skating. Yes, Jeremy had hugged her, but turned his face away when she tried to kiss him. They had walked back to the dorms in silence.

Jeremy hardly said two words to her for the rest of the week in class. In fact, he had said little to anyone. Perhaps he focused on the assignments or did his best to stay away from Greg. He even moved his bench away from Tina and Julie, too.

Now that she admitted how damaged she was, Robin figured he wanted nothing more to do with her. This little visit was definitely a surprise.

Robin shielded her eyes from the sun as she surveyed the lake. "I'm not much of a swimmer."

"At least you could lay out and fry in the sun with Tina and Julie."

"I burn easily," she replied, still shielding the light behind him. "Come closer, so I don't have to cover my eyes."

Jeremy sat down on Robin's blanket, nudging her to move over. "Ah. One of the itchy ones from the dorm."

"Don't tell anyone I took it."

"Lips locked." He gestured, twisting an imaginary key.

'Is that why you wouldn't kiss me?' she wanted to ask. 'Because your lips are locked?' She closed her drawing pad and leaned against the tree trunk.

"What are you drawing?" Jeremy asked, snatching the drawing book and thumbing through the pages. He stopped on one with an angel dressed in flowing robes and a hint of wings. "Whoa! How do you make the folds in the cloth look so real?"

"Practice. I've had a paintbrush in my hand for as long as I can remember." She glared at him when he resisted her trying to snatch it back. They played tug-o-war until he let her win.

Jeremy jumped to his feet and tried pulling on her arm. "Come, throw the ball around with me. We're supposed to be having fun, not working."

Wincing in pain, Robin cried, "Ow! That hurts!" She placed a hand on her shoulder and whimpered.

Jeremy let go. "I'm so sorry. I didn't mean to—"

"I told you. Be gentle with me."

Jeremy sat back down and tried rubbing her shoulder.

She brushed him off.

"What's wrong?"

Seriously? You did not speak to me for three days, and now want to know what is wrong?

"Don't want to talk about it." Was she angrier at him for snubbing her or forgetting how fragile she was? She wished he would just go away.

He kneeled on the grass this time. "I'm sorry. I didn't mean to hurt you," he said, offering a palm of apology Robin couldn't refuse. "You can tell me about... you know..." He pointed at her twisted leg.

"Don't need a whole bunch of sympathy."

ANGEL IN FLIGHT

Just then, a beach ball bounced near the blanket next to Robin. Tom ran up to fetch it. Greg, right behind, pushed him. Tom landed squarely on top of Jeremy, then tumbled onto Robin, knocking her hat off. Jeremy recovered and pulled Tom off her. Robin rolled onto her side in agony.

Jeremy stood and kicked the ball as hard as he could. "You have the whole lake! Take it somewhere else!"

Both knees down, he laid his hands on Robin's leg.

She flinched and rolled to the side.

Loaded like a coil, Jeremy doubled up his fists in frustration, and with one mighty heave, sprang to his feet and lunged at Greg.

Greg lost his balance and fell backward.

Tom ducked.

Jeremy wound up a second time, ready to use all his hundred pounds to leap on Greg, when Robin shouted, "No fighting!"

He remained frozen, but ready.

Greg crawled away. "Geez! Why are you so uptight, man? We're just having a little fun."

Jeremy advanced with a martial arts kind of stance.

"Stop!" Robin screamed and tumbled forward, grabbing Jeremy's swim trunks to pull him back.

Jeremy retreated.

Greg bounced up and stared threateningly into Jeremy's face.

Why didn't Greg strike back? Or at least push him?

Jeremy breathed heavily, but did not flinch. Something had changed in him. Robin had not known him long, and what she had seen so far revealed he was fairly passive. Not this time! Robin knew Greg could inflict serious harm, but Jeremy stood his ground.

Professor Anderson approached. "Gentlemen? Is there a problem?"

Greg pointed at Robin. "Jeremy's *little girlfriend* over here is acting like she got ran over by a truck. Right Tom?"

Tom simply shrugged and took another step back.

Jeremy bristled. "Man, you pushed Tom right on top of her!"

Greg pressed his hand against Jeremy's chest and shoved, making him falter.

Professor Anderson stepped between them when Jeremy cocked his arm to throw a punch. "Look, you two. Knock it off, or I'll have both your parents take you home. Understood?"

Jeremy nodded and backed away.

"Go ahead!" Greg's face turned the same crimson Robin had seen before. "I didn't want to waste my summer at this stupid school, anyway."

Greg slapped the professor's hand away and stormed off. He waded into the lake. Everyone stopped what they were doing as he thrashed about.

"He just needs time." Professor Anderson shook his head. "I thought he'd be better this year," he muttered.

Behavior like that at any other school would get him kicked out immediately. Not wanting Jeremy punished, Robin resisted confronting the professor.

"Why is he like this?"

Dr. Anderson sighed. "He's my wife's grandnephew. Such talent but so troubled. I thought this experience would help."

Now it all made sense. What a dilemma.

"If you could keep that quiet. I don't need the other students thinking I'm playing favorites."

Too late for that. Three of Greg's victims knew the truth and now suffered because of his special treatment.

Once Greg had calmed a bit, Dr. Anderson asked, "Robin? Are you alright?"

Robin rubbed her legs. "I'm better now. Thanks." She picked up her drawing pad and pencils.

"Why don't you put down your things and join the others?"

Pondering her choices of wading in the water, playing catch with Jeremy, laying out with the girls, or playing volleyball, she rocked her body to alleviate the pain. She said, "I appreciate the effort, but I prefer to sit here by myself if you don't mind."

Silence followed as the professor peered down at her and back at the other students.

Please don't insist. Please. She begged with her eyes.

The professor winked at Jeremy and slapped him on the back. "You keep her company?"

Jeremy nodded.

"Good man. Carry on." He motioned for Tom to follow. "Let's go play some volleyball. Greg will eventually come around."

The professor and Tom joined the students slapping the ball back and forth over the net.

"You don't have to stay," she told Jeremy as he planted his butt in the grass next to her.

"You heard the professor. Plus, no place I'd rather be."

She was not sure how to take that. Did Jeremy remain out of desire or obligation?

"That was pretty cool how you stood up to Greg," she said after a while.

Jeremy shrugged. "I guess I kind of lost it. The last time I did that, I wound up unconscious, though."

Then why did he do it? For her? It could only mean one thing—he *did* like her. That gave her a little thrill. "You looked like you were about to give him a karate chop."

Jeremy beamed. "I recently started taking classes from an instructor with a black belt from Japan."

"It looked like you knew what you were doing."

He shrugged and pulled at some grass. "Instinct, I guess."

Professor Anderson took off his white shirt. He was in good shape and super tanned for his age. The teams comprised mostly girls clad in next to nothing.

"I think the professor is a perv."

Jeremy scooted closer and followed her gaze. "Why do you say that?"

"He organized this so he could watch a bunch of young naked girls." She had to admit that she wished she had a body like them, but knew it would never be.

"Are you kidding? He's an art teacher. He sees all the naked models he wants back in the studio."

Robin poked him in the shoulder teasingly. "Is that why you are an artist? So, you can draw naked girls?"

"Uh," Jeremy blushed. "Guys at school pay me to draw pictures of their girlfriends, but the broads have their clothes on."

"Broads? Does anyone even use that word anymore?"

"We do in St. George," Jeremy said with a frown.

"Am I a *broad*?" she asked with a grin.

He shrugged. "I guess not. It's just a saying."

Robin was having way too much fun teasing him. She'd never done that to anyone before and hoped he knew she meant nothing by it. His body language said she had thrown him off balance.

"Now that I'm your *little girlfriend*, are you going to draw me?" she asked, framing her smiling face.

Jeremy hesitated while studying her. "Sure. *Little girlfriend*," he said with the same emphasis. "I need a picture of you with your clothes off, I mean, on." Now *he* flashed a devilish grin. "Unless you want to model for me."

Robin laughed while reaching into her tie-dyed purse. She pulled out a wallet and removed a small black-and-white photograph. "I want you to draw this one."

Jeremy studied it closely, then held it out at arms-length. "Ah," he sighed, like he was holding a cute puppy. "Is this you?"

She nodded.

"How old were you?"

"Five. Kindergarten."

"What are these sticks you are holding?" he asked, pulling the photo closer and squinting. "Sorry. Don't have my glasses on."

Glasses? She had never seen him wear glasses.

"Those are paintbrushes, silly."

"You look really cute in that smock thing."

She shot him a puzzled expression. "Smock? What's that?" Of course, she knew what a smock was. Robin wanted to know how much she could mess with him.

"You know, that apron thing that covers—"

Robin slapped his shoulder. "That's a dress. My aunt always made me wear those. I'm more of a tom-boy. I hate dresses. My dad wanted me to be a boy so bad, so I acted like one. He even gave me a name that could go both ways."

Jeremy's furrowed brow revealed his confusion. "Why would your aunt dress you and not your mother? Did something happen to her?"

Robin watched him attempt to reconcile that in his head. She turned her gaze toward the lake. The tragic events of her youth flashed like a rapid-fire slideshow on the screen of her mind, as they had a thousand times.

Finally, she stated matter-of-factly, "My family all died in a plane crash." She could feel his eyes blazing a hole in the side of her head.

After a long pause, he chuckled nervously. "You're kidding me, right?"

Her eyes closed as she conjured up the last memory of her parents before the accident. That drew a smile to her lips. She opened her eyes to find sadness in his.

"It's too hard to even think about sometimes. I try to remember their faces and how happy we were."

Jeremy was having a tough time remaining focused. "Why, um, how come you weren't with them?"

Robin raised her eyes to the heavens. "I was." Her voice softened. "I was the only survivor."

Despite the clear, blue sky, a cloud of sorrow hung over the two of them. Jeremy moved next to Robin and wrapped his arm around her. She tucked her head up under his chin. At that moment, she realized her hat fell off. She didn't care if he saw her scar. He felt good, and she was not moving.

The embrace continued until Jeremy broke the silence. "I'd like it if you told me the story sometime."

Robin gazed up into his eyes and found sincerity. "My dad was a pilot in the Korean War. He married my mom when he came home, and I was born about six years later."

SHELLY PULSE

5 — Maiden Flight

Summer 1965

Gary Wood opened the passenger door to the family's new Ford Country Squire station wagon. He tipped his fedora to his wife, Sarah, as she walked out of their suburban home. His eyes dipped to her belly, bulging through a tailored summer dress.

She blew him a kiss with gloved hands; his reflection showed in her horn-rimmed sunglasses. Feathers from the fascinator she wore tickled his nose as she brushed past him and lowered herself side-saddle onto the front seat. She swung her legs inside.

"Suitcases?"

"Already in the back," he said, before slamming her door.

A four-year-old Robin Wood waited impatiently by the back passenger door. She tucked her Chatty Cathy doll snugly against her chest and held her little brother, Michael, by the hand.

Gary clapped his hands together. "Okay, kiddos. Let's get in the car. We're going to visit Grandma." Gary opened the door. The kids climbed in. He waited for Robin to move her leg out of the way before closing it.

"I can do it." Robin pulled the door the best she could. It didn't latch all the way. Gary had to give it a shove with his hip to make it click shut. He glanced through the window to find a frown from her.

He whistled as he put on his aviator glasses, took off his bomber jacket, and set it on the bench seat between him and his wife. Pulling a pack of Lucky Strike cigarettes from his shirt pocket, Gary capably flipped his wrist, making two magically appear. He nursed one and offered the other to Sarah.

"Please. I'd like that new car smell to last a while longer."

"My Aqua Velva will cover it up," he said with a smirk, the unlit cigarette bobbing between his lips. Gary then tucked the smoke back into the pack to save for later.

Firing up the engine, he backed cautiously out of the driveway. Gary slammed on the brakes to avoid hitting some children on bicycles whizzing by.

Other children waved at the Woods as they drove slowly down the street past other middle-class crackerbox bungalows, each mirroring the one next door. Robin waved back at her best friend, Olive, sitting on her front porch, elbows on her knees and face buried in her palms.

The trees had little time to mature, so the morning sun peeking up over the Wasatch Front mountain range was strong enough to make Gary pull the visor down. He negotiated the most efficient turns out of the neighborhood's grid, past the new elementary school.

Robin opened a box of crayons and a coloring book she found on the floorboard left from the last trip in the car.

"Michael, if you are going to draw in my book, stay on one page," Robin scolded, annoyed with her little brother. She turned the page and found a fresh picture to fill in. Careful not to touch the lines, she cross-hatched the area with her favorite shade of blue.

"I sorry," Michael replied, looking past her shoulder.

Robin pushed him back.

"I want to see."

"No. Not while I'm coloring."

Michael squatted on the floor and found a stuffed dog to play with. "Fine. I play with Scruffy."

Robin made a face of defiance and went back to her drawing. "Daddy?" she called out, not taking her eyes off the task at hand.

"What, sweetheart?"

"Are we going in the airplane to Grandma's house, or are we driving?"

Sarah peeked over the seat at Robin. "Yes. Daddy is taking us in our shiny new airplane. Won't that be fun?" She smiled at Robin.

"She has a few hours on her," Gary corrected. "It's a 1958, not brand new."

"Do you always have to argue with everything I say?" Sarah asked with a furrowed brow.

Robin put down her coloring book and crayon. She slid off the seat and stood behind her dad. "Can I drive the new airplane, Daddy? Please? You let me—"

ANGEL IN FLIGHT

"Robin! Shh!" Gary hushed her. "That was our secret." He glared at her in the rearview mirror. She plopped back down in the seat and folded her arms.

Looking straight ahead, Sarah said, "No, Honey. Daddy and I have to sit in the front seat of the airplane. You and Michael are going to sit in the back. The view is better from the windows back there, anyway."

Just then, Michael turned over on his knees and peered out the back of the car. "I see a airplane." He shrugged.

"No, you don't. We're in a car, silly," Robin said to her brother authoritatively.

Gary glared at Sarah, then back at the road. "I can speak for myself. I'm the pilot. I say where the passengers sit."

Sarah frowned back at Gary, giving him the cold shoulder. "Knowing you, you'd let her fly the plane the way you let her drive this car. I've seen you stop down the block and make her move off your lap."

The family station wagon pulled onto the two-lane U.S. Highway 89. Gary adjusted his hat and fiddled with the air control vent as he pushed on the gas. "She's got to learn sometime."

"She's only four. And you know how I feel about flying. It scares me. It's not safe."

Gary, distracted by airplanes taking off from Hill Air Force Base, tugged on the wheel at the last second as he drifted over the line into oncoming traffic.

"Flying is safer than driving. And we arrive in half the time. Besides, do you know how many times I flew under fire in Korea? Not once did I crash. On top of that, nobody will be shooting at us. This will be like a Sunday stroll in the park." He chuckled at his own joke.

"I know. I've heard your stories a thousand times." Sarah picked up a Reader's Digest from under Gary's jacket and fanned herself. "Can the next new car have air conditioning?"

"Roll down the window," he said, craning his neck to see the craft overhead buzzing the highway.

"Eyes on the road, dear."

"They are."

Robin hiked her legs up onto the seat and leaned against the door. Michael stood and jumped up and down when he saw some horses. "I want to ride them, Mommy!" He pointed.

"We can't ride the horses. They aren't ours," Robin said.

Michael cried and reached back toward the horses as they disappeared. He bounced higher and screamed, then sat down hard on Robin's feet.

"Ow! You hurt me." Robin kicked Michael hard, which made him cry even louder. Then she threw her doll at him.

Sarah turned around. On her knees, she tried to move Robin's legs off the back seat. "Sit up."

"I don't want to. I had my legs here first."

"Robin. You stay on your side. Give Michael some room."

"Fine!" She swung her legs around and scooted as close to the door as she could. Then she stuck her tongue out at her brother.

"Mommy, she's breathing my air," Michael said.

Sarah turned her attention back to Michael and encouraged him to sit down. He resisted.

"Oh, stop it. She is not. Now, sweetie, you need to sit down. It's not safe to be standing up like that. What if Daddy has to push on the brakes really, really hard?"

Michael glanced between Robin and his mother. He shook his head.

"Son. Don't make me stop this car." Gary's voice was firm and loud.

Michael dropped immediately to his bottom. He snatched Robin's doll, pulled the string, and held it away from her.

The doll said, "Please take me with you."

"Give it back!" Robin shouted.

He threw the doll in the luggage area in the back of the automobile. Robin slugged him while she crawled over the seat to fetch her Chatty Cathy. Michael screamed louder than before.

"Why did you do that?" Sarah reached farther back and pulled Robin by the elastic waistband down into her seat.

"He threw my doll back there," she replied as she cuddled it tightly and closed her eyes. She pulled the string.

"I love you," said the doll.

"I love you too," Robin replied.

Still bent over the seat, Sarah settled Michael, distracting him with a book. She opened it and read a page or two upside-down.

Gary overtook a car that slowed down. The other vehicle's occupants, huge smiles on their faces, looked over as Gary pulled past them. As soon as he got over, the other car sped back up. The driver kept pace in the opposite lane and gave Gary a wink and thumbs-up.

He noticed that Sarah's dress had hiked up and was revealing a little more than it should. He smiled and waved at the other driver. They sped up and pulled in front of Gary before taking another car head-on.

"Honey, you need to sit down."

"I will in a minute. I'm giving Michael something to look at."

ANGEL IN FLIGHT

"Um. I think you are giving everyone plenty to look at."

Sarah tugged at the hem of her dress and tried to pull it down. When she turned to sit, Gary flashed her a lustful smile.

She squinted and slapped him on the arm. "You know that's how it always starts, and I wind up like this," Sarah said, pointing at her belly.

The station wagon turned off the empty highway onto a lane that led into a small airstrip parking lot. Gary parked the car and killed the engine.

Everyone opened their doors and piled out, except Michael; he tried to follow, but Robin slammed the door in his face. He yanked on the handle, but was not strong enough to open it.

Sarah helped him out. "You've got to be more careful. You almost shut the door on your brother," Sarah reproached Robin.

She shrugged and ran after her father.

Gary called out to Sarah, "You two stay put while I go file our flight plan." He headed for the airport office. Robin ran circles around him.

Sarah closed the door behind Michael. Around back, she let the tailgate fall and struggled to pull out the luggage. Once the two suitcases were out and lined up neatly, Sarah sat and spread her legs, taking some pressure off her stomach. She closed her eyes, placed a hand on top of her belly, and felt the baby push back.

After a while, Sarah stood and closed the hatch. She checked her watch. "What's taking him so long?"

Michael shrugged while he kicked a pebble.

Hand on her brow, Sarah measured the distance to a Cessna 170 parked about 100 yards away.

"Ready?" she asked Michael.

He nodded excitedly.

She grabbed both handles, lifted, and shuffled in the aircraft's direction. After three short rest periods, she set the suitcases down in the wing's shade. "It would have been easier and faster to drive," she moaned and sat down.

Michael climbed onto the landing wheel, supporting himself against the spring bar. "Look, Mommy!" He bounced on the hard rubber tire.

"Careful. You'll fall off and hurt yourself." Sarah glanced toward the office. "What's taking them so darn long?" she muttered. She rechecked the time and huffed.

Michael reached up and touched the propeller blade. "What's this?" he asked, patting the flat side?

"That's what makes the airplane go." Sarah stood and picked up Michael, placing him on her hip. "Careful. It can cut you. See." She ran her fingers along the sharp edge of the blade.

Robin's voice carried over the tarmac, where all the other airplanes rested securely. She weaved in and out of them as Gary walked the straightest path to where Sarah was standing.

"That's not ours?" he informed.

Sarah whirled around and examined the craft. She backed up and read the tail number. "Oh. It sure looks like ours." Now she had a confused expression as she searched the lot for what might be the family plane.

"Ours is back here." Gary pointed to one closer to the office. He picked up the suitcases, and the four of them marched off in that direction. "I could have helped carry these."

"You've helped enough already." Sarah patted her protruding belly as she walked beside him.

Gary stuffed the suitcases in the compartment behind the back seat of the aircraft. He loaded Michael into the cabin first, then Robin. "And I thought getting the kids into the car was difficult," he said, fastening the straps that fit loosely on their tiny bodies.

"Yes, dear. You worked very hard while I bathed, fed, dressed them, and packed their clothes for the trip. You opened the door and threw the bags and suitcases in the back. That was difficult, wasn't it?" Sarah slapped his hand away when he pushed her up by her rump. That made them both laugh.

Gary walked around the plane and performed a preflight inspection. Satisfied, he climbed into the cockpit and began the aircraft start procedure. "Oops. Almost forgot to do the run-up." He scanned the instrument panel, aided by his index finger. "Ah-ha! Just as I suspected."

"What?" Sarah asked nervously.

"Everything is just fine." Gary lifted his radio headset and tried to place it on his head, but his fedora was in the way. It fell into Sarah's lap. "Just toss it in the back, honey."

Sarah handed Gary's hat to Robin. Michael snatched it from her and put it on his head, giggling. Rather than blow up, Robin simply smiled.

"Look, Daddy. Michael thinks he's you."

"That's nice, sweetheart. Daddy's a little busy right now."

Gary adjusted the knobs on the radio. "Bountiful traffic, this is Cessna…" He gave them his call sign. "We are taking runway one six for a south departure, Bountiful." He checked all the instruments again as the

ANGEL IN FLIGHT

craft taxied to the end of the runway and turned. He smiled at Sarah and said, "Alright. The runway is ours."

Sarah grabbed whatever she could find to hold on to and closed her eyes. Robin sat up straight and looked out the window. Michael stared at the seat in front of him. Within minutes, the little aircraft was airborne—destination, Ephraim, Utah.

SHELLY PULSE

6 — First Kiss

Summer 1976

"So, was that when you crashed?" Jeremy crawled over by the tree, and Robin laid her head in his lap, so she could see his face.

"No."

Jeremy appeared confused. "When did you?"

Robin stroked his fuzzy face with the tips of her fingers. "You don't shave yet, do you?"

He pushed her hand away and rubbed his face, grimacing at the suggestion. "I shave."

"It's so light and soft against your tanned skin. I didn't mean—"

He shook his head as if to say, 'Don't worry about it.' "What happened next?"

"Patience. I'm getting there. Anyway. I love that feeling when the plane takes off. It felt like I was going to disappear into the seat. Have you ever flown in a small airplane before?" Now she was sure he was aware of her stall tactics.

"Yes. My Uncle Paul, up in Kooskia, has a Piper Cub. It's scary going up in that thing. We take turns because it only has two seats. He has his own landing strip on his ranch." Jeremy squinted. "How did you get to your grandma's house? Could you land there?"

"My dad kept Grandmother's car in the hangar at the airport in Ephraim since she gave up driving. Grandpa had died years before. We would park the airplane and drive to her house a little way outside of town. I loved going there. She had a big garden with chickens and a goat."

"Did you milk the goat?"

Robin screwed up her face. "No. It was a boy goat."

That made him chuckle. "So, it was a *billy* goat?"

"I guess."

"My Uncle Paul has goats. I milk them each morning when we visit. A squirt for the cat, one for me, and one in the bucket."

"Yuck! You like goat's milk?"

"Yes. Love it." Jeremy licked his lips. "So, tell me more about your grandma."

"She's a kind woman. Blind as a bat now. My aunt and I drove down all the time to buy her groceries and clean her house. We finally got her to come live with us."

"When did you start drawing besides crayons?" Jeremy laughed.

"Very funny." Robin smacked him on the leg. "Actually, my grandmother was a talented artist. I remember seeing a lot of her watercolors and oil paintings all over her house. She gave most of her brushes and supplies to me since she can't see anymore."

"Runs in the family?"

Robin nodded. "My dad loved to doodle. I still have a box of his drawings. Mostly war stuff. Pictures of soldiers and airplanes." She stopped talking and gazed into Jeremy's eyes.

He glanced around at all the other students to see if anyone was watching, then bent down and kissed Robin on the forehead.

That was a good start. She sat up and wrapped her arms around his neck, leaving mere inches between their lips.

Jeremy diverted his gaze once more to make sure no one was looking. She drew his attention back with a hand on his cheek, then pulled him into a long, passionate kiss. After what seemed forever, she let go and planted her head in his lap.

That left Jeremy speechless. He combed his fingers through his hair and turned a darker shade of tanned. "I don't know what to say."

"Did you like that?"

He nodded. "A lot."

"We should do that again sometime."

After he regained his breath, Jeremy turned contemplative. "I would like that." He glanced up and down her body.

Robin could read his thoughts had turned back to her injuries. Perhaps he regretted the kiss, and the implied commitment.

"I'm sorry. Maybe I shouldn't have done that."

"Oh, no. I enjoyed it," Jeremy said, lightly touching his lips.

"I'm guessing you want to know about the crash."

Jeremy shrugged. "If you are up for it," he whispered, eyes closed, rooting around her cheek, searching for her lips.

ANGEL IN FLIGHT

Robin was hesitant to pick up where she had left off. Some memories had faded; she had to rely on what her aunt and others had told her. What she recalled of the crash was horrifying and rarely spoke of it.

"I remember it was early winter. My littlest brother, David, was still a baby. My grandmother was desperate to hold him. I remember my parents had a huge fight over whether to drive or fly. Dad must have won the argument. We decided to fly because the roads were already iced up."

SHELLY PULSE

7 — Turbulence

Winter 1965

Gary loaded the luggage into the back of the station wagon and started the engine to warm it up. Several inches of snow blanketed the neighborhood. He returned to the house and prepared the children with coats and hats.

"Can you grab the Christmas presents off the table in the kitchen, please?"

There on the table were half a dozen brightly wrapped gifts for his mother. "I'm not sure all those will fit back there."

"Can we at least try?"

Gary scowled at Sarah and said, "We are at our weight limit with the extra baggage and baby items. And I'm only registering the four of us on the flight plan. That's all we're supposed to have on board."

"David only weighs twelve pounds. And I've lost twenty since we last flew."

Gary shook his head but snatched up the entire stack of presents. He lowered the back window of the car and tossed them in. Raising the window again, Robin startled him from behind with a snowball to the chest when he turned.

"So that's how you operate? Surprise attack?" Gary scooped up some snow and launched one playfully at Robin, who had backed off into the yard. She prepared another ball and threw it with everything she had. It hit him squarely in the leg.

The volley lasted until they heard Sarah's voice call out, "I could use a little help in here with David and Michael!"

"Let's go help your mother." Gary picked Robin up and held her securely in his arms. "Are you excited to fly again?"

Robin nodded. "When can I learn to drive the airplane, Daddy?"

"Soon. When the weather gets nice, and you turn five—just you and me. We'll take her up. But don't tell Mommy. Okay?"

Robin's head bobbed eagerly.

With everyone loaded in the car, the Woods made their way out of the subdivision. Snowmen lined the yards, and a few houses were trimmed with Christmas lights. A few adults and lots of children sledded in the snow.

"I want to play with them," Michael said, peeking through the smear in the fogged-up window.

"We will play in the snow when we get to Grandmother's house. Does that sound fun, sweetie?" Sarah said, holding baby David swaddled in her arms.

Michael said meekly, "Okay."

Gary somehow got all the luggage and packages loaded in the back of the plane. Once his wife and children were all seated, he entered the office to file the flight plan.

They waited at the end of the runway for the tractor to finish clearing a path and took off.

"Pretty!" Robin exclaimed as they rose high above the snow-covered city of Bountiful and headed for Ephraim.

"Yes. It is beautiful," Sarah said, looking down as Gary tilted the plane a little, so she could get a better view. "I've seen enough. You can level out now."

He smiled at her and mouthed the words, 'thank you.'

"What for?"

"Going with me so Mother can see David."

Sarah reached over and patted Gary on the shoulder.

As they rose higher, Gary noticed a massive storm system forming directly in their path. He pressed a button and turned a dial on the radio.

"Cedar City Flight Service Station, this is Cessna. We are on a heading of one-five-zero, over. Need abbreviated forecast. Over."

The speaker on the radio squawked, "Calling Cessna, please hold."

The plane changed its heading slightly, veering deliberately away from the clouds, while Gary shifted in his seat.

"Cessna, we show visibility reducing to less than one mile, light turbulence, and precipitation, winds forecast, 170 degrees at 20 knots."

Gary clicked the mic button. "Thank you, Cedar City." He released the button.

ANGEL IN FLIGHT

Under his breath, Gary said, "The storm's moving toward us." He examined his instruments again.

A look of concern showed on Sarah's rosy cheeks and nose when she glanced over at him. "Everything okay?"

"Ah, yeah. We just have some clouds, but we will not be flying through them for too long."

"We're going through clouds?" Now it was Sarah's turn to fidget in her seat. This time she couldn't grab on to anything because she was holding her infant so tightly.

Gary nodded. "Just for a few minutes." He peered out toward the ground. The clouds obstructed his view. He checked the VOR on the control panel. It read 147 degrees. "Well, at least I got you," he said tenderly while tapping on the instrument.

The tiny plane hit slight turbulence, enough to draw fear in Sarah's eyes.

"Wee!" Michael exclaimed from the back seat. "This is fun!"

"Daddy? Why is it so bumpy?" Robin asked.

"When the wings hit those little bumps where cold and warm air meet, the plane either drops or lifts, depending on how thick the air is. Like potholes in the road. If there's nothing to hold the car tire up, it sinks. Then, when it hits the hard road again, it bounces back up. Understand?"

"Yes," Robin answered softly. "How much longer until we land?" she asked with a notable anxious tone in her voice.

"Not long, Honey. Maybe twenty or thirty minutes. We just have to climb up this mountain somewhere over here, and then we'll be there." Gary pointed toward the windshield, which revealed nothing but solid white.

The plane shuttered violently. Gary placed a finger on the swinging altimeter. He tapped it harder each time.

"Something wrong?"

"Something's clogging the static port. It's what helps it determine the altitude. I'll just switch to in-cabin." Gary pulled a knob on the console, but the altimeter continued to sway. "Huh? That's weird."

"Tell me what's happening! Turn around! Let's go back home!"

"We should be fine. We're almost out of it."

"Is there a problem?" Fear froze on Sarah's face as she held David to her chest.

"Well, kinda, but I got my two VOR's, ADF, my directional and attitude. Those will keep us flying right. I'm turning to 170 degrees to move us out of this weather. It's still clear in that direction. We might have to land somewhere and wait it out."

Gary pressed a button on the radio. "Cedar City Flight Service Station. This is Cessna calling in."

"Go ahead, Cessna."

"We are making a deviation to our flight plan. The weather moved in faster than we thought, and my altimeter is malfunctioning. Going to land at Spanish Fork. Figure fifteen minutes or so."

"Cessna, we'll make a note to your flight plan of deviation."

Gary glanced at Sarah now with an expression of concern of his own. "It's the safest thing to do." He looked down at the bundle Sarah was holding and pulled back the blanket, so he could see David's face. Next, he turned to look at Michael huddled up, thumb in his mouth, and a blanket snuggled up to his chin. Gary's shaking hand found Robin's knee. He patted it.

Robin took Michael's free hand in hers. "We're going to be okay," she whispered.

Michael stared at her, sucking harder on his thumb.

With a tremulous voice and a forced smile, Gary said, "Everything's going to be just fine."

Just then, the plane shook violently. The electronics in the cockpit shut off, and the breaker popped out of the instrument panel. Gary frantically tried to reset the breaker. Now, the altimeter steadied itself but showed signs of sinking. After a third try, he reset the switch, and the instrument panel powered back on.

The clouds thinned. Little doubt remained of the danger when glimpses of the tops of trees passed to their left. When the cloud bank disappeared, an entire forest opened in front of them.

Sarah screamed, "Oh my God!"

Gary pushed the throttle on full and pulled back on the yoke. The ground rose toward them quickly. Doom shadowed Gary's face as he looked out over the engine. His head whipped left as a treetop flew past his window, then another, and another. The motor squealed; the plane shuddered.

8 — The Hero

Summer 1976

Robin broke the bond of Jeremy's arms. The pressure had made it hard to breathe as he held her tighter with each of her words. She sat up, pressing the hat to her head, and leaned against the tree.

"I remember that moment like it was yesterday. The trembling sound of my father's voice. The look of fear on my mother's face. She tried to mask it with a smile when she looked back at me while we were still up in the clouds. I knew when my dad touched my leg, and I felt his trembling hand, there was something terribly wrong. My daddy was never afraid of anything."

Tears pooled in Jeremy's eyes and spilled down his cheeks, which made her cry, too. She reached inside her bag and pulled out a package of tissues. He reluctantly took one, but preferred the back of his arm to wipe his face.

Jeremy's voice trembled. "You don't have to tell me more."

"I don't mind. You are the first guy to really listen."

Jeremy rubbed her back as she wrapped her arms around the one knee she could bend. Robin closed her eyes as he worked his way up her spine. She grabbed her hat to make sure it did not fall off.

When he stopped, and she propped herself against him, she said, "My mom was bent completely over, trying to cover up and protect my baby brother. Michael was crying so hard he couldn't breathe. The noise from the engine and the plane shaking so hard made it impossible to say anything. The last thing I remember was seeing the terror in Michael's eyes and thinking how sorry I was for being such an awful big sister." Robin grabbed Jeremy's hand the way she remembered holding Michael's, interlacing her fingers in his.

"I'm sure he loved you, anyway. That's what big brothers and sisters do. They are mean to you when you are alone, but they'll give their lives to save you. My big brother did the same thing, and if you ask my little brother and sister, they'd say I'm terrible."

"That may be so. But I—" The words failed to escape Robin's mouth.

Jeremy stroked Robin's forehead and pulled the hair from her face that stuck to her tears. He once again cradled her in his arms, gentler this time, as they both stared out at the lake.

After several minutes, he whispered, "How d'you survive?"

Robin closed her eyes. "We barely cleared some trees. I remember my dad yelling, 'Hold on! I'm going to land it in a clearing!' or something like that. I don't remember exactly. By then, I had my eyes closed and ears covered. I remember hearing stories later about how he tried to land it."

"Then, he was a hero for not giving up and striving to save you."

"I hadn't ever thought of it that way, but I guess you are right. The problem was the rough ground. It was on the side of a hill, and there were lots of rocks and tree stumps. So, when we hit, there was nowhere for the wheels to land and roll out. We just stopped. It was like slamming against a cement wall."

9 — Tree Angels

Winter 1965

Robin's body tumbled several times until she came to rest in the recess at the bottom of a nearby pine tree, uphill from the crash. Snow showered down upon her and served as a blanket to insulate her against the cold. Only her head protruded. Propped slightly against the trunk, she had a perfect view of the meadow.

Gary's body had smashed out most of the windshield of the airplane. Robin could see him on top of the rocks, bloody, bent, and lifeless. She tried to sit up, but could not feel her arms and legs.

"Daddy! Wake up!" she called out several times. "Get up! I can't move! Help me!"

A soft, moaning cry reached Robin's ears. She reckoned it was coming from inside the cockpit. "Mommy! Are you okay?" The whimpering continued for what seemed like hours, gradually fading to silence.

The sun came out from behind the clouds and lit up the trees. Snow was missing at the tops where the airplane brushed past before crashing. They looked like the heads of angels dressed in white standing guard before Robin.

Ice crystals swirled overhead from the wind. They appeared to take on a human form, like messengers of hope and comfort.

"Who are you?" she asked these ethereal beings floating above her. They did not answer. Faces suddenly appeared on them, then spun away just as fast. The hems of their robes brushed against her cheek. Although they were made of ice, they felt warm to the touch. "Are you going to take me to heaven?"

A mist flowed over the mountain top and enveloped the meadow. A spectral halo made of all the colors formed a ring around the sun. She loved rainbows and the distinct lines of color they formed. These, however, all seemed to bleed together.

The sky darkened, and flakes of snow descended around her. They were small at first, then grew larger. Although she lay below a tree branch, some flakes found her nose. They tickled, but she could not scratch. She could blink away the ones that landed on her eyelashes.

The tree angels disappeared when the flurry became dense. The tail of the airplane jutted out but gathered little tufts of snow at its edges. Robin could still see her dad's thick black hair a few feet away, but the rest of his body was gradually turning white. The angels covered him with a blanket to keep him warm while he slept.

Robin heard the faint sound of an airplane engine and closed her eyes. She had spent enough with her dad to know the difference between aircraft and cars. Her eyes closed as she listened to the rumble fade into the distance. Perhaps the angels could tell them where they crashed.

Opening her eyes, she called out, "Can you please fly back up and show them?" Robin expected their faces to peek through the veil of falling snow, but none appeared. She said it louder this time. "Hey! Can you hear me? Go get help!" A sensation of well-being overtook her. She closed her eyes and let that warm feeling bathe her body.

After what seemed an eternity, that soothing feeling faded. Pain crept into Robin's extremities. At first, it was cold, like someone was holding an ice cube against her skin. Then it burned. Agony shot up her legs and arms from all directions. Her cries shattered the silence in the little clearing. Consciousness faded as she heard the roar of the airplane engines once more, louder this time.

10 — Storyteller

Summer 1976

Robin surfaced from the depths of her ocean of memories. Her body ached from tensing so much. When she opened her eyes, she found Jeremy staring at her, mouth agape.

"What's wrong?"

He shook his head. "You are a great storyteller."

Robin's chest tightened. She honestly thought Jeremy would be different. Now he was making fun of her.

"I'm not making it up!" she complained, rolling away from him on legs that had grown numb. "No one believes me. I don't know why I even try." She slung her pencils and pad into the bag.

Jeremy stayed her hand. "I believe you," he said, dumbfounded.

"Then, why did you say I was telling stories?"

"I meant, you tell it really well. Every detail. I can't believe you remember all that."

Robin's anger turned to embarrassment. "Are you serious? You believe me?"

"Serious as a heart attack." Jeremy reached into her bag and pulled out her drawing pad. He thumbed through the pages and stopped on one of the angel sketches.

Robin protested and tugged on a corner. She relented when struck by the care he employed to turn and admire each page.

"You are the first person not to laugh after telling the angel story. Except possibly Michael. Even my aunt pats my hand and says I was probably unconscious and dreaming."

Jeremy glanced up from the drawing, confused. "Michael? Your little brother? I thought he—"

"No." Robin shook her head exasperatedly. "The man who found me on the mountain. His name is Michael, too. I didn't tell you that part yet."

Jeremy's attention returned to the ethereal winged creatures illustrated on the pages.

"So, this is what an angel looks like?"

After a long pause, and still not entirely sure Jeremy believed her or was just patronizing, she said, "Yes."

Turning the page, Jeremy said, "Oh. You watercolor, too?"

Robin nodded. "I draw the picture, then apply a wet brush, and it makes the color run, depending on how much water I use."

"You'll have to teach me your technique. This one is incredible." Jeremy extended his arms for a better view and blinked. "I wish I had my glasses."

Robin pried the book from his fingers and stuffed it back into the bag. "You can look at it later. When you have your glasses."

Jeremy stared out at the lake. "So, angels *are* real?" His eyes darted back and forth.

"They are to me." She sensed he believed her and was sorting out the truth for himself.

"Tell me the rest of the story." Jeremy laid back and propped his head on one arm.

Professor Anderson interrupted the moment. "C'mon, kids. Let's go. Time to get on the bus. We've got a long drive back."

How long had they been sitting under the tree? The sun was low in the sky behind them. Goosebumps formed on Jeremy's arms.

"Want to wear my jacket?" She removed a light pink windbreaker from the bottom of her bag.

As the other students march unhurriedly toward the bus as if in time to a funeral dirge, Jeremy said, "I think I'll pass. My shirt is on the bus."

11 — The Cemetery

It was 1:00 a.m. Jeremy followed Tom down the stairs from the second floor of the dormitory. Greg had talked them into meeting him at the cemetery across the street. Breaking the rules could result in their expulsion from the program and going home.

They found the dorm mother's apartment door closed, and all the lights were out but a single bulb over the building entrance. A sign taped to the glass shouted the rule in bold letters, 'All students must be in their rooms and lights out by 10 p.m.'

Tom placed a stick against the doorjamb before it shut. The allure of a midnight raid on the cemetery might garner favor with Greg, Jeremy's number one antagonist. Standing up to him at the lake might have gained a little of his respect. Then again, it might be when Greg unleashed his ultimate revenge on Jeremy for getting him kicked out of the roller rink. Three days of Greg being passively polite to him in class made the situation a little suspect.

Jeremy relaxed when he heard familiar voices off in the distance. He recognized Julie's Valley-Girl accent and Tina's exaggerated laugh.

Robin must be with them. At least, he hoped she was. He wanted to repeat that kiss they had at the lake and perhaps explore it a little more passionately. She had occupied his dreams, both day and night, since that moment. Even more than the intimacy, her story of survival haunted him, and he longed to hear more.

The streetlight lit the way to the entrance of the cemetery. Jeremy followed Tom in the voices' direction as the lamplight slowly waned, and the eerie shadows overtook them. A three-quarter moon hung overhead, turning the granite gravestones into glowing ghosts.

The two boys turned from the paved driveway down a row of headstones. They entered a small grove of trees.

"It's probably not a good idea to walk on the graves," Jeremy said, trailing Tom.

"They're dead, in a cement box, inside a casket ten feet underground. They aren't going to reach out and grab your foot like they do in the movies."

"How do you know?" Jeremy asked, searching the ground around his shoes.

"My mom and dad own a mortuary. Dad embalms them. Mom sews or glues their mouths shut, dresses them, and puts their makeup on. I help dig the graves with a backhoe and then cover them up after the funeral."

"So, you've seen dead bodies?"

Tom laughed. "All day. Every day. We store them in the basement in a fridge."

That thought terrified Jeremy. He now gained a new respect for Tom. In a way, it fit his personality. He showed little emotion, was quiet most of the time, and did everything Greg told him to do.

A flashlight beam landed on their faces. "Who's out there?" Since the laughter stopped, Jeremy guessed Tina was the one holding it and asking the question.

With a spooky voice, he moaned, "It is I, Thomas."

Not to be outdone, Jeremy used his best vampire hiss, "And Jeremy Andrew Kess, here to suck your blood."

"I didn't know your middle name was Andrew," said a voice Jeremy recognized. That gathered warmth in the chilly air. He was so pleased that Robin was bold enough to join them.

It took a minute for Jeremy's eyes to adjust to the darkness after Tina turned off the flashlight. He sat on the grass next to Robin, who reached over and gave him a little peck on the cheek.

"Aah. Isn't that sweet?" The unmistakable voice of Greg Malstrom from the shadows raised Jeremy's hackles.

"Stop it." Julie smacked Greg on the shoulder. "There won't be any of that tonight. We're all going to get along and have fun."

Greg rubbed his shoulder, but shot Jeremy an impudent glance. "I *am* having fun."

"At other's expense," Tina weighed in.

Robin's eyes searched the ghostly faces. "This place gives me the creeps. Do we have to stay here?"

"It's just a cemetery. A bunch of rocks and grass," Tom responded.

"We're sitting on top of a bunch of dead people," Julie said, lifting her hands and inspecting each one.

ANGEL IN FLIGHT

Tom laughed. "There's no such thing as dead people. Only living people and dead bodies. And dead bodies are just bones in a box. They can't hurt you."

Tina scooted over and patted the grass beside her. Tom accepted the invitation and sat.

Jeremy noticed Greg slithered into the shadows when no one was paying attention.

"Still, it creeps me out," Robin repeated.

Julie asked Robin, "Haven't you ever been in a cemetery before?"

Robin diverted her wide eyes toward Jeremy. He could tell she did not want to answer the question, and he certainly would not answer it for her. She had not gotten that far into her story yet.

"Yes. I have family buried in Bountiful and visit their graves occasionally. But I go during the daytime."

"I don't understand why Hollywood makes so many scary movies in cemeteries," Tom asserted rationally. "They always show them at night with lights on. There are never any lights in graveyards."

"And mist! They always show that creeping fog." Tina interjected. They all laughed.

"Boo!" Greg shouted, scaring Tina and Tom from behind, making them jump.

Tina bounced to her feet in a defensive stance while Tom took cover. "Greg! Has anyone ever told you what a jerk you are? I about peed my pants," she shrieked, tugging at the hem of her shorts.

Greg grabbed Tina by the throat with both hands. She struggled to free herself. With a slurping sound, he said, "I'm the ghost of Professor Anderson, and I am going to suck the life right out of that body of yours." He moved in to inflict a full-tongue kiss.

Tom jumped to his feet and tugged at Greg's powerful grasp. "Let go of her now!"

Tina tried to scream. Greg squeezed harder, muffling the sound.

"What? Are you her boyfriend now?" Greg scoffed.

Jeremy added to Tom's effort to free Greg's hold on Tina's throat. Together, they succeeded. She backed away, coughing and choking.

Julie put her arm around her, patting her back softly until she could breathe normally.

Tom pushed Greg. "What are you, insane?"

Jeremy fell in behind Tom, but let the two of them stare each other down.

Greg pushed Tom on the chest. Tom shoved back. Greg took a swing but missed when Tom ducked.

"Grow up, you guys!" Tina wheezed through gulps of air.

Robin inserted herself between the two the way Julie had at the skating rink.

"Stop it!" She stuck a finger directly at Greg's face.

Robin's bravado astounded Jeremy. He glanced at the grass and recognized the effort it took for her to stand. Now she commanded such intense will. She was *not* the Robin he knew.

"You are going to get us all in trouble," Julie warned in a whisper.

Greg reached over Robin and pushed Tom on the shoulder. "I didn't do anything wrong. You all are a bunch of crybabies."

Tom swung past Robin's head and connected with Greg's cheek. When Jeremy saw the flame rise in Greg's eyes, he had less than a second to pull Robin from the line of attack. He leaped and pushed her out of the way, knocking her to the ground. Jeremy caught a fist to the chin and dropped like a rock on top of her.

The world spun as Jeremy rolled off her. Barely conscious, he willed himself to sit, but toppled.

Greg backed off Tom and turned his fury on Jeremy. "Now, you're going to be sorry you got me thrown out of the rink!" He delivered a glancing kick to Jeremy's stomach.

A funny thought entered Jeremy's head. Greg would not miss if he knew how to strike a soccer ball. He laughed deliriously.

"What's so funny?" Greg fumed. He cocked his leg for a second strike.

Julie vaulted in and blocked him. She jabbed a trembling fist at his face. "That is enough!"

"Get... out... of here!" Tina commanded, pointing off into the night and shoving him away.

Greg stumbled on a tree root and fell backward.

"Never come anywhere near us again!" Tina spat, hovering over him.

Greg struggled to his feet and lunged toward Jeremy. Tina nailed him in the crotch with her knee, and he went down again, writhing in pain.

"I said go!" Tina ordered through a clenched jaw, then kicked him in the ribs. "Leave Jeremy alone. If you try it again, I'll crack your head open."

Jeremy staggered dizzily to his feet, slapping at an unseen opponent. Julie tugged on his shirt and guided him next to Robin.

Tina snapped a dead branch from a tree and wielded it high over Greg's head.

ANGEL IN FLIGHT

He shielded his face. "Alright! I'll go. I don't want to hang out with you losers, anyway." He wobbled to his feet and zigzagged his way into the rows of headstones.

Greg kicked at a gravestone, loosening it from its base. It fell after several tries. Then, he toppled over an obelisk, using his whole body.

The gang all gasped in horror when he attempted to strike a third, which did not budge. He fell to his knees in pain.

"Screw you! Screw all you guys! I was just having fun." Greg's voice trailed off into a whimper as he rolled around on his back, grasping his ankle.

"If you think choking someone is fun, go try out for a role in a horror movie," Julie called out.

"Shh. You are going to wake everyone up," Tina directed.

Greg pulled himself up with the aid of the headstone and limped away.

Now fully conscious, Jeremy rolled over to assess Robin's injuries.

"I think I'm okay. You broke my fall," Robin reported as she patted herself down. "I'm worried about you. He clocked you good."

Jeremy rubbed his neck and chin. "I rolled with his punch."

After several minutes, Jeremy stood and helped Robin to her feet.

"Let's try to fix the headstone," Julie said as she walked toward the fallen marker.

"Why? Greg did it. Not us," Tina reacted.

Robin added with a voice of reason, "If he gets in trouble, we all do."

The three girls tried raising the stone back onto its base. Jeremy and Tom joined in. They ultimately got it standing upright with one enormous effort but were unsuccessful in lifting it onto the footing.

"What about that pointy one?" Julie asked.

The five gave all their effort without success.

"How'd he do it?" Tom asked. "These suckers literally weigh a ton. Back home, we have to use a tractor to place them."

"The human body is capable of immeasurable feats if faced with danger or stress," Robin lectured with authority. "When your adrenalin starts pumping, you can do just about anything."

"Where'd you learn all that?" Jeremy asked.

"I read a lot. Our house is practically a library. And, you know—" She drew his eye to her extremities.

Jeremy nodded.

"Plus, that guy is strong. I honestly thought he was going to kill me," Tina said, rubbing her neck.

A pair of bouncing flashlight beams appeared in the distance, coming toward them.

"Hey, kids! What are you doing out here?" a male voice called out into the blackness.

"Run that way," Tom whispered to Julie and Tina, pointing in one direction. "I'll go this way." He turned to Jeremy and Robin. "You guys hide. We'll lure them away."

The two girls ran like the devil through the rows of stones. One flashlight followed them while the other pursued Tom. Jeremy and Robin moved a few rows back and hid behind a large monument. They peeked around it as the lights faded.

"Do you think they made it?" Jeremy whispered.

"I hope so," Robin replied. "If not, I'm dead. My aunt will ground me for the rest of my life."

Jeremy could tell by the behavior of the flashlights joining at the other end of the field that just maybe the others escaped apprehension. The way the beams of light swung around, still searching, gave him hope.

"What do we do now?"

"We sit and wait until they leave."

12 — Integrity, Honor, and Respect

Swirls of alizarin crimson and yellow ochre acrylic paint filled the center of Robin's palette. She blended in a touch of white. Closing one eye and holding up her brush, Robin compared the color on the tip with the model's flesh tone. She applied a small amount to the illustration board propped up on the front of her bench.

A floppy, wide-brimmed straw hat the model wore cast a shadow over half of her face. A stray curl tickled her nose. Brushing it away changed the placement of her hat. Several of the students complained the shadow had moved, making it difficult to continue. The model attempted to adjust the hat but deepened the shadow more.

Professor Matthews studied the students' work, then stepped onto the stage. He adjusted the hat until it reached the original position with coaching from the class.

From behind the students, Professor Anderson lectured, "Class. You shouldn't be too bothered by what you see. You must learn to improvise. You have your original sketch laid out by now, and any changes in her pose shouldn't affect the outcome. Now she is nothing more than a reference for finishing what you started." That triggered groans from a few.

Especially bothered by the changes, Greg threw down his brush. Robin noticed a pronounced limp in his step as he stood and hobbled to the sink with his palette in hand.

Jeremy had a blushing scrape on the side of his chin. His eyes also followed Greg as he shuffled back to his seat. Tom was noticeably distant, choosing to take a position in the room opposite Greg. Not once did he engage Robin or any of the gang from last night's raid.

Robin considered it a miracle that they all made it back to their rooms without getting caught. She had entered a cryptic note in her diary to remember one of the scariest and most memorable events of her life. She also sketched from memory a statue of an angel near their hiding spot. Of course, it had been too dark to make out the details. She elicited a promise from Jeremy that he would escort her back, but in the daylight.

An imposing figure dressed in a midnight-blue uniform entered the classroom. The entire class shifted focus from the model to the police officer.

Robin cringed. She did her best to conceal her fright.

Professor Anderson greeted the officer close enough behind Robin that she could hear him whisper, "What can I do for you?"

"I'm here to investigate a vandalism case that might involve one or more of your students," he said, loud enough for everyone to hear.

Robin froze. Try as she might, she could not move her hand. She stared at the model—brush tip hovering at the surface of the illustration board. Slowly, Robin rotated her head to assess the reaction of the gang. They, too, were motionless. Several of the students stood to get a better look at the commotion. Greg glared at Tom, who shrugged but continued painting. Even the model broke pose to gawk at the spectacle.

"What sort of vandalism are we talking about? The dorms?"

"A report came in early this morning from campus security of screams in the cemetery across the street. They responded in the general direction. When confronted, several youths took off running."

"Was anyone hurt?"

"They searched the area for victims but found none. But they found this."

Robin could not help herself. She turned when the officer handed over a Polaroid photograph of the toppled stones.

Her heart raced as she looked up into the officer's eyes and smiled. He smiled back. At least if his investigation led to her, he might show mercy since she was innocent of the crime.

Robin's gaze swept back on the others, who avoided eye contact. Now she hoped Jeremy kept his bruise concealed.

"Let's go into my office," Dr. Anderson said with a note of worry.

The two men disappeared behind the closed door.

The professor steadied himself on the corner of his desk. He gestured for his guest to sit.

"I prefer to stand," the officer said, patting his gun and other gear hanging from his belt.

Professor Anderson employed the reading glasses hanging from a chain around his neck. "What am I looking at here?"

"They pushed two headstones over. It appears others tried putting them back, unsuccessfully."

He returned the photo. "You think this was the work of our students?"

The officer flicked the photo with his fingernail. "The campus officers observed a juvenile male fleeing toward the dorms. We can't be sure, at this point, he had anything to do with it. Mrs. Walker, the dorm mother, said all students were in bed, lights out by ten."

He nodded. "Those are our rules."

"By the time they caught up to him, he was already inside, and the door locked. Walker also states only your students occupy her building. The enrolled summer students are reassigned to other housing. That means at least one of yours was out past the ten o'clock curfew."

The professor's eyes narrowed. "I see. How can I help? Would you like to address the class?"

"I can do that."

Greg raised a fist to Tom when Professor Anderson and the police officer entered his office. He formed the words, 'I'm going to kill you.'

Tom shrugged. "I didn't say anything."

Jeremy squirmed when Greg stood and wove his way toward him. "Did you call the cops?" he hissed.

Jeremy shook his head.

Greg glared at Tina. That rage, Robin had seen so often, flared.

"Where I'm from, we don't call cops. We take care of business ourselves," Tina said defiantly.

"Who did then?" he asked, looking up and down the row.

"Go sit down," Julie ordered. "And shut up!"

"If something happens, I'm taking you all down with me." Greg clenched his teeth; the veins on his neck bulged.

"I have no idea what you are talking about," Robin said with a shrewd smirk. "Did you do something wrong and need to blame someone else?"

The uninvolved showed their bewilderment.

"Turn around. Mind your own business," Tina threatened them while drawing little circles in the air.

Professor Anderson emerged from his office. The law enforcement officer followed him to the stage at the back of the classroom. He dismissed the model. The guitar she held as a prop fell from her hands, making a harsh sound when it hit the floor. Everyone stopped what they were doing and set down their materials.

The policeman held the photograph high enough for everyone to see. Tom squinted at the picture while Greg turned away.

"If any of you know who committed this vandalism in the cemetery last night, I would appreciate you coming forward. You may remain anonymous." He bowed toward the professor. "I'm sure your teacher would be happy to relay the information to me."

The officer wandered among the benches, showing the photo to each one. Robin was sure he was assessing every reaction. She caught Julie and Tina sharing glances from the corner of her eye. Jeremy stared straight ahead. Greg faced away toward the window.

Tom raised his hand. "What kind of damage was done? I can't see it from here."

The officer stepped forward and handed it to him.

Tom sat straighter. "Why do you think it had anything to do with one of us?"

"Following up on a lead."

"What time did it happen?" Tom maintained his composure like a reporter firing questions at a press conference.

"Sometime after one o'clock."

"We're all in bed by ten." Tom handed the photo back to the officer.

The room filled with chatter.

Tina rubbed her neck. Looking more closely, Robin noticed significant purplish marks forming under her flesh.

When another question distracted the officer, Robin whispered, "Tina, button up your shirt. Your bruise is showing."

Julie gave a confirming nod when Tina glanced her way. Tina sunk back and tugged on her collar.

The offer announced, "We take desecration of graveyards seriously in this town. If one of those belonged to your ancestor, you would want the culprits punished for the crime."

Most of the students nodded, including Tom. "I work at a cemetery. That would not be tolerated," he added.

Way to throw him off your scent. Robin smiled at Tom admiringly.

With that, the officer gathered up the photo and stuck it in his front shirt pocket. "You all have a nice day."

Professor Anderson led him through the door and outside. As soon as the door latched, Greg slithered through the benches, knocking knees and toppling easels. He grabbed Tom by the t-shirt and raised his fist. Everyone in the room gasped.

"Don't you dare say a word! I *will* kill you!" His words blazed white-hot.

Tom put up his hands in surrender. A smile curled on his lips.

Greg glanced around the room. All eyes trained on him.

"Do the right thing, Greg," Tina said. "If you don't, I'll tell them you strangled me. We're talking an assault charge on your record." She pulled down her collar to reveal the bruise. "Your rich lawyer daddy won't be able to defend you."

Greg knocked Tom's painting across the room, stomped back to his bench, and swept his supply box onto the floor, scattering his brushes and paints in all directions.

"I'm out of here." He marched for the door. It opened as he reached for the handle.

The police officer stepped in and said, "Son, why don't you come with me."

Greg's head drooped. Then he looked back at Robin and the gang. Was that genuine remorse? Because of his actions or for getting caught? She was not sure.

Tears trickled down his cheeks when the voice of Dr. Anderson from outside said, "I'll be calling your parents."

Robin swung her leg around off the bench and pushed herself up as all the other students rushed to the window. Jeremy made space, so she could watch as the officer escorted Greg away.

The students, except Robin and Jeremy, scattered back to their seats when Professor Anderson returned. Robin could not move fast enough.

"Please return to your seats," he said.

Jeremy tucked his arm in hers as they maneuvered their way.

Dr. Anderson paced for several minutes, scratching his chin. Robin was sure his eyes were swelling with tears of disappointment.

"When I convinced the board to let me start this program, I made one promise." He stopped, faced the class, and stared each student, one by one, in the eye. "That promise was each of you would leave here, not just as the best professional artists Utah has to offer, but having learned honor, integrity, honesty, and respect. Respect for each other, for each other's artwork and property. In that mission, I have failed." He hung his head, pulled a handkerchief from his back pocket, and wiped his eyes.

A deathly silence descended on everyone present. Robin peered through watery eyes at Jeremy, moved by those words. Tom froze like a statue. Julie gushed tears. Tina slumped with her arms folded; a gloomy disposition enshrouded her.

'Respect for each other's artwork' echoed in Robin's ears. Then why did he tear up Jeremy's homework in front of the class? Maybe he learned a lesson himself.

"If there is anyone who cannot commit to living that code of professional artists, I ask that you gather your things and go home now." He scanned the room. No one moved, except Tina, who raised her hand.

"Does that mean the program will be canceled?"

"It depends on what the cops find out. For now, I want you all to do the best work you've ever done."

The mist of suspicion and doubt lingered as he ordered the model to return to her place on the stage.

13 — The Inner Self

The girls' dorm mother, Mrs. Olson, opened the door to her apartment by the building entrance, startling Robin.

She followed Robin's gaze out the window. "Waiting for someone?"

"Yes."

Before the inquiry into the cemetery incident, Mrs. Olson was extraordinarily stern with all the female students and strict about the rules. Now she had become overbearing, and Robin dodged her attention whenever possible.

"Who are you waiting for?" she asked coldly.

The probing nature of her question left Robin hesitant to answer. "One of my classmates. We're supposed to work on an assignment together."

Two other female students pranced past in tiny silk shorts and midriffs.

"Ladies!" Mrs. Olson called out, halting the girls mid-stride.

"Yes, Mrs. Olson?" one of them asked.

She regarded their clothing disapprovingly. "You know that violates the dress code."

One girl glanced down with a frown, then shrugged. "What do you mean? It's hot outside."

"Unless you are participating in a sporting activity, your shorts are to reach mid-thigh and your midsection covered." She raised a deliberate fleshy finger back down the hall. "Go change!"

The other whined, "We are playing football. That's a sport."

"March!"

Robin shrunk beside Mrs. Olson and cowered when the belligerent girl sneered.

"You sound like my mom!"

A furtive curl crept into the corner of Mrs. Olson's lips. "That's why they call me dorm mother. Now go!"

The girls obeyed and shuffled down the hallway.

Robin stood frozen. She expected Mrs. Olson to find something to scold her for.

"I'm glad I don't have to worry about you," Mrs. Olson said, looking Robin up and down. "Modesty and virtue become you."

That relieved the anxiety building in Robin's chest. "Thank you."

If her legs had not been so scarred, she would not dress so 'modestly,' as Mrs. Olson put it. She had a pair of shorts and wore them in her fenced backyard at home, where no one could see her. The doctor had said that some sunshine was healthy.

A toddler in nothing but a diaper appeared in the doorway to the apartment. Robin stooped and offered the back of her hand to the child as if he were a puppy. The baby acted shy at first, then ran to her.

"What is your name, little man?"

He mumbled something unintelligible and held up a finger.

"I one."

"His name is Scotty, after his father."

Robin lifted him into her arms and placed him on her hip. "Hello, Scotty, who is one. My name is Robin."

The dorm mother's face softened, and she made little effort to hide her surprise.

"Hey, you are good with kids."

"Thanks. I love them. I want to have a ton of them someday."

Mrs. Olson narrowed her gaze. "How would you like to babysit for us this Friday night? I can't remember the last time we went on a date."

It was true. Robin loved kids and often babysat for her neighbors back home. Since her aunt never married and her siblings were killed in the plane crash, she longed for a little brother or sister. In a way, she felt it was her atonement for being so mean to her brother Michael and resenting her baby brother, David, for *stealing* all the attention.

"I'd love to." Robin poked Scott in the tummy. "Would you like me to babysit you?" He hugged her. "I guess that means yes."

Jeremy opened the entrance door. He wore athletic shorts and the half-tee with the illustrated soccer ball as promised.

Mrs. Olson gave him the once over with a disapproving scowl.

The two girls she had sent to change returned. One wore longer shorts, the other warm-up pants, and both had changed to full-length t-shirts. In their hands hung gym bags. Smirks painted their faces.

"Is this better?" one of them asked, sprinkled with a little teenage attitude.

"Much better. Yes."

The girls pushed through the door. Robin could still hear them laughing even after the door closed. She knew as soon as they were away from Mrs. Olson's watchful eye, they would strip off those pants and stuff them into their bags.

Mrs. Olson turned her attention back to Jeremy. He fidgeted uncomfortably with his art box and portfolio in hand.

"I'm not your dorm mother, but—" With pursed lips, her eyes drifted to his bare legs and stomach.

Jeremy followed her gaze. "What's wrong?" He frowned.

"I'll explain later," Robin said, patting him on the shoulder.

"What can I do for you, young man?" Mrs. Olson asked, standing erect and jutting out her pudgy chin.

"I—"

Robin came to his rescue. "We are working on our homework together. I'm helping him redo one of his assignments."

"Classmate? I didn't know it was a *boy*," she said with a tinge of accusation.

Robin winced.

"And *where* are you doing this?" she demanded, hands now on hips.

More like asking permission, Robin said, "In the kitchen."

Mrs. Olson grimaced at her watch. "You have two hours. Quiet time is at nine o'clock and lights out at ten." Grabbing Scott from Robin's arms, she ordered, "No hanky-panky up there!"

She left no doubt in Robin's mind that she meant business.

Stepping forward and standing next to Robin, Jeremy said resolutely, "Yes, ma'am. I'll take good care of her."

"You better. She's a sweet girl."

Robin felt her face glow. Compliments were rare since she had turned into an ill-tempered teen. Margaret was weary from caring for her all those years and now focused attention on Robin's grandmother.

Jeremy's eyes probed every detail of Robin's face. He'd done that once before, and it made her a little uncomfortable.

"Yes, she is beautiful."

The heartbeat in Robin's head surged. The blush in her cheeks grew red-hot. She could not bear his piercing stare any longer and diverted her gaze.

Mrs. Olson chuckled. "Oh, to be young again. I remember how that felt," she sighed, clicking her tongue and shaking her head. "You two go do your homework. I'll check on you after a while."

It was Robin's turn to escort Jeremy. Down the hall, they paraded, arm in arm, to the stairwell. They turned back to find Mrs. Olson still glaring. Robin waved and smiled. Mrs. Olson nodded and disappeared into her apartment.

"Is she always so strict?" Jeremy asked as they ascended the stairs.

Robin held on to the railing and navigated each step. "Nothing gets past her now."

"How were you able to sneak out the other night?"

"They were out of town for two days. A substitute checked on us, but left at ten. And yours?"

"Mrs. Walker lets us do whatever we want. Mr. Walker even comes out and kicks the soccer ball around with me. He's the one who told us about the stick-in-the-door trick. But not to get in trouble, or the stick would disappear, which it has."

"So, you *do* have to be back by ten, or they lock you out?"

A mischievous grin gleamed on Jeremy's face. "We found another stick."

Robin laughed.

Jeremy set his things on the kitchen table once they reached the common area at the end of the hall.

"I'll go get mine. Be right back."

Two doors down the hall, Robin entered her dorm room. She inspected herself in the mirror. The hair on the back of her head was still in place. A little extra lip gloss and blush on her cheeks freshened her glow. She felt giddy. Did he really think she was beautiful? Now she laid a hand on her chest and felt the beat of her heart. It was pounding.

Was there anything in her closet more appealing than the burnt-orange blouse and blue jeans? No, all her clothes were drab. Aunt Margaret shopped for her clothes in the ladies' department where she worked. All her shirts were white, or tan and the pants were black or gray. This was her only pair of blue jeans, but they were too hard to put on. Plus, it would take too long to change. She slammed the closet door. Color, that's what was missing!

Robin picked up her art stuff and returned to the kitchen.

Two other students searched the refrigerator and cupboards for food to prepare for their dinner.

"You two going to hog the table?" one asked.

ANGEL IN FLIGHT

"We're doing our homework," Robin replied defensively.

"You're supposed to do that in your room. This is for eating and recreating," said the other girl, turning on the television in the corner next to a well-used foosball table.

"We were here first. Plus, the light is out over my desk," Robin argued.

"No boys allowed in the dorms."

"Well, we need a place to eat."

Jeremy gathered his things. "We can go over to mine if you want."

Placing a hand on his arm, Robin said to Jeremy, "No. We were here first." She laid her items out to claim the rest of the table. "They can either sit on the couch or go to their rooms."

The tennis-match-like exchange of angry glances made Jeremy's head swing. Brushing past one girl defiantly, Robin filled a cup with water at the sink, then sat down.

The other two girls banged dishes and slammed doors to be as loud and annoying as they could.

"Just ignore them," Robin urged.

Touching only the edges, Jeremy gently picked up the project she was working on. The current assignment was to illustrate 'The Inner Self.'

"This is disturbing," he observed.

It depicted a nude girl rolled in plastic wrap, struggling to free herself. The surface of the skin on her legs and arms appeared to be distorted.

"Was this intentional, or did the acrylic paint dry that way?" he asked, pointing at the parts of the flesh peeking through the plastic.

"What does it say to you?" she returned, mimicking an answer she once heard an artist give an admirer. Robin expected this piece might lead to the *big reveal* of all her superficial flaws, but she did not care anymore. She was growing weary of hiding them.

He shrugged. "You've painted the plastic folds the way you do the angels' dresses. It's really cool." Jeremy narrowed his focus. "Why does it look like the skin is sliced up? And she looks like she's suffocating."

Suddenly, Robin regretted choosing this way of illustrating her *inner self*. Would her good attributes be enough to hold his affection and be blind to her outward faults?

"She's struggling to break out—knowing she's capable of so much more but restricted by her physical limitations."

"If she grew some long, sharp nails, she could pierce through the plastic."

The corner of Jeremy's lip turned up slightly when she held up her hands. Her nails were unpainted and short from chewing them.

"I know. It's a nasty habit." Now Robin was self-conscious about her hands and tucked them up under her thighs.

He showed her his nails. "I need to clip mine. Maybe you can bite mine for me," he said jokingly.

Robin's face wrinkled. "Ew! Disgusting." She pushed them away. "Look how dirty they are."

Jeremy laughed so hard she thought he would fall off the chair.

The two other girls both groaned.

"That is so gross," one howled.

"Let's go eat in our room," said the other, picking up her plate, fork, and glass.

They left.

Robin snickered. "You know how to clear out a room."

"I do my best." Jeremy turned his attention back to Robin's assignment, studying the face. "She looks panicked."

"She's feeling suffocated, trapped. Even if she had nails, it would be a struggle to break free." Pushing her piece to the side, she said, "Let's have a look at yours."

The illustration depicted the figure of a young man, transparent like a clear plastic mannequin. Inside the torso area was another human-like shape, stretching its arms and legs, pressing on the outer shell.

Jeremy picked up Robin's piece again and set it next to his. "They are incredibly similar."

Drawing a circle with her finger around the midsection, Robin commented, "Yours looks like he's pregnant. The little one inside looks female. See? She's got big hips and boobs."

"No, he doesn't. That is supposed to be the real him, trying to get out. Those are muscles in his legs and a big chest because he works out a lot," Jeremy groused.

"If I didn't know any better, I'd say you are trying to express your feminine side."

Now visibly irritated, Jeremy whined, "No, I'm not!" He mimed an imaginary wall between them.

Robin played along, feigning effort to pierce through that wall, and poked Jeremy in the stomach. Mockingly, she said, "I'm sorry. Did I hurt your little male ego?"

Relaxing, Jeremy grasped her sleeve and pulled her toward him. "I'll show you my male ego if you show me your female—"

Robin creased her lips with a finger. "Shh. Mrs. Olson could come in at any minute."

ANGEL IN FLIGHT

His other hand crept up her arm, then gently pulled her closer. Their eyes locked. This time, she could not look away.

The setting sun cast a warm glow through the window onto his golden hair. His eyes were bluer than she'd ever seen them before. Bent forward, she could feel his hot breath on her lips. Closing her eyes, Robin waited for contact.

The kiss was gentle and sweet. She had forgotten about Mrs. Olson, and the world around her disappeared into that moment. His hands crept ever higher up her arms, all the while drawing her closer and closer to him. Their chairs slid nearer, and knees touched. Lips probed each other as their heads shifted from side to side.

When he stopped to draw in oxygen, Robin opened her eyes to find his twinkling.

"You *do* have a masculine side," she said. "You are a great kisser." She closed her eyes again and puckered for round two.

His chair scooted beside hers; their hips touched. Jeremy's arms, wrapped around her, felt soothing and safe. As the kiss grew more passionate, he pulled her to him even tighter. She winced and moaned slightly when the twisting of her back was more than she could bear. He let go a little of her shoulder. His hand found the back of her neck, so she could not move her head, even if that was her desire.

The kiss ended with their foreheads pressed together. His eyes intensely lured out her soul, and there was nothing she could do to stop him. Robin ignored all that her aunt had warned her about boys and their intentions. She would not deny herself of Jeremy's affection.

Jeremy's fingers crept up through her sticky hair. A slight furrow appeared on his brow when she pulled back. Instinctively, Robin grabbed his wrist and withdrew from his embrace.

"What's wrong? What did I do?"

Robin moved her chair away and probed the back of her head.

"I don't want you touching me there." She tried smoothing the disturbed clump covering her bald spot.

With outstretched arms, Jeremy protested. "Where? I didn't do anything wrong."

"I mean, I don't want you touching the back of my head."

Lowering his arms, Jeremy's voice softened. "Why not?"

Backing away farther still, Robin used both hands to pat it down. "I have a bald patch, and I don't want anyone to see it."

"Oh really? I didn't feel one." Jeremy's expression turned from frustrated to inquisitive. "C'mon. Let me see."

"No. It's horrible!"

"I don't care. It won't bother me. I promise. Just let me—" Jeremy got down on all fours and, with a playful grin, crawled toward Robin like a leopard stalking its prey. With a hand on her extended leg, he drew closer.

That made Robin giggle nervously. "Why?"

"Because. I care." He reached out to touch her face.

Robin pushed his hand away. "No."

"Please."

She stopped resisting.

Enticing her in for a comforting hug, Jeremy whispered in her ear, "It's part of your story. But it shouldn't define who you are."

"You are a freak. You know that Mr. Jeremy Andrew Kess?" Burying her face in his shoulder and wrapping her arms around his neck, Robin braced herself for humiliation.

He lightly stroked her hair. "Another day."

Pushing him back, Robin stared unblinkingly. "The broken glass from the windshield scalped me. They had to sew it back on. It's pretty ugly."

With the intensity of a movie actor uttering his iconic line, he said, "There is nothing about you that is ugly. Just the things that happened to you."

"That may be so. But I—"

"Shh. Some other time."

Jeremy stroked Robin's forehead, brushing hair away from her face. His finger traced her eyebrow, nose, chin, and stopped on her lips. He kissed them. "How did you survive?"

ANGEL IN FLIGHT

14 — Angel Michael

Winter 1965

When Robin opened her eyes, it was night. The sky was crystal clear. An icy breeze kissed her nose and cheeks, the only part not buried in the heavy blanket of snow. Light, reflecting from a three-quarter moon, lit up the little meadow with the brightness of the daytime sun.

The faint outline of the airplane broken in half was visible under a thick layer of fresh powder.

"Daddy?" Robin called. She could no longer see his head. "Did the angels take you?" Looking up in the sky, she imagined where heaven was beyond the stars and hoped he was there, watching over her.

"Mommy? Are you awake?"

No response came from the gaping hole in the side of the fuselage where a door used to be.

"Michael? Can you hear me?"

The meadow remained silent. Snow blanketed the tops of the trees where the airplane had struck. Gone were Robin's angel friends. She felt alone. What she wouldn't give to see her little brother, Michael, again, even if he was annoying. She wished she could wrap her arms around her daddy's neck and hear him tell her that everything was going to be alright.

Robin had never experienced these emotions of fear and loneliness. Her body was numb, and it felt as though it was not part of her anymore— a little like when she dreamed at night. She loved the sensation of soaring like a seagull or diving deep in the water like a dolphin. The difference was, in this nightmare, she could not move. Fantasy frequently took her to the faraway lands spoken of in the books her mother read to her. This adventure was not one she would have ever hoped for.

Voices carried through the forest. Robin saw flashlights bobbing up and down between the trunks of the trees. Her pulse quickened. The angels showed them where to find her. She closed her eyes and offered up a little prayer of gratitude to the now unseen spirits.

"I found the tail! Over here, men! This is it!" The rescuer's shouts echoed off the trees.

The beam of his flashlight lit up the broken tail section. The familiar numbers Robin had heard her father speak into the microphone became visible. That's how she had learned to read—identifying them on the side of each craft they saw.

The other rescuers waded through the snow, following the beam of light's path toward the downed airplane.

"No sign of a fire, sir," one called out.

The man with the flashlight gestured wide circles around the little meadow. "Watch your step, boys! Keep your eyes open for dangerous debris or victims. They could be scattered all over the place the way this thing broke apart!"

Someone shined a light into what remained of the cockpit. Robin's first thought was they wouldn't find anyone because the angels took them all.

"We have a body!" shouted one man.

"Another one over here! Probably the pilot!" hollered another.

They cleared away the snow, revealing the familiar dark hair of her father.

Tears melted the snowflakes that skirted the corners of Robin's eyes. "Daddy," she softly cried, but no one heard her.

Several flashlights trained on Gary's lifeless and contorted form. One man pulled off his glove, bent down, and touched Gary's neck. "Solid as a rock." He put his glove back on. "My guess is he died on impact."

"There's movement!"

The men rushed back to the cockpit.

Just then, an airplane flew overhead, low and slow. The men all shined their lights up at the plane, which dipped its wings back and forth like a teeter-totter.

"Female. Still warm. Has a pulse."

Those words had meaning. "Mommy?" Robin mustered enough strength to move her lips.

"Get a stretcher over here!" a commanding voice broke through the cold. "Let's extract and place her on a board. But be careful!"

ANGEL IN FLIGHT

Three men used brute force to pull back the wrinkled door to the cockpit. Moments later, they freed Sarah's body from the harness and laid her out on the stretcher.

"Tie that head down. I don't want it flopping all over."

One rescuer stole a towel from a rucksack and delicately tied it to one side of the board, draped it across Sarah's forehead, then fastened it to the other.

"What's that she's got a hold of?" the commander inquired, pointing at Sarah's arms, holding something tight to her chest.

Sarah whimpered softly as the rescuer attempted to pull her arms apart.

"Something wrapped in a blanket." The man sat up. "A baby, sir."

"Dammit! What are people thinking, transporting an infant like that? A little turbulence could knock that child right out of her arms." The commander shined a light down at the wrapped bundle. "Check it for a pulse."

"I'm afraid there isn't one, sir."

"Get her out of here."

One tried to remove the deceased child from Sarah's arms. She whimpered louder.

"Let her keep it."

The man threw a blanket over Sarah while two other men lifted each end of the stretcher.

"Get her off the mountain, now!"

They took off running through the snow.

"Flight plan says there were four souls on board, sir," said one of the two remaining men to their commander.

"Gentlemen. We have one more body to find. Let's pray for one more miracle."

The men moved cautiously toward the tail section a few yards from the cockpit. "Possibly over here," said one man.

Probing the snow, they found nothing. Toward a punctured section of the tail, the man lifted the rear flap. "I see a shoe." He quickly trenched down through the snow. "We have a body. A boy. About two, maybe three. Afraid he didn't make it."

Michael's name formed on Robin's lips as she observed the men bow their heads as if in prayer over his body. She did not want to witness any more of the tragedy. It was already too horrifying to watch them carry her mother and baby brother away.

"Gentlemen. Thank you for your effort. Never a pleasant experience. That makes four. Dawn comes in a few hours. We'll come back at first light," the commander said, pointing toward Gary.

The men draped a blanket over her father's body. A beam of a flashlight surveyed the area and flashed across her face, temporarily blinding her. The others packed up their gear and started down the hill. The man with the flashlight hesitated, then followed.

"What about me?" Robin squeaked.

The man stopped and placed a hand to his ear. "Did you hear that?" he called to the others.

"No. Hear what?"

"I could swear I heard a voice."

Robin was so weak she could barely make a sound. "I'm over here."

"There it is again. A little girl's voice."

"I didn't hear anything."

"From over there. Under those trees."

Again, his flashlight blinded Robin, and she closed her eyes.

"Is there someone over here?" he yelled.

The commander's voice roared across the clearing, "What on earth are you two doing?"

"Michael thinks he hears something, sir!" called out the other man.

"It's me. Robin," she whispered.

The man dropped his flashlight in the snow, creating an eerie glow that lit the little space up under the pine tree.

"I found another one!" he screamed, dropping to his knees.

The other two men joined him.

To Robin, their faces seemed like the angels she had seen swirling around her before. Tears welled up in her eyes, blurring her vision. She tried blinking them away, but that only made it harder for her to see.

"Shall I go fetch another stretcher?" a man asked.

"No time for that. Find another blanket," the commander ordered.

"We're all out, sir."

Through gritted teeth, the commander hissed, "Get them off the victims." He nodded toward the deceased.

"Yes, sir!"

By the time he returned with the two blankets, the others had thoroughly cleared the snow off Robin's body.

The rescuer inspected each part and shook his head. "It's a wonder she's still alive."

ANGEL IN FLIGHT

"The angels saved me," Robin whispered, now able to see the face of the man who came back for her.

"Angels?"

"Yes. There were lots of them." Robin bobbed her head about as if pointing with her nose.

"Thank god for those angels, Robin."

Robin blinked. "What is your name?"

The man looked up at his commander, who nodded. "My name is Michael. Nice to meet you."

"Just like my brother. Did you find him?"

Michael wiped a tear away and glanced up at the others.

The commander interrupted, "Let's put you onto this blanket, young lady." He pointed at one end. "You. Take that side."

The other man ducked under the branches of the tree. Together, the three men pried Robin's twisted body from the snow and gently placed her on the blanket. They covered her with the second one. Each grabbed a corner, lifted, and waded through the drift, retracing their steps down the hill.

SHELLY PULSE

15 — Angels in White

Dr. Richard Young examined the worst of the car crash victims. The emergency room gurneys and waiting room filled to capacity. This small-town hospital near the highway inherently received more patients than it could typically handle during winter. The unexpected storm dumped a lot of snow, followed by freezing rain.

Nurse Pearl Hillman pleaded with the uninjured family members to either stay in their cars or move to the other waiting room on the other side of the hospital. An orderly used his large frame to herd the crowd through the door.

"Thank you, John," said the nurse.

"You are welcome, ma'am," the orderly replied, clapping his hands like he was dusting them off. "Anything for you."

The nurse grinned and patted him on his enormous shoulder. "Help me wheel this one into that room." She nodded toward an open door.

He did as she ordered.

Standing by Dr. Young's side, Nurse Hillman asked, "Who's next?"

Speaking as though the patient could not hear, he said, "I think this one can sit. Let's free up the bed."

The nurse helped the portly man off the gurney. He placed his injured foot on the cold tile floor and lost his balance. She struggled to hold him upright.

"John! I need your help!"

Orderly John rushed to assist the patient to a chair.

"Thanks again!"

"Don't move anyone without me, you hear?" he scolded.

"Yes, sir!"

A gust of chilled air and powdered ice enveloped Dr. Young when the emergency room door opened.

The doctor shielded his face. "What you got?" he inquired of the man dressed in a dark green uniform and helmet.

"Air crash victim, sir." The rescuer propped open the door. Two equally clad men stomped their feet as they entered, hands on either side of a double-pole stretcher.

"Put him right here." Dr. Young patted the vacated gurney.

"She's a her, sir." The soldiers laid the soaking-wet stretcher on top of the clean, dry sheets.

Dr. Young beckoned John. "Get that patient out of the exam room. We're going to need it."

The bewildered look said John did not know where to move the patient.

Keeping his temper in check, Dr. Young ordered, "Through that door and out into the hall, for now. Warmer in there."

John jumped into action.

The doctor drew back the blanket to find Sarah's eyes swollen shut, her face blue, nose and lips purple. "How long was she out there?"

"Cedar City lost track of them about nine hours ago. An hour just to come down off the mountain."

The doctor shook his head. "Vitals?"

The soldier rested a hand on her leg. "Blood pressure when we first picked her up was 110 over 60. Best read we could get. Pulse weak. Low fifties. Couldn't gain access with her arms occupied."

The soldier pulled back the blanket further to reveal Sarah's lock on the bundle. Moving to the other side, he lifted a corner to uncover her feet.

The patients in the room all gasped in horror at what they were witnessing. The soldier covered her back up.

Dr. Young examined her blackened toes. "No shoes?"

The soldier shrugged. "Must have fallen off at impact. Somewhere at the crash site."

"The worst case of frostbite I've ever seen," he sighed. "She needs a bigger hospital. Not sure we can do anything for her here and doubt she would survive the trip." The doctor brushed his knuckles against Sarah's cheek, bowed his head, and offered a silent prayer.

"All the roads are impassable for fifty miles," added one of the other soldiers.

The doctor summoned Nurse Hillman. "Get Dr. Collins in here."

She nodded but said, "He just went off a twelve-hour shift."

Dr. Young lowered his voice and spoke deliberately, "Call to see if he made it home safely and beg him to come back. Please."

ANGEL IN FLIGHT

"Yes, sir."

On cue, she and the orderly pushed Sarah into the exam room. Then the nurse lifted the receiver on the wall in the hallway and dialed.

Glancing around the room at the other half dozen patients, all wide-eyed and wanting, Dr. Young felt powerless. Only once before, on the battlefield, had he suffered this depth of helplessness. Putting on a reassuring smile, he stepped toward the exam room.

The soldier stood in the doorway. "Doctor. We received a radio message from our team still up on the mountain while we were in transit."

Dr. Young rubbed his eyes, then peeled back the blanket covering Sarah. It fell to the floor in a heap. "Yes?"

"One more found alive. A little girl. Maybe four or five. Should we instruct them to transport to another hospital, if they can?"

Hanging his head low, he scuffed the wet floor with his shoe. The doctor then peered up over the rim of his glasses out the window at the falling snow. "You saw the roads. What would be your judgment?"

"No other place to take her, sir."

"There's your answer. We'll stabilize them, and when the weather breaks, transport up to Salt Lake."

"Yes, sir."

The soldier stood a little straighter and, resisting the urge to salute, let his arm dangle. Pivoting on his heel, he disappeared from view.

"How's she doing?" the doctor inquired of Nurse Hillman.

"We were able to remove the child from her arms. And—" Breaking down and sobbing, she turned her face away.

The baby blanket still swaddling the lifeless infant lay on a table next to the window.

John, from the corner of the room, stepped forward, putting an arm around her.

"She expired within a moment after," he said.

Dr. Young stroked Sarah's wet bangs, then examined the length of her body.

"Nothing stronger than a mother with a child in her arms."

Unfurling a sheet from the cupboard, John covered Sarah's body. He and Nurse Hillman lifted her onto the gurney and wheeled her out.

The doctor well used his time and helped another car crash patient. Nurse Hillman returned to his side.

"How are you holding up?" asked Dr. Young.

"I'm sorry about that," the nurse said with eyes red but dry.

"It's been a long night. About to get even longer. Her five-year-old daughter is on the way at any minute now. Do you think you can handle it?"

"I heard. Yes."

"Good."

Suddenly, the door blasted open. "Who's in charge?" a commanding voice boomed while snow swirled around the tall, imposing figure.

Dr. Young whirled around and met him halfway.

Two soldiers entered right behind the commander, carrying a blanket with two ends tied together on each side.

"Is this the girl?"

The commander barked, "Yes. I want you to save her. Got it?"

"I'll do my best."

The commander tapped the doctor's chest. "That is not the answer I was looking for."

Nurse Hillman grabbed the lead soldier's arm and pulled him past the others toward the awaiting exam room. "We'll get to it right now, sir," she assured the commander.

"That's the spirit."

The nurse had dismissed the orderly and had cut most of Robin's clothes off when Dr. Young entered. A warming lamp to the side of the exam table cast an orange glow across Robin's naked body. He methodically examined every inch.

"Bleeding?"

"Lots of lacerations, but I didn't find any. It all seems to have stopped."

Robin opened and batted her blue eyes at Dr. Young. "Can I see my mommy?"

Astonishment painted their faces.

"After a while, dear," said Nurse Hillman.

Mildly caressing her cheek, Dr. Young said, "I'm amazed you're even conscious with all these fractures." He glanced at Nurse Hillman. "Can we take any vitals?"

The nurse shook her head. "Cuff too big and no place to—" She glanced down at Robin's contorted appendages.

Robin smiled at the doctor when he shined a light into her eyes. "Just like the angels," she whispered.

Dr. Young chuckled. "Angels?"

"They shined a big light on me."

"Oh. You mean the soldiers who rescued you?"

She gave her head a slight shake. "No. They were angels."

That made the doctor smile. "They sure can sometimes be. Does anything hurt? Can you feel any pain?" he asked, touching her legs and arms.

Robin shook her head again. "It used to hurt. Not anymore."

The doctor and nurse shared a moment of distress.

"Can you wiggle your toes?" Nothing moved. He took in a deep breath then deferred to Nurse Hillman. "Did you get through to Dr. Collins?"

"Yes. He's on his way."

Dr. Young closed his eyes and bowed. "Thank you."

"Is my mommy okay?"

Nurse Hillman stroked the top of her head. "Yes. She's going to be just fine."

That drew a scowl from Doctor Young. "She's cold as ice. Let's warm her up," he said, placing his warm hand on her cold stomach, just below what seemed like a plowed field of deep cuts and abrasions.

Robin tried lifting her arm. She closed her eyes and shrieked.

"No, honey. You need to lie still."

"I want my mommy," she bleated.

The doctor stepped to the door. "Let me know when Dr. Collins arrives."

Nurse Hillman nodded.

As Dr. Young made his rounds, checking on the other patients, the door opened again. In walked the soldier who had delivered Robin. He approached and extended his hand. Dr. Young shook it.

"How's our little girl doing?"

"Waiting for the surgeon. You are?"

"Private Michael Smith. I'm the one who found her."

Dr. Young placed a hand on his shoulder and pulled him over to a corner for a little privacy. "Do you know if she has any other family?"

"I believe you have her mother."

The doctor closed his eyes and shook his head. "Lost her just before you got here."

"The pilot, Gary Wood, was, I'm guessing, her father. He was pronounced dead at the scene."

Dr. Young rubbed the side of his face. "Gary Wood, you say?"

Michael nodded.

"Captain Gary Wood?" insisted the doctor.

He shrugged. "I'm not sure. I do know he's a pilot."

"I may have served with him." Dr. Young stretched and yawned. "Not what I wanted to hear." He eyed Michael up and down. "Got any medical training?"

"Yes, sir. I'm enrolled in medic school and certified in search and rescue."

"Can you stick around?"

"Yes, sir."

"Good man." The doctor patted his arm. "I'm going to need someone to look after all these." His gaze swept across the room.

The doctor left Michael standing in the ER with a dazed expression and returned to the exam room.

"Dr. Collins is in the operating room and waiting," said Nurse Hillman.

"Let's go."

The nurse and orderly lifted Robin off the exam table and back onto the gurney with a concerted effort. Robin's eyes followed their movement as they thrust forward through the door and down the hall, Dr. Young by her side.

Michael scurried after them until they came to a large door marked 'Surgery.'

Nurse Hillman held up a hand to Michael. "I'm afraid this is as far as you go."

"Yes, ma'am. Will you let me know how she does?"

Dr. Young stopped and said, "I promise to keep you informed." He pushed through the door and was about to disappear when Michael grabbed the sleeve of his lab coat and turned him around.

"Please. I would like to stay. My commander authorized it," Michael said with a quivering voice.

"Alright. As soon as Dr. Collins is up to speed, I'll join you back in the ER. Do what you can to locate next of kin."

Michael's head bowed in gratitude as he pivoted on his heel and returned to the swinging doors.

After changing into an operating robe and donning rubber gloves, Dr. Young joined the others. Robin's frail body splayed out on the operating table. Her eyes fluttered as Nurse Hillman placed a mask too big for her face over her mouth and nose. Robin then glanced around at each of the medical staff dressed in white gowns. She said something the doctor could not understand. He nudged the mask slightly to the side.

"What's that, sweetheart?"

"You all look like the angels too."

"You are the angel."

They exchanged smiles as he replaced the mask.

Nurse Hillman inserted an IV needle into the least injured leg. That drew a muffled yelp from Robin.

"That's a good sign," Dr. Young said.

When Robin's eyes closed, Dr. Collins went to work suturing the open wounds. "Once she's sewn up, we'll need some x-rays. See what we're dealing with."

"I agree. We've counted at least seven fractures," Dr. Young replied.

SHELLY PULSE

16 — Spinster Margaret

Gauze partially obstructed Robin's vision when she opened her eyes. All she could see was a whitewashed high ceiling above her and a single light fixture hanging from a chain in the middle. Moving her head to survey her surroundings proved impossible. Something clamped her head in place.

Robin panicked; her chest heaved as shrieks stuck in her dry throat. Something muffled the sound. Eyes darting up, down, and sideways, she strained to glimpse something, anything. At least up on the mountain, she had a view of the entire meadow. Now nothing but painted plaster.

"Help," she whimpered.

A woman's face, framed by short wavy black hair, black horn-rimmed glasses, and a wool hat, slid from the side into view. That startled Robin. She tried to focus, but the image blurred through her tears.

"My goodness, you are awake."

The woman's voice sounded familiar to Robin, but she remained unsure of her identity. Her perfume was strong.

Robin's nose itched. She tried scrunching it to make the tingle go away.

"Good morning, honey."

Once the tears drained, Robin could see her better. It was Aunt Margaret, her father's sister. Margaret lived a mile from them, and they often went to her house on Sundays to visit. She was a single woman and had no children.

Robin's mother had always referred to her as a *spinster*. She remembered asking her momma what a spinster was. The answer surprised her. 'A woman who was not good-looking enough to attract a man's attention. And when she passes a certain age, no man will want her.' She thought that comment was mean and did not understand why her mother would say that about Aunt Margaret. Her aunt was one of the most beautiful women she had ever seen.

Again, Robin strained to move her head to see who or what else was in the room, but it would not budge. She sensed the presence of another warm body next to her and could hear breathing.

"Lie still. You are in a cast, so you don't injure yourself further. Let me go fetch the nurse," Margaret said.

The image of her aunt disappeared from view, and Robin heard a door open and close. Just then, the head of a man popped into view. That familiar face made Robin smile. It was Michael.

"Boy, am I glad you are awake. I'd give you a hug, but…," He glanced down her body. "… they have you wrapped up like a mummy."

Mummy? The sound of that word reminded Robin of her mother. "Where is mommy?" she tried to ask, but no sound came out. Only her lips moved.

Michael's countenance turned dreary, and he looked away.

Robin knew something was terribly wrong. Adding up all the factors in her head, she quickly concluded that her momma probably died. Mother had often said Robin was 'too smart for her own good.'

"Your surgeries went well. The doctor said, because of your age, you should heal quickly."

Surgeries? Robin did not know what that word meant. She guessed it had something to do with fixing her after the accident.

The accident? All the memories of the crash came flooding back. She remembered how scared she was and her father's trembling hand on her knee.

The hours lying in the snow, shivering until she could feel nothing, made her aware of how much pain she felt now. How she longed to be back outside again, covered by the blanket the angels had placed on her. If only her head and legs would stop hurting.

"I brought you something," Michael said, disappearing from Robin's view. He returned with a stuffed bear almost as big as her. Brushing the bear's nose against her cheek tickled. That made Robin smile. He set the bear next to her in the bed and brought back a vase filled with flowers, holding it up where she could see. "Your grandmother sent these. She says she can't wait to see you."

Grandmother? Robin loved her grandmother and now wished she was at her house playing with the goat, chasing the chickens, and romping in the snow.

ANGEL IN FLIGHT

Snow? Oh, how she loved snow. One of the last memories was the snowball fight with her father in their home's front yard. What she wouldn't give to be back there now.

Robin heard the latch on the hospital room door open. Leather-soled shoes scuffed the polished floor, telling her someone larger than her aunt approached. She now had to rely more on sound and smell than on sight. The scent was musty, more like Grandmother's attic than Aunt Margaret's perfume.

She felt a hand applying pressure on the exposed part of her leg. Then, that same icy hand touched her upper arm free of a cast. An unfamiliar older man's face came into view. He had a bald head; only a few strands greased back over his crown. A short gray mustache lined his upper lip. He looked familiar, but she couldn't be sure.

"Hello, young lady. My name is Dr. Young. And this is Nurse Hillman."

Robin could strain her eyes far enough to one side. A fleeting glimpse of a tiny woman with a funny white hat buried in a nest of reddish-brown hair registered in her vision.

"You may not remember us. You were in a lot of pain when you came to our hospital a few days ago," she said.

A few days? Had she been asleep for that long? It seemed like only a few hours ago when they whisked her off the mountain into a big truck.

"You are doing so well," the nurse said. "You are a strong little girl and so brave."

Robin blinked once; her real voice still eluded her. She wanted her mother, but she was not sure if she was still alive. Momma would have come for her by now.

The nurse's face remained in her field of view while she fidgeted with the bandages on Robin's ears, making it easier for her to hear. Other voices echoed off the ceiling from the corner of the room.

"Another few days, and we can move her to Primary Children's Hospital up in Salt Lake. They'll be able to perform the remaining surgeries and give her the care she needs."

"Thank you, Dr. Collins," Robin heard her aunt say.

There was that word again—surgeries. Robin imagined the worst of this nightmare was not over and meant more pain. As the aching in her body grew, she wished to go back to sleep in the snow on that mountain.

The room brightened. Robin guessed the sun came out from behind the clouds. Figures of light danced on the ceiling. She did not understand how they got up there precisely, but they had to be some kind of reflection off the melting ice and snow outside. Those figures reminded her a little of the angels she saw floating above her in her darkest moment.

"What are you smiling about?" Michael asked when the nurse stepped away, and his face greeted her again. She glanced past him up at the ceiling and pointed with her eyes. His gaze followed.

"Angels."

"They certainly look like them, don't they?"

Failing at her attempt to nod, she blinked twice instead.

The muffled speech faded to silence as the door closed. Whatever they discussed was not meant for her ears.

Mother and Father had argued behind closed doors. They never knew how often she listened. Distinguishing the words from the emotion taught her a lot about their meaning, even though she didn't understand them. Being denied information about her medical status left her wondering what would happen next.

The door opened. Robin could hear the tap-tap of the narrow heels of her aunt's shoes—one thing she remembered about her aunt—how well she dressed. Margaret always wore a dress or skirt and sweater over a blouse, even when it was hot outside. A matching hat completed the ensemble when she left the house.

"Darling," she heard her aunt say while resting her hand on an unbandaged part of her arm. "I've spoken with the doctor, and it looks like you will be going to a hospital near my home. I'll be able to spend the evenings with you there. When you are released, you'll be coming home to live with me. Would you like that?"

Did she have a choice? That shattered like ice any hope her mother survived. Living with her aunt meant she'd still visit Grandmother. She could think of no one else. Robin blinked twice, hoping she understood that meant *yes*.

"Of course, we don't have to worry about that right now. You've got a long road of recovery ahead of you. I'll be with you every day until you can come home with me. I'm fixing up a bedroom for you. I'm sure you will like it."

Robin wanted her old bedroom. Yes, they lived in a small house. She remembered her aunt's house was bigger, with lots of books, and it had a big backyard where she could play.

Aunt Margaret planted a kiss with cherry red lips on her forehead. "I love you."

Only two people had ever said those three words in that way, and she would never hear them spoken by her parents again. The term felt strange,

ANGEL IN FLIGHT

out of character for her, in fact. She had never uttered them to her before. Why now?

"We will have so much fun together. I'll buy lots of dresses for you to wear and you can start school next year."

Dresses? She hated to wear dresses. Surely her aunt could bring all her clothes from home. Home? What would happen to her house? That was where she wanted to be. She hoped her best friend, Olive, would come to visit her.

Michael brushed her cheek with the back of his fingernails. The two smiling faces looking down at her turned dark when the sun went behind another cloud.

He said, "You take care, and I'll come and check on you whenever I get time off. Does that sound good, my little angel girl?" Michael asked.

She squeezed her eyes shut twice and smiled. Now Robin was sure he understood.

SHELLY PULSE

17 — Cracked Heart of Glass

Summer 1976

Halfway through the riveting end to Robin's tragic story, Jeremy had dragged her over to the couch to get more comfortable. Her head lay in his lap while he caressed her hair with one hand and let his other rest on her stomach, just below her folded arms.

Jeremy said, "I had to stay in bed for three days after a running injury. I can't imagine what it must have been like to be stuck in bed, in a body cast, for months."

"It was terrible. The worst part was the smell. No one could bathe me. The doctor offered me a piece of the cast as a souvenir. My aunt says I plugged my nose."

Jeremy wrinkled his, then laughed. He could only imagine that nasty smell.

The clock read 8:35 pm. "So much for finishing homework."

"I'm sorry. I got a little carried away."

"I'm not. I understand now why..." He glanced down the length of her. "I mean—"

"I know. Why I take so long to walk up the stairs? Why it takes so long to put on my pants?"

"No. Why you are the most amazing artist I have ever met."

Robin's eyes narrowed. "There's that silver tongue again." She reached up and drew him in for a kiss.

Jeremy thought he heard footsteps in the hallway and quickly pushed Robin up off his lap. "I don't want you to get in trouble with Mrs. Olson."

Robin sat up and eyed him mischievously. "I have an idea. We have twenty minutes. Maybe I can talk Mrs. Olson into letting us back in after we watch the sunset."

The couch was too low for her to push herself to her feet. Jeremy helped her up.

"Do you think she will?"

"If not, we can try the stick-in-the-door trick." Robin giggled.

Just then, Mrs. Olson peeked inside as if trying to catch them in the moment of doing something they ought not to be.

"How's your homework coming along?" she asked with a disappointed tone.

"Great!" Jeremy said. "I'm learning more and more from this master artist."

The blush in Robin's cheeks returned, like when he had told her she was beautiful. He had also realized how smart and talented she was.

Mrs. Olson looked down at the two paintings on the table. "Did you do these?"

"I did the one on the left," Jeremy said proudly.

Mrs. Olson frowned. "This is what they are teaching you kids here?"

Jeremy's puffed chest shrank.

Robin interjected, "It was an assignment to illustrate our *inner self*."

Mrs. Olson shook her head and scowled as she found a drawing pad to cover them. "They should teach you to draw something more appropriate, like a pretty landscape or a meadow with horses. These are disturbing." She rubbed her eyes like she was trying to rid herself of the images now emblazoned in her retinas.

"Mrs. Olson?" Robin started, looking up at the wall clock.

"Yes, hun?"

"Would it be alright if Jeremy and I went up to the grassy hill and watched the sunset?"

The dorm mother glanced at her wristwatch. "Fifteen minutes until quiet-time."

Robin tilted her head pleadingly with her hands in her pockets. "I know. But it always sets after nine o'clock. My window faces north, so I never see it. I've heard it's gorgeous up there."

Jeremy covered his mouth to keep from laughing. How could anyone ever say no to this girl? Her poor aunt must be made of stone to rebuff her constant pleading.

Mrs. Olson appeared to be having a two-sided conversation in her head.

"I promise we'll be back by ten. I'll go straight to bed. Oh, and can Jeremy help me babysit on Friday? I really don't want to be alone."

ANGEL IN FLIGHT

Babysit? Jeremy didn't want to babysit! Especially on his last Friday night in Logan, Utah. He had plans to hang out with the gang at the local burger joint. Curfew began at eleven on Friday.

Mrs. Olson sized him up and down again. "Only if he wears pants and a real shirt."

Jeremy expected her to say no! "Wait. I didn't know about any babysitting."

Bouncing on her toes, Robin patted him and said, "His name is Scotty. He's as adorable as can be. You'll love him."

"The kid you were holding when I walked in?"

"Yes. He's so cute!" she squeaked.

Jeremy blinked several times. He often babysat his two younger siblings as his parents worked and traveled a lot. They were finally old enough to take care of themselves. The last thing he wanted to do was babysit somebody's kid. However, Robin's face, all lit up like that, was irresistible.

"So? Are you going to help me or not?" she asked, her face dead serious.

Mrs. Olson's now sported amusement.

"Only if you promise not to tell anyone."

That made Robin laugh. Poking him in the stomach, she kidded, "He doesn't want anyone to know about his feminine side."

Robin glanced expectantly back at Mrs. Olson as she grabbed Jeremy's hand. Without waiting for an answer, Robin pulled him toward the door. "We'll be back at ten. Don't lock us out."

They were already out the door and halfway down the hall when Mrs. Olson called after them, "You two behave yourselves!"

"We will!" Robin replied with a grin.

Although they were about the same height, Robin felt Jeremy's strength as she nestled between his legs in the tall grass. She laid her arms over his that were wrapped around her waist. With her head propped back against his shoulder, she turned and kissed his chin. She found it salty and made a slight spitting noise.

"Did you shower today?"

He groused, "Yes. Why?"

"You taste... sweaty."

Squeezing her tighter, he said, "We played a little soccer after class, and you know how hot it gets in that classroom."

The golden glow turned orange, then pink, as the sun sank behind the mountains.

"You were right. It is beautiful," Jeremy said. "I like mornings best. I've always wanted to paint the sunrise over the red hills of St. George."

Craning her neck, Robin saw a sliver of the twilight reflecting in his eyes. "Why don't you?"

"I suck at painting clouds, and I want to capture that contrast of the bluish-purple against the orange glow of the sunrise. You know how it turns that pink and red streak at the lower edge. I've tried, but it always turns into a muddy mess."

There were no clouds in the sky tonight, only the golden glow at one end and darkening at the other. They laid down next to each other, arms interlocked. Stars were already piercing through the indigo shroud when Robin asked, "Who broke your heart?"

"What do you mean?"

Robin let that question hang in the widening space between them. Now she regretted bringing up the subject again. "You said your heart got broken. You know, *Heart of Glass*."

"Oh. That." Jeremy let go of her arm and sat up.

Robin used his elbow to pull herself upright. It was her turn to comfort him. She rubbed his back that had cooled in the grass.

"I've done all the talking. Your turn."

A long pause followed as Jeremy checked the red glow of his LED watch. "Girl at school." Another pause followed while Robin waited for more. "And another girl from Richfield."

"Wait. Two girls?" She stopped rubbing. In fact, she shuffled on her hands over where she could look directly into his face. "Two at the same time?" Her voice trembled with disbelief.

Jeremy nodded.

"You two-timer!" Robin slapped him on the shoulder.

A horrible question crossed her mind. Was he still dating someone else back home? It was possible. When the summer was over, he would go back, five hundred miles away. Then something else occurred to her. Tina might steal him away. She quickly dismissed that thought. Tom and Tina had sat next to each other on the other side of the classroom all week.

Now curiosity took over, and she pressed further. "Did they know about each other?"

"No. At least not until Richfield's basketball team came to St. George."

Hiding her shock was impossible. "Was she on the team?"

Jeremy continued to look up at the stars, avoiding her inquisition. "She played saxophone in the band."

"What happened?" Robin placed a hand on his fidgeting fingers to calm them.

"They both walked up to me in the bleachers. Each took turns slapping me in the face."

Robin suppressed a giggle with the back of her hand. She tried picturing two angry girls beating the crap out of him, but the image was too comical and frightful at the same time to conjure.

The frown made it clear that Jeremy did not find anything about the story amusing.

"I'll bet that was embarrassing. How did they find out about each other?"

"The out-of-town girlfriend happen to ask the local girlfriend, who was volunteering as an usher, if she knew me and where she could find me. Of course, the local girlfriend wanted to know why."

Tears of mirth gushed from Robin's eyes as she tried to suppress her laughter.

Jeremy didn't see the same humor she did. He grumbled, "They made me take them both to dinner. Emptied my wallet."

"Ooh. Two girls." Robin imagined Jeremy sitting at a fancy restaurant, one on each side, ordering the most expensive thing on the menu, leaving him broke. Served him right! "You are a devil. So, which one broke your heart?"

That drew Jeremy's attention back to Robin's probing eyes. "Both. But now I have you. I don't need to wear that shirt anymore."

Robin's heart softened. She could tell the experience was truly painful for him. There was more to the story, and she'd leave it for another day.

She crawled up on his lap and sat side-saddle, her arms wrapped around his neck. "Mrs. Olson wants us back by ten."

Jeremy held up his watch and pressed the button. "We're already late."

"I'm hungry. I didn't eat anything tonight. Let's go get something. You only have to buy dinner for one girl. Not two."

Pleased he took it good-naturedly, Robin pulled him in for a kiss on his lips this time. "Mm. Not as salty." She jabbed him in the stomach, still tense from laughing at her last joke.

He helped her up.

"How are you going to get out?"

"I'll wait until Mrs. Olson is asleep. I'll meet you by the back door. You find the stick."

18 — Double Root Beer Float

Checking the time so often depleted the battery in Jeremy's Casio. The last image on his watch read 11:17 p.m. before it faded.

"C'mon, Robin. It closes at one, and we still have to walk there," he muttered to himself while leaning against a tree in the dark.

The drive-in burger joint was only a few blocks away, but it would take at least half an hour at the pace Robin walked. Maybe she got caught by Mrs. Olson. Or perhaps she stood him up after confessing his two-timing affair. He twirled a twig between his fingers.

When Jeremy was about ready to give up on Robin, he heard a hushed voice behind him.

"Where have you been?"

Robin appeared in the dim light of a far-off streetlamp.

"Right here." He pointed a stick at the back door.

"That's not mine." Nudging Jeremy to face the building next to it, she said, "That one is."

Jeremy groaned. "I'm sorry. They all look the same from the back."

Despite the dark, Robin's scowl said she was no longer in a playful mood.

He held up the twig. "Do you still need this?"

"I used a hairbrush. Now you have to buy me two burgers and make it a double root beer float." Robin lifted his arm and made him drape it over her shoulder. "This time, I'm not waiting for you to take the hint."

Jeremy wondered how she would be cold wearing a thick sweater over her long-sleeved shirt. But when a gust of wind blew up his half-tee, he wished he had worn something warmer. He pulled her in closer to siphon off some of her body heat as they strolled to the end of the street.

Tom and Tina sat next to each other at one of the picnic tables outside the drive-in restaurant. Across the table, Jeremy was shocked to find Julie with Adrian's arm wrapped around her.

"Isn't that the guy she dumped because she wouldn't put out?" Jeremy queried Robin while they were still out of range.

"I think so. The local girl must still be nursing her butt back to health," Robin joked. "Which reminds me. How's that fine one of yours recovering?" She pinched him down there.

Jeremy's squeal announced their arrival to the others. To make room, they all moved around and invited them to sit. Robin, with Jeremy's assistance, slid her legs under the table next to Julie.

"Double burger and a root beer float?" Jeremy confirmed with Robin.

"No. Two double burgers." Pulling out a ten-dollar bill, she held it out. "I was just kidding about having to pay for me."

The others waited for Jeremy to take the money.

"Nah." Jeremy waved it off. "I can cover it."

Shrugging, she put the bill back in her purse and said, "Then make it a combo with fries. Don't forget the sauce and two scoops of ice cream."

The laughter grew faint behind him as he made his way to the order counter. By now, she would be telling the story of his two girlfriends. Pulling out his wallet, Jeremy counted just enough change to pay for her order and a small hamburger for himself. Maybe she wouldn't be able to eat it all, and he could clean up the leftovers. He leaned against the counter and looked back at the gang while swatting at the flies attracted by the fluorescent tubes overhead.

Robin smiled and waved at him.

He gave a halfhearted smile. What had he gotten himself into? Melancholy suddenly gripped his chest. The summer program would soon be over. How could he keep a long-distance relationship going with Robin? The last time resulted in disaster.

This meant forgoing dates with local girls. The town was small, so there were few to choose from. Even so, if the opportunity to ask a girl out presented itself, he must turn it down. Otherwise, it would be cheating, and he didn't want to go through that again. Would he have to break up with her before they even got started?

Jeremy suddenly missed Robin, and he hadn't left yet. He plotted how he would convince his parents to let him drive up to visit her. There was no way she was traveling to St. George. She lacked a license and probably could never drive with her right leg being so weak. Perhaps someday she could buy a car with hand controls.

The girl behind the counter called his name through the window three times before Jeremy realized his order was ready. Hands grasping the tray, Jeremy stumbled on a curb, spilling part of her float.

ANGEL IN FLIGHT

When he set the tray in front of Robin, and she unwrapped her hamburger, Tina asked, "Where is a little girl like you going to put that big thing?"

Pointing at her belly and chomping off a huge bite of the burger, she said with her mouth full, "Right here." Sauce drizzled down her chin, and she wiped it with the back of her sleeve.

Jeremy had shared only a few meals with Robin. This was the first time he had ever seen someone eat like her. The others raised their eyebrows and gasped. Robin was halfway through her first burger and working on her float before he unwrapped his.

Adrian grabbed one of Robin's fries and threw it at Tom. "Miss your roommate?"

"Who, Greg?" Tom threw it back. "Not really."

The fry missed its target. Adrian reached for another. "I thought you two were best buds."

"No. He was good at bullying me and everyone else into doing what he wanted. Most of the homework he turned in was mine. He added a few of his touches, signed his name, and turned it in." Tom reached for another fry off Robin's tray and threw it back at Adrian.

Robin slapped his hand when he went for a second. "Excuse me. Those are mine." She stuffed a handful in her mouth and let the ends dangle out while she chomped.

Not very lady-like, but it was funny and endearing. Jeremy was sure she did not behave this way at home. Knowing what she had told him about her aunt, that would have been unacceptable.

Robin took a drink of her float, leaving a milk mustache. She turned to Jeremy and pursed her lips. "Kiss me."

Everyone laughed but Jeremy. He shook his head and handed her a napkin. She took it but, before he could react, she'd smeared a trail of foam across his lips and cheek.

He snatched the napkin back and wiped it off.

"Ah. That was sweet," Julie said.

After wiping her mouth with the napkin remnants, Robin grabbed him by the neck and pulled him in for a proper kiss. Everyone at the table fell silent.

Jeremy had never kissed a girl in front of others and was stunned by her audacity. One more side of her he had never seen. It was decision time. Should he dive right in or leave her wanting? He closed his eyes and met her halfway. The kiss lasted through the whistling and clapping.

"I guess you guys *are* an item now," Tina said.

Robin beamed. "We are!" She stuffed another French fry in her mouth and chewed loudly. Picking up another, she shoved it into Jeremy's mouth.

"How long have you two been sharing spit?" Adrian asked.

The others groaned.

"Gross." Julie slugged him in the abs.

"Since the lake," Robin offered readily. "He's the best kisser."

"I don't remember seeing you two making out." Tina slurped the last of her soda and handed the empty cup to Tom. "I'm still thirsty."

"Me too," Julie said, handing her empty to Adrian.

"We weren't making out," Jeremy protested. "We were just—"

Robin glared at him.

"Talking," he finished.

Robin's smile returned. "Kinda hard to talk when I had my mouth on yours."

Where did she learn how to talk like that? Jeremy wondered. She had told him how much she loved to read. Maybe the books were those steamy romance novels. Then again, her aunt would not approve of such things. Perhaps she hid them in her bedroom.

When the two boys wandered off to refresh their ladies' drinks, Robin asked Julie, "I thought you two broke up?"

Julie waited until Adrian was out of earshot. "Shut up," she hissed.

"What did I miss?" Robin asked eagerly.

Tina burst in, "He came back begging after that other girl dumped him. Julie is going to torture him, make him think she likes him again, then dump him on the last day of classes."

Robin frowned. "That's cruel."

"What he did was cruel," Julie said. "You don't make out with me, then when another girl throws a Frisbee at your feet, dump me and go running off with her. Not cool."

Jeremy jumped into the discussion. "Looks like you and Tom are getting along," he said to Tina.

Her dark eyes flashed, revealing what he interpreted as longing and jealousy. Hopefully, he misjudged.

"Kind of. My dad has someone from our tribe lined up for me back home, and I don't want to disappoint him or break tradition. The son of some wealthy ranch owner."

"If you like Tom, why would that matter? He knows how to work hard and could learn to ride a horse," Julie said.

"This whole summer has been nothing but a temporary fling. We'll all go home and never see each other again," Tina declared solemnly.

ANGEL IN FLIGHT

The bank of fluorescent lights turned off one by one around the outside of the drive-in. The last thing to go dark was the sign overhead, leaving the three couples in nothing but the light of the streetlamps and the stars.

Robin belched when she set down the last half of her burger. "Want it?"

"Thought you would never ask." His little burger was not enough to sustain his sixteen-year-old appetite. It took him about two bites to make it disappear.

Adrian and Tom returned with the drinks. The six of them began their slow journey back to the dorms.

Julie pressed the button on her watch. "Oh, no! It's two o'clock in the morning? We are so screwed. How are we getting back in?"

"I blocked the back door," Robin said as she plodded along.

Jeremy noticed Robin's limp was a bit more pronounced than before. Instead of putting his arm around her, he switched sides and held it out for her to lean on.

The rest of the gang ran ahead into the night, leaving them behind.

Robin asked, "Are you going to Winter Conference?"

Winter Conference? His astonishment conveyed he didn't know what she was talking about.

"The brochure was in the packet. Didn't you read it?"

Either it was hiding, or someone forgot to include one in his packet. Plus, reading was not his thing. That was how he got into trouble with his first assignment. Words on a page were either blurry or backward. That was why he liked to draw. The three-dimensional world made more sense to him. To Jeremy, a picture was worth more like a *million* words.

"When is it?"

"During winter break. In Park City."

He felt the corner of his lip curl and not into a smile. "Doesn't it snow a lot there in the winter?"

"Yes. That would be the point. I love the snow."

"You do? After all you went through?"

Robin closed her eyes and drew in the cool night air. "Yes. The big flakes remind me of the angels."

Jeremy liked snow, to a point. He had fond memories of playing at his uncle's house in Idaho. His classmates all bragged about their ski trips, but he had never done more than tubing down a gentle slope.

"Do you ski?" He realized what an ignorant question it was.

"About as well as I skate. I have to hold on to the rope on the bunny hill. I've been once. Sledding is better. The neighbors used to pull us on a toboggan behind their pickup. That was fun."

The image of Robin dressed in a ski parka and pants popped into Jeremy's head. He could picture how the ski boots would support her legs, much like the high-ankle skates. Her long brown hair pulled back in a ponytail sticking out of a beanie framing her sweet face made him smile.

Stopping under a streetlamp, he took Robin into his arms. "I'll bet you are cute all dressed up for the snow."

"It's when I'm happiest." She pulled him in tighter. "Do you think you can go to the conference?"

"I'll have to see. How much is it?"

They continued their journey toward the dorms.

Robin laid a finger on her chin. "I think the whole thing costs $350. That includes lodging, food, and ski lessons if you want them."

"I'd definitely need them. Never been before."

Just the thought of sliding down the hill with his feet crammed in thick plastic boots and long sticks clamped to them made him anxious. Jeremy preferred his bare feet to be planted on the desert soil of St. George.

It had taken every ounce of energy to cajole his parents into letting him attend the summer art program. Like Robin, Jeremy's art teacher visited his house to convince them they would not have to pay a dime. How would he talk his parents into paying for a week of fun and frivolity in Park City?

"I'll have to put in extra hours at the shoe store."

"I hope so. I'm going to miss you."

Leaves crunched under their feet, signaling the end of the summer. Stopping under a tree, Robin spun him around to face her. Jeremy had to feel her face in the dark to find her lips. The kiss was long and meaningful. He wondered if that would be one of their last.

"I'll miss you too."

Those words were true.

19 — Playing House

Mrs. Olson showed Robin the stack of clean diapers and the pail to deposit the dirty ones. Instructing her on little Scotty's feeding and sleeping schedule came next. The baby food jars and utensils lined up like ducks in a shooting gallery on the kitchen table.

"Leftover casserole in the fridge if you get hungry. Or make yourselves a peanut butter and jam sandwich." After lifting the lid to a bread box, Mrs. Olson pulled out a jar of Jif and placed it next to the loaf.

"Do you have any cereal?"

Mrs. Olson frowned. "For dinner?"

Jeremy mimed the shape of an enormous box, then pretended to pour its contents into his mouth. "I ask Santa for a case of cereal for Christmas every year."

The chuckle told Robin Mrs. Olson was warming up to Jeremy. "I can't reach, but there might be some up there. Milk is in the fridge."

A chair from the table acted as a ladder for Jeremy to climb. The frown confirmed he was not fond of Cheerios, but that didn't stop him from taking them down.

Mr. Olson stood by the door, tapping his watch. "We've got to go now, or we won't be done in time for the 7:45 show," he growled.

That is why Mrs. Olson was so grumpy all the time. The husband left without holding the door or escorting her to the car.

Robin glanced back at Jeremy and hoped that if she ever married, someone would still want to romance her, even after they had a whole passel of kids. Of course, all that wouldn't matter if she ended up a *spinster* like her aunt.

"You two behave yourselves. Stay out here and don't let anyone else in," Mrs. Olson lectured. She put on a sweater, grabbed her purse, and ran after her spouse.

Scotty toddled after them, nearly catching his fingers in the slamming door. Piercing screams followed. Robin snatched him up. A minute or two later, Scotty calmed, and she distracted him by wrapping his 'blankie' around his head and playing peek-a-boo.

"How many of those did you say you wanted?"

"At least a dozen."

Robin imagined her baby brother Michael's face every time she opened the blanket. The giggle and wide smile with just two bottom teeth tugged the last memories of him out of the dark edges of her mind. A flash of the last time she saw Michael burst into view when Scotty stopped laughing. She squeezed her eyes shut and set him down.

"What's wrong?"

Opening her eyes, she discovered him pulling back her bangs and lifting her chin.

"I'm fine," she said, trying to convince herself more than Jeremy.

Blankie in hand, Scotty waddled away with thumb nestled snugly in his mouth. Robin chased after him, and Jeremy chased after Robin.

When they reached the hall, he spun Robin around and pressed her against the wall with his whole body. "What happened?"

His breath was hot against her forehead. Robin stared right into his lips. Why was Jeremy so much taller? She glanced down at his feet; he had on platforms.

"You've never worn those before."

Until now, she had only seen him in Adidas brand shoes, shorts, and shirts. Now he wore bell-bottomed slacks and a button-down silk shirt with a wide collar. My, he was handsome.

"You got dressed up for me?" She thought maybe that would distract him.

"No. Mrs. Olson."

Robin frowned. Why would he dress up for her?

"Dress code. I didn't want her sending me back to change."

Now Robin remembered the warning. "But you are too tall." She reached for his neck. "How am I going to kiss you?"

Lifting her off her feet, he said, "Like this." He pinned her to the wall.

Feet dangling an inch from the floor, she giggled. It had been a long time since someone carried her, but never to kiss her. At least not like that.

Aunt Margaret was not the most affectionate person. Yes, she had held Robin in her arms and rocked her to sleep, but hugs were rare.

It was indeed a strange sensation being suspended in the air. "You are stronger than I thought."

"I ate my Wheaties before coming over."

That made Robin laugh. "You can put me down now."

After kissing her, Jeremy's brow drooped, and he shook his head. "Not until you tell me what just happened."

"Michael. My brother."

"It looked like you were having a seizure, locked up and kind of contorted."

Going for a second kiss, Robin turned away. Jeremy let her down. She slapped him on the shoulder and wandered into the bedroom to find Scotty.

"I did not."

The clomp-clomp of Jeremy's heels said he was right behind.

"You aren't supposed to be back here. Go take off those stilts."

Child found and scooped up in her arms, she returned to the living room to discover Jeremy, shoeless and lying on the couch. She could swear he'd unfastened the top two buttons of his shirt, as his smooth tanned chest was now showing.

"I called my parents last night."

A sensation of hope twined up in Robin. "What for?"

"To ask if I can go to the conference. I read them the pamphlet."

With Scotty now seated in the highchair, she slipped the stainless-steel tray into the slot and locked it in place. She wrapped a bib around his neck and tied it in the back. Opening the jar of whipped peas proved difficult; she held it out to Jeremy.

"Open. Please."

When Jeremy jumped up, she could nearly see his belly button. He *had* unbuttoned his shirt. Robin was not sure what he intended and was not taking any chances. The dorm mother could walk through that door at any moment.

"Um. You might want to do that up. You don't want Mrs. Olson to get the wrong idea."

The baby food jar snapped open easily for Jeremy. The chair made the same screeching sound as the benches in class when he pulled it out. He sat next to Robin. She placed a spoon in Jeremy's palm like a nurse handing a scalpel to a surgeon.

Jeremy opened his mouth wide to encourage Scotty to do the same. In went the first scoop. Scotty wrinkled up his face and spewed it out all over his silk shirt.

"Hey! What'd you do that for?" Jeremy frowned, set down the jar, and searched the kitchen for a towel to mop up.

Choking through heaves of mirth, Robin stated the obvious, "I guess he doesn't like peas."

"Can't blame him." Jeremy spat in the sink. "It's nasty stuff. I wouldn't want to eat it either."

Cracking open a jar of peaches, he tried again.

"Mm."

Motor-like sounds accompanied one spoonful after another, descending like a helicopter into Scotty's mouth. His little feet kicked with delight.

"He likes these."

"Where'd you learn to do that?"

"Little brother and sister. They are about seven and eight years younger. I learned to change diapers, and Mom always made me take baths with them to save on water. That was until I found a floatie."

Robin scrunched up her nose. "What's a floatie?" Then it dawned on her. The laughter returned so hard her stomach hurt. "Are you kidding me?"

He shook his head.

"You like kids, don't you?"

The shadow on his face disturbed Robin.

Jeremy picked up the notes Scotty's mother had left and read aloud. He reached for another jar and opened it.

His not answering made something shrink in Robin. What made him not want them?

"Kids are fine in small doses. I was expected to babysit a lot. My older siblings were almost grown and gone when my younger ones were born. Mom and Dad worked all the time, so I got stuck with them."

The image of having a dozen kids with Jeremy shattered. Of course, she was unsure how many her fragile body could sustain, but even at sixteen, she knew she wanted to be with a boy who liked and wanted children.

"You seem to be doing fine now," she said hopefully.

Breadcrumbs sprinkled like snow on the metal tray. Scotty shoved each one in his mouth as fast as Jeremy dropped them.

Robin pulled a baby bottle from the fridge. The clock on the wall read ten past eight. "Time for Scotty to go night-night," Robin said, handing the bottle to Jeremy.

Scooping him up in her arms after changing his diaper, Robin cradled and rocked the child in her arms as he sucked the bottle dry through labored gulps. When it came time to burp him, she struggled to lift and hold him against her shoulder.

"I can do this part." Jeremy snatched the dry diaper from off Robin's shoulder and draped it over his own. He wandered around in circles, bouncing him and rubbing his back.

"I think you have to do it harder to burp the bubbles out," she instructed.

Jeremy glared at her as he continued the gentle push-rub movement. Scotty let out a resounding belch accompanied by a stream of curdled milk, which luckily remained mainly on the burp rag.

"Not good for their organs or spine when you pound on them too hard."

"You sound like a doctor."

"Wanted to be. It's hard for me to read. Grades aren't good enough."

What a giant leap from artist to doctor. Both were worthy but entirely different disciplines. Robin had spent enough time in hospitals and operating rooms to know that Jeremy had what it would take. His compassion for others, plus his talent at precision drawing, would have made him a skilled surgeon.

When Scotty's eyes drooped, Robin led the way back to the nursery. She placed a hand on Jeremy's shoulder as he laid the sleeping infant in his crib and covered him with the blankie. The two of them, arm-in-arm, gazed down on Scotty's peaceful face and stroked his head.

"You are amazing," she whispered.

"Thanks."

Robin left the door to the nursery open a crack as she followed Jeremy back into the kitchen.

"Hungry?" he asked as he opened the cereal box.

"There's some casserole in the fridge." She pulled out a glass pan wrapped in aluminum foil.

Peeling back the cover, Jeremy peered inside and turned up his nose. "Looks like dog food."

Robin sniffed it. "Smells good." She spooned some in a plate and placed it in a microwave oven on the counter. The kitchen soon filled with the scent of noodles, cheese, and ground beef while Jeremy filled a bowl with Cheerios and poured milk. He looked over longingly at Robin's dish.

"I'll have a little." Milk trickled down his chin as he slurped spoon after spoon into his mouth.

"Where are your manners?" Robin chided.

"Hey! The way you downed that hamburger and those fries the other night, I was scared to put my lips anywhere near your mouth."

Robin grabbed his hand and gradually lifted it to her lips. She kissed the back of it. "You better watch it, Mr. Kess. I'll take these fingers right off like they are French fries. Two things I have are a strong jaw and sharp teeth." She bore them and chomped.

He yanked his hand away.

The first spoonful of casserole went into Robin's mouth. She waved her hand in front of her face and made huffing sounds. "Hot!"

Jeremy handed the milk carton to Robin. She chugged, leaving casserole stains on the spout.

"Now you have to drink all of it."

She did. With one mighty, continuous gulp, she polished off the rest, wiped the milk mustache with the back of her sleeve, and belched.

The look on Jeremy's face was nothing short of stunned and amazed. "I bet you don't do that when your Aunt Margaret is around."

Robin shook her head. "Being here with you, I've never felt so free."

"Do I need to burp you too?" Jeremy asked, setting down his bowl and reaching for the stained diaper hanging over the back of the highchair. He draped it over his shoulder and held out his arms.

The diaper fell to the floor as she buried her face in his neck. She felt secure and loved as he performed the burp-push method on her back. They danced affectionately to no music but their own in that tiny kitchen.

A brief child's whimper down the hall broke the silence. Robin waited for another cry, but none came.

"Must be dreaming." A moment later, she asked, "What did your parents say?"

"What they always say."

"What's that?"

"We'll see."

Withdrawing from his embrace, she tugged on Jeremy's hand, pulling him over to the couch. "Do you think you can convince them?"

"I'm pretty good at it. They are worried I'll miss Christmas."

"Will you come up with the money?"

"I think so. We are going to a shoe market in Salt Lake as soon as I return home. Sales will be good again once we replenish stock."

"Shoe market?"

"Yes. The shoe manufacturers come to a hotel and display next year's models. My parents spend all day going from room to room checking out all the styles, then place an order." Jeremy's attention drifted away.

"What's wrong?"

After a while, Jeremy said softly, "That's where I met the girl from out of town. Her parents also own a shoe store."

A twinge of jealousy burbled up. A finger on Jeremy's chin brought the focus back to her. "Will she be there this year?"

"Probably. Our families always eat together."

Confusion and hurt made Robin's chest heave. The pounding of the blood in her ears made it difficult to hear. "How long does this market thing last?"

"About three days."

Not only did they have less than a week remaining in the program, but a chance also existed Jeremy might get back with his ex—even if it was only for three days. The image of him in someone else's arms frightened her.

Robin finally found someone who could overlook her flaws. She admitted to herself for the first time that she was in love with Jeremy Kess.

He touched a tear that had escaped the corner of her eye. "I'm going to ask my dad if I can drive up to visit you. Bountiful isn't that far from Salt Lake."

Snuggling back into his arms, Robin fell silent. All she wanted now was this moment to last forever. "I want a picture of you."

"Why?"

"In case I never see you again."

SHELLY PULSE

20 — Love, Jeremy

Like Tina and Julie, she was too busy bidding farewell to her boyfriend with her lips. Robin had said her goodbyes to the few students she had gotten to know. Many of the students left early on the shuttle to the airport. Most parents picked up their children curbside at the dorms.

Wearing a wide-brimmed hat tied about her chin and sunglasses, Aunt Margaret motored up in a Buick. Jeremy opened her driver-side car door to help her out. Lowering her sunglasses to the tip of her nose, she eyed him suspiciously when he stuck out his hand to shake.

"You must be Robin's aunt. So nice to finally meet you. You are all she talks about."

Taking his hand briefly, she said, "Pleasant to make your acquaintance. You are?"

"Oh, sorry. I'm Jeremy," he said, whacking his chest.

"Well, Jeremy. I hope you behaved yourself while you were here."

Jeremy progressively turned three shades of red.

Robin glared at him.

To Robin, Margaret said, "We must be going. Your grandmother has a doctor's appointment at two."

Jeremy held out his hand again to Margaret. She frowned and didn't extend hers.

"Keys?"

"Why?"

"Trunk?"

"Oh."

After snatching them from Margaret's hand, Jeremy grabbed Robin's suitcases and set them behind the car. Curious, Robin followed.

"Stay back," he ordered.

"What are you doing?"

Blocking her view, he opened her suitcase and slipped something inside. Trunk lid slammed shut, Jeremy reached out to hug her. All he got from her was a hand to shake.

"Why not?"

"She could be spying on us."

Robin was right. Her eyes were framed in the rearview mirror.

Aunt Margaret had already sat behind the wheel when he returned the keys. "Thank you."

He shut her door.

She started the engine and pushed the sunglasses up higher on her nose.

As Jeremy walked her to the other side, Robin mouthed the words, 'I'll miss you.'

Jeremy repeated them back and closed the passenger door once her legs were inside.

"Buckle up!" He slapped the window frame.

"I will."

Robin turned and waved as the car sped away.

The tone in Margaret's voice was more like an interrogation than sincere interest. "He seems like a nice boy. Did you two get along well?"

"Just a boy who was actually nice to me," Robin said, looking out the window as they descended the canyon road leading out of Logan. She tried to hold back, but the tears flowed.

"What's wrong, dear? Didn't you have a good time?"

"I… I had a wonderful time. I made lots of friends and will miss them terribly."

"Good for you, sweetheart."

The rest of the journey home was mostly silent, with an occasional question. Robin told her about babysitting Mrs. Olson's child, but was careful not to talk about Jeremy. Nor did she mention the cemetery, skating, or other activities that might have gotten her in trouble.

When they arrived home, Robin opened one of her suitcases to find a large manila envelope sandwiched between two pairs of pants. On one side, Jeremy had written in beautiful calligraphy the words, 'Do not bend. Open carefully.' She closed the lid quickly before her aunt spied it.

"Do you need help putting away your things?" she asked, pointing at the suitcase.

Adding a little too much teenage spice, Robin sniped, "I packed them. I should be able to unpack them."

ANGEL IN FLIGHT

Helping her in with the second piece of luggage, Margaret lifted it onto the bed. "I'd like to see some of your work. Do you have any you'd like to show me?"

Robin was horrified. She wanted to be especially selective of the illustrations her aunt saw. The more *sensitive* ones hid toward the bottom.

Eyes lighting on the paintings of a seated boy holding a soccer ball, Margaret said, "He looks an awful lot like Jeremy. You did this?"

She nodded proudly. "Yes. He modeled for the class. Many took turns. But not me."

Margaret held it up to the light streaming through the sheer curtains. "I had no idea just how good you are." She sighed.

Robin showed her a few more. She confidently talked about the pigments used and the assignment's objective of each. Professor Anderson had hired professional models.

Her aunt would not have approved of a man and woman dressed in leathers mounting a Harley-Davidson motorcycle as an appropriate subject. Nor would she have allowed her precious niece to draw a nearly nude woman with hairy armpits. Those illustrations remained in the trash bin at the dorm. The janitor would probably find a use for them somewhere.

"I suppose it was worth the money sending you to that school."

"Does that mean I can go next summer? If I'm accepted, of course."

Margaret hesitated. "We'll see."

We'll see? Robin had never heard her say that before. It was either yes or no, very direct and concise. Had she been talking to Jeremy's parents?

"I'm glad you're back. Are you hungry?"

"Starving. Anything but peanut butter."

Margaret smiled. "I'll make your favorite grilled tuna sandwich."

Happy to be back in her bedroom, Robin lay on the bed for a moment and admired her angel drawings. Several of her new paintings joined them. Jeremy and his soccer ball hung right next to her bed. There he could be with her, watching over her.

As she put away her washed and folded clothes, she ran her fingers over the blouse that had gotten stained. The colors were still there, but faded. Now she wished she had left that one unwashed.

Moving to her desk, she inspected the mysterious manila envelope. "What have you given me, Mr. Kess?"

Opening the flap revealed the backside of a green Crescent brand illustration board they used in class. The photo she had given Jeremy spilled out when she shook it.

"Lunch is ready!" Margaret called from the kitchen.

Robin tucked the envelope in the lap drawer and closed it. The photo went back in her wallet, right next to one Jeremy had given her. It was last year's school picture of when he was in the tenth grade. He looked so young. She wished she had one of the two of them together.

"Be right there!"

Grandmother Helene rested against the arm of her wheelchair beside the dining room table. Robin kissed her on the forehead and patted her hand before she sat down. She laid an illustration she had painted next to Helene's plate.

"I made this one for you. I know how much you like the angels with dark hair," Robin said. "She has real wings and a green gown."

Helene squinted at it, then shook her head. "I wish I could see it better," she muttered. "Thank you, darling. Did you have an enjoyable time?"

"Yes, Grandmother. I learned so much."

"Wonderful. I'm happy someone is carrying on the talent."

A sense of tension pervaded the room when her grandmother's face portrayed disappointment toward Margaret.

No, her aunt did not possess artistic ability, but excelled at cooking and had an eye for fashion. She loved her kitchen and spent half of her days off from the department store baking bread and desserts while planning meals and making shopping lists. Since there were just the three women in the house, plenty of leftovers got wrapped up and shared with the elderly neighbors.

"Slow down, there, little one," Margaret restrained Robin. "What's the rush? Food is to be enjoyed. Together."

Eager to return to that envelope in her bedroom, Robin had all but finished her sandwich. Her aunt had not even sat down to eat.

"Sorry. I'm so hungry and happy to be home."

Robin really was. Usually, she ate like a bird and picked at her plate. She often got reproached for wasting food. Having prepared meals on her own for nearly two months, she appreciated a home-cooked meal. She even ate the carrot and celery sticks.

When Margaret finished her sandwich, Robin asked, "May I be excused?"

"You just got home," Grandmother complained. "Why don't you sit with me a while and tell me all about your trip."

A groan almost escaped. Robin loved to sit for hours listening to stories of how hard life was homesteading at the ranch. Now the property was sold, and the money was used to pay for her care. Few tales remained untold.

"The class started with thirty-three students. One boy was sent, I mean, had to go home early. The boys were separated into one dorm, the girls in another. I shared a room the first day with a girl, but she moved. So, I was by myself the rest of the time."

Hearing that seemed to displease Margaret. "You didn't tell me you were alone the whole time. I hoped, having a roommate, you would become accustomed to sharing."

Funny. Before the plane accident and Grandmother falling ill, Margaret had lived alone from the time she left home. Robin was not going to point that out.

"Oh, there was plenty to share. I had to get up early to use the shower and bathroom. Everyone stole my food. I caught a girl drinking out of my milk carton once."

Disgust curled Margaret's lip. "I hope you threw it away."

"Yes, I did. And when she got a new carton, I—" Robin stopped herself. Margaret would disapprove of taking revenge. "Anyway. We all sat on these benches that looked like rocking horses, so we had something to hold our drawing boards. We painted all day in class and did our homework in the dorms at night."

Margaret informed Grandmother, "Robin met a very nice young man. What was his name again, dear?"

Was it that obvious? How did her aunt know it was serious? Had she called the professor? Now Robin's head was spinning, and she took the last bite of pickle. That made her mouth pucker.

"Which boy?"

Margaret smiled. "The one who had his arm around you and carried your suitcases out of the building."

"You saw that?" Robin shook to the core. Now she knew for sure her aunt would not let her go to Winter Conference, let alone next summer session.

Her aunt matter-of-factly recounted, "I got lost and pulled into the driveway behind the buildings, and while I was backing out, I noticed the two of you under a tree, kissing."

Robin hung her head. She wanted to bolt for her room and never come out. Anytime now, she'd hear the words, 'you're grounded.' Margaret seldom grounded her, but when she did, it was for something she deserved. The two big ones were pulling a girl's hair and biting a boy on the arm for hitting her in the face with a snowball.

Grandmother's surprise turned to a smile. "He kissed you?"

She felt her face flush. If only she had eaten her sandwich more slowly. Her stomach churned. Expecting a stern reprisal, none came.

Robin nodded. "His name is Jeremy."

"I can see why you like him. He's about the same height as you," Margaret offered.

The calm response was unnerving, as Robin expected the tide to change at any moment. "Yes. He's a lot shorter than the other boys."

"Where does he live?"

"St. George."

Margaret's rigid shoulders grew slack. A look of relief washed over her expression. "That's quite far from here."

Now it was Robin's turn to slump. It *was* far. *Too* far, in fact. That reminder dashed her hopes of ever seeing him again.

"He is going to be in Salt Lake in about a week. He says he might drive up and see me." Might as well put it out there, in case he showed up unannounced on her doorstep.

"He has a license?" Margaret asked, as if shocked that someone Robin's age was capable of driving a car.

Why wouldn't he? Robin was about the only one at school who lacked driver education.

"Yes. He grew up on a farm in Idaho and has been driving since he was eleven."

Margaret raised a brow and sipped her tea. "I see."

"May I be excused now?"

Done with this interrogation, Robin wanted to go to her room, bury her head under a pillow, and cry herself into next week.

Margaret breathed an 'uh-huh,' into her cup.

The dining room filled with chatter as Robin placed her dishes in the sink. The whispers between the two matrons were too muffled for her to hear. She speculated they would gossip about Jeremy for days.

At her desk, Robin opened the top drawer. She reached into the envelope and removed the illustration board. Turning it over, she discovered Jeremy's color interpretation of the small black-and-white photo.

A giddy smile stretched across her face. It was the finest of all the pieces she'd seen him do. He had captured perfectly the shy expression on the child's face—her face.

Robin peered inside the envelope again. Two more pieces of paper emerged. One was a photocopy of the pencil study Jeremy had done first.

ANGEL IN FLIGHT

She was unsure which she liked better, the painting or the drawing. The other sheet had a brief note inscribed in gorgeous penmanship.

> *I hope you like this one. I stayed up all night. You can send the one you do of me in the mail if you still want to. You never finished telling me the story about what happened after you got out of the hospital. Maybe I can call you sometime after long-distance rates are low or you can write to me. I can't wait to see you again soon. Love, Jeremy.*

He said, 'Love, Jeremy!' That made Robin's heart sing with delight. She immediately opened a lower drawer, pulled out a stack of stationery, and began to write.

SHELLY PULSE

21 — Two Brushes

Autumn 1966

A feeling of summer extended into autumn, even though the leaves on the trees along the Wasatch Front turned golden, amber, and crimson. The season had passed with few visits from friends. Olive was the only girl who had come to *play* regularly—dressing dolls and coloring. The casts Robin wore made it difficult to do much else.

Robin was excited to return to school. All that remained to support her healing bones was a leg brace. Margaret insisted Robin learn to walk again and refused to let her use a wheelchair.

She held Margaret's hand as they plodded into the courtyard of the kindergarten. Each step was painful, but Robin was past crying. The agony had withered to varying degrees of annoyance.

The teacher approached exuberantly. "My name is Mrs. Greene. I'm thrilled to finally meet you, Robin," she said, stooping to her eye level.

She smelled of the same strong perfume her aunt Margaret wore, but a bit more floral. And she had breath so bad it made Robin's eyes water.

"We are going to do a lot of fun things today—all kinds of art projects. Your aunt tells me you like to draw and color. How does that sound?"

Robin nodded eagerly.

Margaret stooped, tucking the tail of her coat under her knee to protect her nylons. "Listen to your teacher and do exactly as she says. Alright, my dear?"

This time Robin let her head bob, not quite so enthusiastically.

Margaret stood. She brushed down her coat, straightened her collar, and patted her hat to be sure it was still in place. "Child, Aunty must go off to work." She hesitated by the door.

Placing a hand over the big pink bow covering Robin's scar, Mrs. Greene herded Robin over to the corner of the courtyard where several easels stood. Robin picked up one of the many thick-handled paintbrushes laid out on a table. Encouraging her to hold it like a pencil, the teacher repositioned the brush. Robin's pudgy little hands couldn't grasp it tightly enough. She let her put it back the way it was, bristles down.

Tearing off a wrinkled sheet of paper from one easel, Mrs. Greene said, "You can dip the brush in the paint and apply it right here."

Robin guided the tip of the brush first into the blue liquid. Lifting it, some spilled onto the ground.

Margaret, who remained a few yards off, gasped.

"It will wash. It's only tempera," Mrs. Greene said, directing Robin's hand.

After a few strokes, Robin learned how to dip and apply. What would be better than one brush? Two! She picked up the second one in her other hand.

"Just one at a time," Margaret admonished from the other end of the courtyard.

Mrs. Greene lifted a finger, shushing Margaret, then waved her off, signaling her to leave. "She's doing great," she whispered.

Robin dipped both brushes at once, one in the blue, the other in the red. She created straight lines with one and swirls with the other simultaneously.

A gulp of amazement emerged from Mrs. Greene's lips. "I've never seen anyone do that before. You are remarkably coordinated."

Margaret pulled a small camera from her purse and approached. Crouching down at Robin's level, she said, "Smile."

Robin stared into the lens and shyly laid a brush against her cheek. The shutter snapped in the camera.

Putting it back in her purse, Margaret rose and admired the image forming on the paper. "Very well done, child."

Robin beamed.

"I'll be back after a while." Margaret put her white gloves back on.

"We'll take good care of her, Miss Wood. You need not worry about a thing," Mrs. Greene said. "She'll love playing with the other children."

Margaret frowned. "Be careful. She can't stand for long periods."

The teacher smirked as if to say, 'I didn't just start teaching yesterday.' She shook Margaret's gloved hand, then led her to the door.

"I'll be back at five o'clock."

ANGEL IN FLIGHT

"That'll be fine. We are here until six." Mrs. Greene laid a hand on Margaret's fine worsted wool and said, "I promise you. She's in safe hands. We are well versed in handling children like her."

Margaret, head held high, pivoted and departed.

Children suddenly showed an interest in what Robin was painting and surrounded her.

One nodded at Robin's leg. "What is that thing?"

"I dunno. Looks like broomsticks holding it together," said another.

"Look how she holds the brush," said a third. They all three laughed.

The instructor rushed to intervene. Wedged between Robin and the other children, she said, "Let's be kind. She has endured a terrible accident and is still recovering from her injuries. Please speak nicely to her."

Each of the faces exhibited acceptance and understanding. The children continued to ogle Robin's leg as she curled in on herself in a protective stance, causing her to drip paint on her dress.

A student advanced and stared Robin in the eye. "Hi. I'm Charlie."

Robin lowered her arms, still gripping the brush handles so rigidly her knuckles turned white.

"Hello."

"What are you painting?"

Contemplating the figure with wet paint dripping where it was too thick in places, Robin said timidly, "An angel."

Another student elbowed Charlie out of the way. "It doesn't look like one." She pointed. "It doesn't have wings."

Charlie, vying for the best view, shouldered her to the side. "How do you know what an angel looks like?"

"I saw them in our bible at home. They have halos. That one doesn't have a halo." The girl drew a circle in the air around the blob-like head.

"Real angels don't have wings." Robin's voice, though soft, was confident and unwavering. "I saw them."

When the girl huffed, the others laughed. "How? Did you go to heaven?" she mocked.

Robin frowned and raised her voice. "No. I was on a mountain."

"Angels have wings like this." The girl flapped her arms like a bird as she wandered in a circle around the courtyard. Stopping again and pointing at the painting, she said, "That's not an angel."

Tears welled in Robin's eyes. When the teacher saw her wield a brush like a knife, she stepped between them.

"That wasn't very kind," she reproached the other girl. Holding out her arm straight, she ordered, "March! Go in there and sit at your desk. I want you to think about what it's like to be nice."

The girl stomped off, slamming the door behind her.

Charlie dipped his finger into the yellow paint and drew an ellipse over the figure's head. "Now she has a halo." He wiped his hand on his blue and red striped shirt and ran off. The other children fell in behind.

"Robin, darling. Are you alright?" she asked while pulling up a chair to sit beside her.

Setting the brush down, she tried wiping away some tears. The teacher pulled a handkerchief from the pocket of her apron and blotted the rest. She looked up at the easel. "That's a very fine angel you are painting."

Brush in hand again, Robin continued to fill in what would be the dress with the yellow paint. With the red and blue mixed, she formed a line that resembled the ground. The figure seemed to float in the air, casting a shadow.

"Is this your first time painting?"

Robin nodded. "I only color with crayons at home."

The expression of awe and wonder was unmistakable.

Next, Robin painted a darkened area on the ground that looked a bit like a prostrate child's body.

"What is that?"

"Me."

"That's you?"

Robin nodded.

"With an angel floating over you?"

Robin turned away. Here came the skepticism she had gotten so many times before. This same scene from different angles filled many pages of her sketchbook. Her aunt encouraged her to fill in the spaces in her coloring book or draw something else, like horses or puppies. No! She wanted to draw angels. The world needed to know they were real!

22 — *Friend* is Good

Summer 1976

The bedroom art gallery developed through the years. A few winged creatures had crept into Robin's collection—butterflies, fairies, dragonflies, and one bird. They were not her favorite, but Olive liked them.

Robin's eyes traced the circles and lines of that original tempera painting she had done in kindergarten. She was still mad at Charlie for ruining it with that stupid halo. Wiping it off with a damp cloth would have damaged the paper. Margaret had it professionally framed under glass, making it impossible to try.

Artwork covered two entire walls from floor to ceiling, one just from the summer class. Her favorite was the Jeremy painting of her.

"I miss you, Mr. Kess. When are you going to call me?"

A calendar said the end of August was near, which meant Jeremy was at the shoe market right then. Did he go? Did he take back his ex and forgot all about her? Had he gotten her ten-page letter and drawings she did of his ninth-grade school photo?

Robin's penmanship was not as good as Jeremy's, but he loved the little hearts for dots she drew over the letters *I* and *j*. She counted fifty-two in the last letter she wrote to him. In fact, his name filled one entire page in her drawing journal, just so she could practice the little heart over the first letter.

The last entry from a week ago far exceeded the capacity of the book. It was time for a new one. Robin had a lot on her mind and needed to pour her heart out to someone, even if they were only lines on paper.

The clock radio on the nightstand next to Robin's bed read 10:45 a.m. Time for the mailman. She grabbed a drawing pad, an HB pencil, and an eraser.

SHELLY PULSE

Grandmother was asleep in her La-Z-Boy. Blind, but her hearing was still crystal clear. Careful to open the front door quietly, Robin tried not to wake her. It was no use. The hinges needed grease, and it squeaked so loud it woke her with a start.

"Sorry, Grandma. Going to check the mail."

"It hasn't come yet, dear."

Of course, she would know that. Grandmother sat by the window and listened for him every day. Margaret wound and calibrated the cuckoo clock on the wall regularly, so she always knew the time. The mailman, Mr. Clark, was just as punctual as that clock.

"I'll wait for him outside."

"Jeremy hasn't written to you yet?"

No. Jeremy had not. Grandmother knew that because she had that same question yesterday and the three days before. She was as eager, if not more so. Of course, Robin would read the letter first before sharing it, in case she had to censor certain parts.

Stepping down Grandmother's cement wheelchair ramp, Robin held onto the rail with one hand and tucked the pad under the other. She sat on the edge of a brick planter box in the front yard and opened her drawing pad. A few days had passed since she last felt like sketching.

Robin had begged her aunt to drive her to Salt Lake to buy more illustration board, but Margaret was putting in extra hours at the department store. Someone had to look after Grandmother. Robin would return to high school soon, which meant working fewer hours.

Excitement built when she heard that familiar rumble from the Jeep engine drawing near. She waved at Mrs. Jones next door, who was also waiting for her mail.

"Has he written to you yet?" Mrs. Jones called out.

Man, does word travel fast around here!

Besides her culinary skills, Margaret was good at sharing gossip with all the neighbors. When she wasn't in the kitchen or caring for the two in her charge, Margaret was out delivering covered plates of her newest confection. It was like currency to acquire the latest news.

Robin shook her head. "Maybe today, Mrs. Jones!"

That letter had to come, or she would go crazy. The sleepless nights were more than she could handle. School started next week, and all hope of seeing him before the Winter Conference evaporated.

The mailman put his truck in neutral and set the parking brake. "Hello, young lady," he said with a mild rasp in his voice. He had delivered mail to the area for over thirty years and knew more about everyone's business than her aunt.

"Hello, Mr. Clark." Robin leaned against the mailbox that was permanently rooted in the cement sidewalk.

"Are you waiting for this?" He held up a thin white envelope.

It was addressed to her in Jeremy's trademark calligraphy. 'Do not bend,' screamed in bold red letters next to the address. Robin grabbed a corner. Mischievously, Mr. Clark tugged back.

"Careful. It says not to bend it," Robin snapped.

Letting go caused Robin to lose her balance. The mailbox stopped her from falling.

"He must be quite special. Mrs. Ward says you met at some kind of art school. Your aunty thinks he's very handsome."

Handsome would not be a word to describe him. He had the typical teenage acne. And he was very tan under that mop of bleach-blond hair.

"Yes. He's pretty cute."

Mr. Clark handed Robin the rest of the mail, released the brake, and waved as he moved on to Mrs. Jones' residence.

Robin set the bundle addressed to her aunt on a credenza by the front door. Forgetting her grandmother was even in the room, she opened the one from Jeremy.

"Lordy, lordy, child. Come sit next to your poor old grandmother and read to me what the young man has to say." She gestured for Robin to sit on the couch next to her.

Pouring over the words quickly, Robin already noted a few things she didn't want to share aloud. Her stiff leg stretched the length of the couch; the other dangled over the edge when she sat sideways to read by the light of the window.

"Dearest Robin."

"I like the sound of that," Grandmother said with an approving tone.

"I can't believe art school came and went so fast. I had no idea how fun it was going to be, well, except for Professor Anderson tearing up my homework and almost—"

Robin stopped. She would not read the rest of that sentence, '… and almost getting arrested for knocking over headstones.'

"I'll leave that part out. It is sort of personal."

The top of her dentures clicked. "Uh-huh."

"I wanted to give you a drawing I did of an angel. It's not even close to as good as yours, but I tried."

Peeling back the letter, she uncovered a drawing of a figure dressed in long flowing robes, hovering in the air over a snow-covered mountain, arms spread wide, and looking up into the heavens. The likeness of her was striking. He must have done it from memory, having never given him a recent picture.

Robin described the rendering in detail to her grandmother.

"Sounds like the young man has quite a lot of talent."

Nodding to herself, knowing Helene couldn't see it, she said, "He does." She set the drawing on the sofa cushion.

Continuing, she read, "I hope I'm able—"

Oops. Robin did not want them to know they were planning to meet in Park City.

"What was that?" The expression in her milky eyes told Robin to *spill it*.

"He is trying to convince his parents to let him go to Winter Conference. I'm afraid Aunty won't let me go—"

"If Prince Charming is there?"

Robin shrugged and laid back in the throw pillow. "Yes."

"I don't see the harm in it. He's a good boy, isn't he?"

Define good. Jeremy was a good artist and an excellent kisser. So far, he hadn't tried anything too naughty. Though, she was a little bothered by his uncertainty regarding children.

"Yes. He is."

Next, she read, "I'm sorry I couldn't visit you while we were in Salt Lake. Dad said it was okay, but my mom didn't want me crashing the car. She also didn't want to be left stranded. Mom never misses an opportunity to go shopping in the big city. She already has an entire store full of shoes in two closets and came back with even more. I ended up watching my little brother and sister the whole time. Again! Boring."

Grandmother laughed heartily. "A woman can never have enough shoes."

But Jeremy mentioned nothing about that girl from Richfield. Was she there? Did he see her? Are they back together, and he doesn't want to say? And if he did, how much kissing could they have done with him babysitting his siblings? Plenty if he bribed them enough.

She read on. "We have family up by where you live and might visit them soon. Maybe I can talk my parents into letting me stop to see you. Write to me. I'd love another one of your drawings. If there is something else you want me to draw or paint for you, let me know. Hope all is well.

Tell your grandmother and Aunt Margaret hello for me. Your friend, Jeremy Kess."

Your friend? That's it? No 'Love, Jeremy?' Now I'm just your friend? Robin let the letter fall unceremoniously into her lap.

"What a sweet, sweet boy," Grandmother remarked.

She obviously couldn't see the look of disappointment seizing Robin's face. A gloomy cloud formed over her. She couldn't believe she spent all that time and emotional energy to just be his *friend*.

Forcing a positive note in her voice, she said, "Yes. Yes, he is."

Examining his angel drawing more closely, she had to acknowledge his effort was exceptional. Maybe *friend* was a more elevated title than she gave credit. *Friend* is good. At least she had that.

After folding the letter and flattening the drawing, Robin kissed her grandmother on the forehead. "Is there anything you need?"

"No, darling. I'm fine right here."

Grandmother was used to spending her days sitting in that chair by the window. Once in a while, she wanted the television on for company. A radio tuned to her favorite music station on a table next to her kept her entertained. Now, too many commercials blasting from their speakers made them unpleasant.

"I'll be in my room if you need me."

She retreated to her sanctuary. The new drawing became enshrined next to the soccer ball painting on the ever-shrinking wall space. When she grew up and got a place of her own, she would need a mansion to house all her art.

Robin reread the letter. Why did that word bother her so much? She was too young to be anything else, she supposed. Of course, 'girlfriend' *did* contain that word. And signing his letter, 'Your Boyfriend, Jeremy,' would have sounded weird. She tucked the letter away in the top drawer under her journal.

A newspaper clipping, hanging out of one of the earlier diaries, caught her eye. Robin opened to that page. The entire article fell open, and she reread it like she had a hundred times.

The story told of a four-year-old girl named Robin Wood, rescued from the side of a mountain by a soldier named Michael Smith. He was very young in the picture, not much older than she was now. His visits to the hospital after the crash and surgeries were frequent. Michael had visited her home many times to check on her progress. She guessed he was in his thirties by now.

Her aunt was a little older than Michael. That didn't stop him from spending a lot of time chatting with her when he visited. Several times he stayed for supper and did not leave until after dark.

When she was about ten, Robin secretly hoped her aunt and Michael would fall madly in love and marry. Then, Michael could be her sort-of dad.

For a few years, Michael did not call on them when he was overseas. The mention of his name on her lips dwindled, and his letters stopped altogether.

One picture in the article was of the clearing where the plane had crashed. The photo was of the meadow covered in snow, and no evidence of plane debris appeared. Robin tried to guess which tree in the scene was the one she laid under. She had never been back to that spot and wondered what it was like today. How hard would it be to reach that spot?

That evening, while setting the table for dinner, Robin asked, "Have you heard from Michael lately?"

"No. Why?"

"Just wondering."

Margaret stopped stirring the pot of mashed potatoes and set it to the side. She wiped her hands on her apron and faced Robin.

"You haven't talked about him in years. Why now?"

"I told Jeremy about him, and I found that article about the crash. It made me think of him. He used to visit all the time."

Margaret spooned the potatoes into a large bowl and set it, and a gravy boat, full to the brim, on the table. Out from the oven came the most delicious meatloaf Robin had ever smelled.

"I think the war took a lot out of him. Last I remember, he was headed for Germany or Indonesia or some such place. Would you like me to call him? Perhaps he is back now."

That conjured images of him in exotic foreign lands—the handsome and daring young soldier rescuing little girls from burning buildings or sinking ships.

"Yes. I would like that."

Robin helped her grandmother to the table and filled her plate with peas, potatoes, a slice of bread with butter, and a wedge of the meatloaf, which she cut into small pieces. She placed a fork in her hand.

ANGEL IN FLIGHT

Grandmother could still make out shadows, so she was still good at landing food in her mouth. Someday, Robin would spoon-feed her like Jeremy did with little Scotty.

"Jeremy must be very special if you told him about Michael and the accident," Margaret stated after her third bite.

"Yes. And he didn't laugh when I told him about, you know, the angels."

Robin observed Margaret's reaction to that last part. No, she never laughed exactly, but she had made it clear how silly a thing it was to believe in.

"I'd like to visit the crash site."

Margaret stopped chewing and glanced up from her plate. The frown told Robin she thought it a poor idea, which usually followed with a statement of, 'Maybe when you are older.'

Her reply shocked Robin. "I guess if we are going, we better make it soon. Before cold sets in and it starts snowing. It is a fairly high altitude. You might not—"

What? I might not walk well enough to make it there? The glare dared her to finish that doubting declaration.

"I'll phone Michael tomorrow from work. It won't be a long-distance charge. If he's in town, perhaps he'll remember where it happened."

SHELLY PULSE

23 — Perry!

Everyone in the eleventh grade had grown several inches over the summer, except Robin. Stuck at under five feet, she was probably not going to grow much more. Like walking among giants, all she saw were the students' backs as she wove her way through the hall.

Besides her core required classes, Robin had to pick an elective of either art or a language. It was no surprise she chose art again.

After the first ten minutes of class, she thought perhaps she had made a mistake. The new art teacher spent the entire time extolling the virtues of the master painters from the Renaissance. Robin found the subject boring and lost herself in the doodles of her new journal.

Tucked inside the middle was a copy of the drawing Jeremy had done of her as an angel. She pulled it out and studied it.

The teacher cleared his throat. "Miss Wood. Is there something you'd like to share with the class?"

She folded the picture and sat up straight. "No."

Towering over her, he picked up the drawing and unfolded it. Was he surprised because it had to do with art, the subject of the class, or that it was so well done?

"Did you draw this?"

Robin shook her head.

"Who did?" He searched for a signature.

To avoid attention, she preferred the back of the class. Fortunately, with the last name of Wood, she often found herself assigned there. The last thing she wanted was to discuss Jeremy.

"A friend."

Concern formed on his face. "It sure looks like you. How old is your friend?"

All the students in the room faced Robin. "Seventeen."

Relief replaced the concern, and her teacher held up the drawing for the class to witness.

"See what you are capable of doing? One of you could emerge as the next Michelangelo or Da Vinci." He handed the drawing back to Robin. "Excellent friend to have. Pass along my admiration of his work, will you?"

Robin nodded. He obviously had not seen hers yet. Not that she was better than Jeremy, just different styles.

Professor Anderson's words echoed in her head, 'There are those who can do art and not teach. Then, some can teach but not do. Lastly, a few can do both. You are lucky to learn from teachers who also get paid in the real world for their work.' She wondered if Mr. Page had any such talent.

"Please tell us all which is your favorite classical painter, Miss Wood," the teacher admonished her from the back of the room.

Robin could not tell exactly how close he was, but his heat radiated against her back.

Names churned through her mind. She was not sure about the classical ones, but she had met a few contemporary artists at summer school. Professor Anderson had flown in several big-name illustrators to lecture the class.

"I don't know, but I like Henry Foster. He's probably my favorite."

"I'm not familiar with that name. What century was he from?"

"The twentieth."

Some students laughed.

"What do you like about his work?" The teacher strolled up the aisle. One hand folded across his chest while his chin rested on the knuckles of the other.

"The simplicity of the wash over gesso and opaque strokes of paint at the point of focus. It draws your eye to the subject. I love how he uses contrasting colors of the same hue. Freaks out my retinas."

Robin remembered the man fondly. He was not much taller than her and showed a genuine interest in her work.

The teacher whirled around. "Are you sure you are in the right class?" This time, *everyone* laughed. "Perhaps you should be teaching it."

Robin's face flushed as she shrunk back in her seat.

When a student expressed him or herself as too knowledgeable about a particular topic, it often drew teasing from the other students. Not this time. The countenances facing her appeared to admire her. Maybe the eleventh grade was that magical time when the immaturity of children transformed into well-mannered adults. She liked that.

ANGEL IN FLIGHT

Finally, someone diverted Mr. Page's attention. "When do we get to draw?" a female student asked.

"Are we going to draw nude models?" asked a boy, making his buddies titter.

He reminded Robin of Greg and his posse. Noting this guy's face, she vowed to avoid him at all costs. She knew his type, and he spelled trouble.

Mr. Page expressed little amusement. "I shall answer Melonie's question. First of next week. I want you all to understand the history of art—from the time our cave-dwelling ancestors drew stick figures with charcoal all the way to the greatest painters of the present."

Melonie's head drooped.

Feeling the same way, Robin wanted to spend her time creating, not wasting it on meaningless history. Perhaps Melonie would make a good friend and homework partner, the way Jeremy had been.

Combating drowsiness in this, the last class of the day, Robin stretched her good leg under the desk. She accidentally knocked the other student's books onto the floor, causing quite a clatter.

Mr. Page peered up from the lectern and lowered his reading glasses. Robin sat up a little straighter, pretending to listen. She didn't want a repeat of before.

The boy in front of her turned around and smiled.

Oh, no! It was Perry! She didn't recognize him. She thought she had escaped his ever-present attention this year. My, how he looked like Jeremy. He was taller but had the same hair, and devilish grin.

"May I see the drawing?"

When Mr. Page pressed the button on the slide projector to the next image, Robin slipped the picture to Perry. Maybe if he knew she had a boyfriend—and not just any boyfriend, a talented one, as a matter of fact—he'd leave her alone.

"Be careful with it," she whispered.

He secreted it between the books he had picked up from the floor.

She immediately regretted that—now she had to explain what it meant, her as an angel.

The bell rang. Every student jumped up and gathered their books, except Perry.

"Don't forget to read the first chapter of the text by Wednesday. I want you to be able to identify the name of the painting and the artist of each of the pictures," Mr. Page called out as the students clogged the exit.

Perry handed the drawing back to Robin. "That's pretty good. Who is he?"

Flustered, she weighed the consequences of her response. After three attempts, the words finally came out. "My boyfriend."

The momentary flash of jealousy vanished. Perry's sneakers skidded on the floor, making a squeaking sound as he shuffled away.

Did she say the right thing? How she wished Jeremy lived closer. All she wanted was to roam the halls holding his hand. People would see how happy she was, and Perry would leave her alone. Now all they saw was misery.

Mrs. Jones readied to leave after caring for Grandmother when Robin returned from school.

"How was your first day back?"

"Fine."

Robin was wary of divulging more. Only one gossip was more extravagant than her aunt and the mailman, and that was Mrs. Jones.

"Good. I took the liberty of bringing in your mail. It's sitting on the kitchen table." Mrs. Jones was as giddy as a schoolgirl just invited to the prom.

Robin knew something was up. Another letter from Jeremy had arrived. She wanted to rip into it but was sure Mrs. Jones would, like her grandmother, want to know all the details.

"I'll read it later," she said, pretending to be disinterested.

Mrs. Jones acted dejected. "I'll have to wait to hear all about it from Margaret." She slammed the door a little harder than usual when she left.

The thump of the door woke up Helene. Robin was hoping for a little quiet until her aunt returned home from work. Now she must sit with her and chat.

She slipped the letter from Jeremy between her schoolbooks. Hopefully, Mrs. Jones hadn't told Grandmother about it.

Robin kissed her grandmother as usual, then sat on the sofa beside her. The room remained quiet for a long while. Robin studied every line of her face as she stared blankly into the tidy parlor lined with bookshelves. Eyes drifting to her left hand, Robin noticed that her grandmother still wore her wedding ring, even though her grandfather had passed long before she was born.

Searched her memory. "How did you and Grandpa meet?" She told that story a thousand times, but it meant something now.

ANGEL IN FLIGHT

It appeared as though Helene could suddenly see again. She smiled and directed her eyes toward Robin.

"His family moved west during the Great Depression and settled in the valley. They homesteaded a farm next to ours."

She twirled the gold band tips of the fingers of her right hand.

"He came to school on the days he could, but was mean to me. Pulled my hair. Called me names. Once he ran up and rubbed snow in my face. My momma became angry when I told her, so she marched me right over and demanded an apology."

Robin covered her mouth in surprise.

"Did he say he was sorry?"

"No. His mother denied her little boy was capable of such poor behavior. I remember her accusing me of trying to gain attention," Grandmother said with a chuckle. "That started a feud between our two families. We were always warring over property lines and whose dog got into which chicken coop."

It suddenly struck Robin where she got her storytelling skills. Wanting Grandmother to get to the point, she fidgeted with Jeremy's letter. The second regret of the day—asking about Grandpa.

"Did he ever apologize?"

"Yes. Years later. When he proposed marriage on my eighteenth birthday, that made both of our parents furious. They refused to pay for the wedding."

"What did you do?"

"Your great aunt Martha gave us some money, and we eloped to Salt Lake. We lived with her for two years until your daddy was born. That softened both of our parents when they got word that I was pregnant. The depression ended. We returned to the ranch and built us a little log house."

Grandmother let out a heavy sigh and closed her eyes. Either she was tired, or Mrs. Jones didn't tell her about the envelope from Jeremy.

Robin thought about asking her more, but let that wait for another day. Right now, reading the contents of that letter was all she could think about. She patted her hand and went to her room.

At her desk, she turned on her little pink ceramic lamp and opened the letter.

Dearest Robin,

That looked good to her eyes and sounded terrific to her ears when she repeated it aloud several times.

Thank you for your last letter. I can't believe school starts next week. Mr. Bower is letting me put together more bicycles to earn money for Winter

Conference. He increased the amount he pays per bike from $8 to $10. Business is picking up. I work there on Saturday mornings. It usually takes me two hours. I've got it down to an hour and a half. He said he's going to let me fix and tune bicycles soon.

I still have to work at the shoe store after school.

My parents still won't answer me about Winter Conference. I barely got them to let me run the first 50-mile leg of the March of Dimes race to Salt Lake. They wouldn't let me go all the way. I'm sure it's because they know you live there. They found out about the incident with the two girlfriends. I told them all about you and the great time we had. They think I should 'take a break' from girls for a while. But they do love your painting of me and the angel drawings.

Anyway, I hope school goes well, and I can't wait to hear from you again. I've enclosed a crosshatch drawing I did of you with ink from the picture you sent. I'm practicing with that now. Take care.

Love, Jeremy

P.S. Thanks for telling me more about what happened after the accident. It's incredible what you have gone through.

He said, 'Love, Jeremy!' Whatever gloom had followed her around the last few days vanished. Now Robin couldn't wait to tell him about what happened in class today. She took out a short stack of paper and wrote. Her hand cramped about the time she heard the front door slam.

Helping to gather brown paper grocery bags from Margaret's arms while she took off her jacket and hung it up, Robin stuck her nose inside a bag and sniffed. Fish? Cheese? Something smelled foul. Very few of the dishes her aunt made she disliked.

"What are you making?"

"A French dish I've wanted to try. I saw it in a magazine last week." Margaret donned an autumn-print apron. "Will you be my taste tester?"

Robin cautiously agreed. "I guess so." A broccoli casserole she had made once turned her stomach. Hopefully, this one was better.

"Can I help?"

Margaret eyed Robin suspiciously. "Sure. I need a 9 by 13 glass Pyrex down in that cupboard." She tapped the cupboard door next to the olive-green stove that matched the refrigerator. "What's going on? How was your first day? What happened?"

Relating the events of the day in detail, Robin's chatterbox took over. Her aunt was good at opening her up. She was a good listener; she had to be with long-winded storytellers in the house.

ANGEL IN FLIGHT

The fish casserole was in the oven to bake for forty-five minutes at 275 degrees before Robin finished her monologue. "Mrs. Jones brought in the mail. I think that's it."

She cleverly extracted more by remaining silent and starring unblinkingly down at Robin. "And—?"

Robin could not help herself. "Jeremy wrote to me again." One half of her was angry at the other half for telling, but she knew her aunt would eventually find out. Robin did not want her going through her things.

"Again? I must have missed the last one. How is he doing?"

She had only read it to Grandmother. "He's working hard. Had to watch his brother and sister. His mom wouldn't let him drive up. She needed the car to go shopping for shoes."

Lifting her eyebrows, Margaret said, "A woman can never have enough shoes." She took off her apron and draped it over a chair.

Robin laughed. "That's what Grandma said." She stared down at her own sneakers with the loosened strings.

"Now don't you go getting any ideas," Margaret said. "Those are all you ever want to wear. You will need a sturdy pair for next weekend, though."

Puzzled, Robin asked, "Next weekend?"

"Yes. Michael is coming to take the two of us up to the mountain."

Robin was overjoyed. She struggled to decide which was more thrilling, seeing Michael or going back to where they crashed.

"Really?"

Margaret nodded.

"Michael is coming here?" she repeated even more excitedly, pointing with two fingers toward the floor.

"Uh-huh."

Robin wrapped her arms around her aunt's middle and squealed with delight. "You called him?"

"Yes. He still remembers right where it's at. He'll bring one of his army buddies with him to help carry you up the hill, if necessary."

That thought was a little humiliating, but whatever it took, she had to make it there. If Jeremy had been strong enough, she would not have minded wrapping her arms around his neck and letting him trudge up the mountain. She might have even climbed on his back. That image lingered, making her smile.

"When?"

"Saturday. I switched days with Gladys. Will you mind sitting with your grandmother on Sunday?" She peeked around the corner at her mother, dosing in her soft chair.

"Of course. Yes." Robin was so excited she could hardly contain herself. "We should get a camera."

"I'll bring mine."

24 — Climbing the Mountain

The cool air stiffened Robin's arthritic hand, making it hard to hold on to a pencil. She sat on the cement steps outside the front door, longing for summer while tracing the outline of an image through the paper. Memory offered up the meadow scene from all those years ago. She had tried drawing airplanes a few times but had difficulty getting the wings' perspective right.

Gary, Robin's father, was an expert at rendering all kinds of military hardware, from tanks to guns to boats. He was especially good at drawing aircraft. This time, for Robin, it was more about depicting the broken parts. A little hump off to the left of her sketch represented where her father lay blanketed by the snow.

A blue Ford pickup pulled into the driveway behind the Buick. It was Michael! She set down her drawing pad and pencil and hobbled as quickly as she could to greet him.

"Boy, look at you go!" Michael said when he stepped out and slammed the door.

Jumping into his arms, he lifted her. She held onto his neck so tightly, he struggled to breathe.

"I was wondering if you were ever going to come back." He set her down. Robin disappeared under his coat as he wrapped it around her shoulders with his muscular arm. She looked up at him. "Where have you been?"

"Just about everywhere. I got promoted, but my commanding officer sent me traveling all over."

Robin grabbed his left hand dangling in front of her. She noticed it still had no ring on it. "Haven't you got married yet?" She hoped the answer was 'no.' But she would have been happy for him, anyway.

"Not yet. Came close a couple of times."

They reached the front steps, and Robin picked up her pad and pencils.

Margaret wiped her hands on her apron when she opened the screen door to let them in.

Michael stood still when his eyes met hers.

Robin found the silence between them rather amusing. She sensed there was an attraction, but neither of them would admit it.

Deep and sultry, Margaret finally said, "So wonderful to see you, Michael."

"It has been way too long." He bound up the stairs with one leap. Reaching back, he held Robin's hand as she maneuvered the steps. He had to duck through the door.

"I hope you are hungry. I made breakfast."

"Starving. Happy for a home-cooked meal. Those army rations are growing a bit tiresome." Michael crawled in front of Grandmother and drew her hand into both of his. "You must be Helene I've heard so much about."

"Yes. You are Michael. The angel who saved our little Robin." Grandmother reached up and caressed his face. "Bless you."

"Thank you, Mrs. Wood. She's a strong and talented child. I'm sure she takes after her grandmother in many ways."

She patted his hand while he stood.

Michael had aged since Robin last saw him. He was still fit, but his short hair was thinning and sported a bit of gray about the temples. It was not as dark as she remembered her father's, a more pleasant chestnut brown, about the same color as hers.

Margaret called from the kitchen for everyone to gather in the dining room. Michael and Robin helped Helene to her feet; they escorted her to the table, each taking a hand. Her aunt ceded the chair at the head of the table to Michael and hovered beside him.

It occurred to Robin that Margaret had jet black hair. Did she color it just for Michael's visit? Her lips were particularly red. She was wearing a rather tight-fitting blouse for a Saturday morning. Pants? She'd never seen her aunt wear trousers before, except to work in the yard pulling weeds.

When Margaret spooned scrambled eggs onto Michael's plate, she moved quite close to his shoulder. After the third helping, he stayed her hand. She was not leaving much for the rest of those seated at the table.

"I can make more."

"This will be plenty."

ANGEL IN FLIGHT

Robin took what remained and divided it into thirds, one for each of the other plates.

"No, dear. You eat it. I'm not that hungry this morning."

Michael helped himself to four sausage links. "You better eat up. We have a long hike today."

Margaret smoothed out the wrinkles in the legs of her pants. "If I eat all that, I won't be able to move."

Robin and Michael shared a knowing smirk when Margaret entered the kitchen with the empty bowl and returned with a plate of biscuits, hot from the oven.

She was about to slice open one of them, butter on a knife at the ready, when Michael took it from her and said, "I know how to do it."

Margaret's hand lingered a long moment before she relinquished the knife.

My, oh, my, Aunt Margaret had a crush on Michael. All this time, and she did not know. Why had she never talked about him the way she did of Jeremy? Her aunt was a beautiful and smartly dressed woman. She could date all the time. Now it occurred to Robin that she was hoping Michael would sweep her away into that enchanted land of romance. She let out a little giggle.

"What's so funny?" Margaret asked as she sat down.

It was Michael's turn to spoon two sausage links onto her plate. She gave him the signal to stop when he went for the third.

"I'm just happy."

"Uh-huh."

"How long are you here for?" Robin asked Michael.

"I have the option of retiring. I've been in the army for almost fifteen years now. My commander is trying to sign me for another five. He says I have a good chance of making colonel someday."

His wide grin showed a set of brilliant white teeth framed by a square jaw.

Margaret's countenance fell suddenly to her plate. Robin could tell that answer disappointed her.

"Have you decided yet?" she asked, looking wistfully into his eyes.

"No. My cousin works at a bank and thinks I would make a good branch manager. My uncle wants me to go sell life insurance with him."

"Do any of those appeal to you?" Margaret brightened.

Even Grandmother had placed her misty gaze on him, as though she could see him clearly.

"I could do that. But I don't like desk work." He held up his large, powerful hands. "I'm more cut out for physical labor. You might as well put me in a cage if I can't keep moving."

Robin remembered her friend Tina and the land her family owned up the canyon. "I know someone who needs a ranch manager. You wouldn't be far."

"A real ranch? With horses and cows and such?"

Robin nodded.

He pursed his lips and narrowed his focus out the window. "That wouldn't be too bad."

"What else would you do?" Margaret steered him away from the idea of the military.

"I worked on a lot of trucks and tanks. I could be a mechanic. Diesel mostly. Good money."

"I'm sure there's plenty of that around here with all the industrial growth in North Salt Lake," Margaret said expectantly. "I know a lot of wives of business owners in my line of work. I'll ask around."

"That would be great."

Robin had never seen her aunt so contented in her life. She cut and carefully placed small bites of sausage in her mouth so as not to smear her lipstick.

"Well, squirt. You ready to go up to the mountain?"

Robin jumped up from the table. "How far is it?"

"Couple hours to the trail-head parking lot. From there, maybe half-hour hiking. It's a little off the path, but I've got maps. We'll find it." He cocked his head; his eyes traced the outline of her slightly bent leg. "You up for it?"

Now Robin was nervous, scared, eager, and overwhelmed all at once. The big breakfast she ate churned. The thought of trying to step over rocks and fallen branches worried her. "What if I can't?"

Michael lifted his arms and flexed like a bodybuilder. "I carried you out of there; I can carry you back in."

Robin laughed, as did Margaret.

"Yeah, but I weighed 30 lbs. Now I weigh, um, I'm much bigger now." She sat back down.

"Why the sudden interest?" Michael asked, glancing back and forth between Robin and her aunt.

Margaret declared, "Robin has a boyfriend."

He raised his eyebrows. "She does?"

ANGEL IN FLIGHT

Embarrassed? Angry? Why did her aunt bring up Jeremy? Her face felt red-hot, and her hands trembled. What did that have to do with her wanting to go back there?

Talking about it with Jeremy made her face her darkest memories and pain. It could have been anyone else, even her best friend, Olive. Robin wanted to leave the table.

Margaret glared at her. Letting her fingers touch Michael's arm lightly, Margaret's gossip motor revved.

"She met a young man at art school and shared her experience with him. He had apparently taken a great interest in the details of where and when it happened. And he doesn't seem to be bothered by her... you know—"

Being crippled? Robin wanted to say. Because she had scars and broken bones? Because she couldn't walk as fast as other people?

"Sounds like a nice young man," Michael said, placing a hand on Margaret's.

"He writes to her about once a week. They want to meet at some art conference thing this winter in Park City."

"Are you going?" Michael asked Robin.

She shrugged and deferred to Margaret for an answer.

"I haven't decided yet. What do you think?" Margaret asked, leaning in closer to Michael.

"Sounds like fun. I know how much she likes the snow."

They talked as if Robin were not even in the room. Margaret told him all she knew about the summer program she attended and the pictures they drew for each other.

"Honey, why don't you bring some of your drawings and show them to Michael."

Taking her time pulling thumbtacks out of each one, she gathered a few off the wall. A recent drawing was of a soldier, with a hint of wings, carrying a child in his arms. That one she handed to Michael when she returned to the table.

"I did this one for you."

He held it close and didn't utter another word for several minutes. The moisture forming in the corners of his eyes said enough.

"You did this?" he asked, wiping away a tear with the back of his sleeve.

Robin put her arm around his shoulder. "Yes."

Michael set the picture down and pulled her in close. "It's beautiful. You are a very talented young lady. I'll cherish it forever."

Margaret clapped her hands once. "I'll clean up, and we better get on the road." She began clearing the table. "I prepared lunch for later."

"What about Grandma?"

"Mrs. Jones will be over to check on her. I told her all about our little adventure. She hopes to meet Michael if we have time." Margaret patted Michael on the shoulder as she returned to the kitchen.

Michael boosted Robin up into his truck, where she positioned herself behind the gear shifter. Margaret's feet remained rooted where she stood and arms folded when he went around the front to get in. He returned. Michael seemed a little uncomfortable pushing her up into the truck with a hand on her thigh.

Once seated, Margaret smiled. Not one of her stiff saleswoman smiles, no. It was the real thing, warm and welcoming. Robin rarely saw that one.

"Thank you, kind gentleman," she said with a pucker.

The hesitation said Michael wasn't sure how to read those lips. He grinned, bowed, then slammed the door.

After placing the picnic gear and sack of food in the truck's bed, Michael climbed in and started the engine. Robin noticed the curtains of two of the houses across the street parted at the motor's rumble. Mrs. Jones waved from her front porch as they backed out.

Margaret rolled down the window and shouted, "Thank you for checking on her. We should be back before dark, and I left plenty of food in the refrigerator."

"We'll be fine. Have a good time." Craning her neck to catch a glimpse of Michael, Mrs. Jones smiled and nodded her approval.

Michael did most of the talking during that two-hour journey. He told of all his assignments, both in the States and overseas. Robin laughed most of the time until her aunt spoiled the festive mood with her burning question.

"Did you shoot anyone?"

"Fortunately, no. My job was to keep the machinery moving. I was nowhere near the action."

"Did you know anyone who got killed?"

A long pause followed. Michael reached down behind the stick shift and opened the ashtray. He was about to pull out a cigarette from a pack stowed in there, but changed his mind.

ANGEL IN FLIGHT

Robin didn't know Michael smoked. Of course, she was about ten or eleven the last time she saw him, and he never did in front of her. Apart from the vague memories of her father always with a cigarette hanging from his lips, she knew of no one else.

She glared up at him. "You smoke?" Robin asked with a tone of disapproval.

He looked down at her apologetically. "Sometimes. When I'm nervous or upset. Which doesn't happen very often."

Robin deduced that her aunt's question caused him to feel the latter and hoped Margaret wouldn't push further. But she did.

"Were they close friends of yours?"

"Uh-huh. One I bunked with at boot camp. Two others I served with along the way." Michael scanned the horizon through the windshield. "What a beautiful morning."

Margaret wanted more details, Robin could see. She would get none. Not now, at least.

Sensing the same pain she experienced losing her family, Robin leaned her head on his shoulder to comfort him, the way she would if her father were still alive. Michael kissed the crown of her head, right in front of the bow and rubber band, holding her hair back in a ponytail. She remembered the many times he'd done that when she was a child lying in a hospital bed.

The truck turned off the highway and lumbered up an old logging road. A light skiff of snow lined the edge on the north side.

Robin asked, "Is there going to be snow up there?"

"Some. There was a light dusting overnight, but it should be melted by now."

Robin was not sure which way she hoped. If it had snowed, then she could experience it like it was at the time of the crash. Another part of her wanted it dry, so she could explore and change the picture in her head.

They parked next to a battered sign that read, 'Woodland Hills Trail.' Michael hopped out and came around to help Margaret out of the truck first. She did not waste the moment and fell into his arms, sliding down his large frame to the ground. He was more than a head taller than her, and she had to tilt her head to keep her eyes locked on his. He smiled and let go, holding out his hands to catch Robin.

Sliding to the edge of the bench seat, Robin half-launched, half-fell into his arms, letting him catch her the way her dad did when she was little. He stumbled backward, but stayed upright.

Teasingly, he said, "You are definitely not five anymore."

"Is it very far?" Robin asked when he cautiously set her on the ground.

Michael's gaze traced the outline of the tops of the trees. "No. Just up that ridge."

"Have you been up there, you know, after the crash?"

Michael's eyes turned misty.

Robin puzzled over that response. Why would that make him sad?

"We had to go up there several times to clean up. I helped with the investigation, escorting the boys from the aviation board. That went on for two months."

Perhaps he had to help retrieve her father and little brother's bodies and didn't want to talk about it. That elevated him in her eyes to a whole new level.

Margaret looked down at her feet. "I should have worn sturdier shoes." She had on a pair of sneakers, just like Robin's, but brand new. She must have forgotten Robin needed some.

Robin grew tired of her old ones and wanted something different, anyway. Jeremy could suggest a pair. The next letter would include that question. He had mentioned clogs as an alternative since they lacked the need to lace. For now, she would make do with her ratty old tennis shoes.

"You'll be fine." Michael slammed the door, grabbed the food, picnic gear, and blanket from the truck bed, and headed up the trail. "We'll take the longer route. It's not as steep."

Partway up the hill, they reached an open area with lots of wildflowers. Most had withered and dried, but a few sunflowers remained. Robin methodically stepped over some fallen branches and picked some. She wrinkled her nose when she discovered the sticky sap oozing from the ends. Wrapping the stems in the sleeve of her jacket, she wiped her hands on her jeans. Robin then added a few wild daisies she could reach and rejoined the others, who patiently waited.

Margaret had taken Robin to the cemetery each December to visit her family's graves. They always stopped at a florist shop to buy flowers. Robin knew her mother's favorite flowers were roses because she got excited when her dad brought them home. Her aunt sometimes brought a bucket full of soapy water and a brush to clean the headstones. Today, these wildflowers would suffice.

When they reached the top of the hill, Michael set down the items he was carrying and unfolded a map. He traced the route with his finger for Margaret and Robin to follow.

"Right over that line of trees." He glanced up from the map. "You two doing alright?"

ANGEL IN FLIGHT

"There is no trail," Robin bleated. All she saw were rocks, gullies, and fallen trees.

"I know an easier way."

A little farther and the three reached a precipice overlooking the meadow below. The path down was a little steeper and made of sharp gravel and loose dirt.

"I don't think I can." Robin's voice trailed off tremulously.

Michael set down the things he was carrying at Margaret's feet. "Wait for me here. I'll carry her down and come back for you."

Margaret's red lips bent into a grateful smile.

Arms hooked around his neck, Michael scooped Robin up. She rode in the cradle he made with his arms. One foot in front of another, he slid down the side until they came to flat ground. That left a cloud of dust that made Robin choke and her eyes water.

If it had snowed overnight, there was no evidence. The sun was bright and high in the sky, a little toward the south. Robin recognized the general direction she was facing. She had studied the map of that mountain range many times over the years.

Towards her home in Bountiful, she could see a massive bank of clouds. One in the center rose miles into the air. A breeze breached the seams of her jacket, and she wrapped it around herself.

Girlish giggles echoed through the meadow. Clinging to Michael, Margaret descended, her feet dancing uncontrollably down the gravelly slope. He slid ahead to catch her. Face-to-face, he locked her in an embrace when they reached the bottom.

Breathless, she gazed up into his eyes. "That was fun! And you are so strong," she said between gasps.

"Going up will be easier than coming down." His eyes turned away.

Margaret did not weigh too much more than Robin. He could have just as easily carried her. Why he let her struggle was a mystery.

This resembled a family outing. Robin could sure picture the two of them as her parents. Just not letting go of his hand showed how much her aunt liked him. Now she had something to blackmail her aunt with if she ever brought up Jeremy again.

Pulling out the camera, Margaret began snapping photos. First, she had Michael and Robin pose together. Then she put the camera in Robin's hand and said, "Make sure we are in the frame and push this button."

"I know how to take pictures," Robin snapped with more attitude than her aunt deserved. She set the flowers on the blanket.

Margaret tucked her arm in Michael's and laid her head against his shoulder. What had been the meadow, now dotted with young pine trees and scrub oak, made for the perfect backdrop.

Robin took her time to frame the shot with the right balance of people, horizon line, and trees. She applied the golden ratio she'd learned at art school. When she thought it was perfect, she held her breath, pressed the button, and the camera fired.

"Looks like we have a professional photographer in the family as well," Michael said.

What did he mean by *family*? Did he include himself in that statement?

Robin handed the camera back to her aunt and picked up the flowers. The breeze blew harder now and almost knocked her over. She pulled the hood up over her head to cover her ears.

When the breeze stopped suddenly, tranquility descended on the area, giving Robin a sense that this was hallowed ground. Without prompting, she reverently walked toward a flat spot. Using the treetops the plane hit as a point of reference, she oriented herself to the site.

A little frustrated, she looked back at Michael. "I can't figure out where we crashed and where I was."

Stepping over rocks, he wound his way through the young pines. "Right about here is where the cockpit came to rest." He moved a little more west and stood on a stump and pointed down. "Here is where the tail broke off." Facing Robin, he said, "And those three trees right there next to where you are standing is where I found you."

The distance to where Michael was standing surprised her. How did she fly so far? It had to be at least a hundred feet, possibly more. No wonder she was so seriously injured.

She estimated where her father laid covered in snow. Margaret joined Michael and watched as Robin sat at the spot and glanced around. She peeled off the sunflowers from the bouquet and laid them at her feet.

Closing her eyes, she faced the sky. "Thank you, Daddy. I love you and miss you." She let the moment envelop her like a hug from the angels. If she didn't know any better, she could swear they were present, swirling around her, giving her assurance and comfort. The breeze returned, caressing her face. She felt droplets of rain and opened her eyes.

There were no clouds! When it happened again, she wiped her face. They were not her tears. Was it her imagination? Angels!

When Robin turned, she found Michael with his arm securely wrapped around her aunt's shoulder.

ANGEL IN FLIGHT

Mascara smeared as Margaret tried to wipe away tears. She whimpered through awkward snuffs. "I promised myself I wasn't going to cry."

The moment was poignant. It was then Robin realized how much Margaret had lost in that crash. Gary was Margaret's only brother. Oh, how much she had sacrificed. For her. For her mother, Helene. Maybe that is why she never dated or married. Gossiping with her friends and neighbors about their lives was how she coped with her own tragedy. Compassion filled Robin's soul.

Robin struggled to her feet and joined them in the moment of sorrow.

"Thank you for being such a wonderful mother to me," Robin said, squeezing Margaret affectionately.

There. Robin said it. Never had she called her *Mother*. That title had always been reserved for the one who bore her, the one she had only known for a few years. She now allowed herself to share that honor with the one who gave so much without obligation.

"Thank you, dearest one. You've always been so special to me." Margaret produced a handkerchief from her pocket and wiped her face and nose. "Don't look at me. I'm a mess," she said, turning away from Michael's grasp.

"You are as beautiful as you ever were," he breathed.

Beautiful? That made Robin's heart leap. He called her beautiful! She wished there was someone else to capture the three of them together with the camera. Deciding to try taking it herself, she reached into the bag, pulled it out, and made sure it was wound to the next frame. Before Margaret could say no, Robin aimed the lens at them and pressed the shutter. She hoped it got them all in the shot.

Margaret whined, "Why did you do that?"

"Because I always want to remember this moment."

She snatched the camera from Robin and threatened to open the camera's back.

Knowing that would expose the film, Robin yelled, "No! I want them."

Michael came to the rescue and retrieved the camera. "I'm with Robin. I want a copy too." He set it back in the bag.

"Then, I want another without looking like a raccoon."

Robin climbed on the rotting stump where Michael said the tail section was. She let the daisies drop where she guessed they found her little brother.

Michael picked them up and said, "He was more back here." He kneeled and laid them out straight.

Now it was his turn to cry. Robin hopped down, put her hand in the middle of his back, and rubbed tenderly.

"Were you the one?"

He nodded. Through sniffles, he said, "That was probably the hardest thing I've ever had to do. I stayed until I knew you were going to live. My team came up here the next morning. Then—" He choked.

"Shh. You don't have to talk about it."

Margaret lugged the sack over and set it by the big stump. She unfurled the blanket and laid it out in a flat spot. "Is anyone hungry?" She handed Michael and Robin each a sandwich wrapped in wax paper.

After each had eaten, the edge of the storm cloud edged out the sun. The wind whipped up seeds from nearby weeds, sending them floating through the air, reminding Robin of snow. The temperature dropped, sending a little chill through her. Michael helped her to her feet.

Robin wandered toward the trees where Michael said he had found her. Her memory said the branches were a lot lower, hanging right above her body. Now she could easily stand under them. Perhaps someone cut them off. Evidence suggested the snow was deep here. It was a wonder she didn't sink and get lost in it.

Leaning against the trunk reminded her of time spent with Jeremy at the lake. Now she wished he was with them. Someday she would bring him, and they would sit right there and tell more stories.

The darkening clouds masked the sky. The wind blew the blanket away when Margaret stood.

Michael chased after it, then gathered up all the items. "I think we better head back."

One foot over the other, he pulled Robin and Margaret up the slope.

With a last look back over the meadow that had claimed the lives of her family, Robin found strength in knowing her father did all he could to save them.

She turned around. It also occurred to her how close they were to the top. If her father could have pulled back on the yoke a little more, they might have cleared the summit—a few feet, is all.

Life was so fragile. Something so small could change the course of one's life forever.

A single snowflake fell. Robin gazed up and saw a thousand more. Closing her eyes, she could feel them cascade down her cheeks. Her angels had returned.

25 — Patch of Ice

The calligraphy on today's letter from Jeremy had peculiar loops and dramatic flourishes she'd never seen before. He had invented his own font! Mr. Clark, the postman, remarked how lovely it was but challenging to read.
"Never seen anything like that in all my years of delivering the mail."
"He's a showoff," Robin agreed.
Turning on the light over her desk, she pulled out the letter opener that had been her father's. Not wanting to damage it, she cautiously sliced one edge. She puffed into the envelope, making it balloon open. Her father had always opened his mail that way.
Unfolding the contents, Robin read,
Dearest Robin,
That never got old. She skipped to the bottom of the second page. Yes, two pages! More than she'd ever gotten before. It read:
Very Truly Yours, Love Jeremy.
Wow! That left no doubt in her mind where they stood. The beat of her heart quickened both in her head and in her chest. She had not felt that in a while. Now she returned to the first page.
My parents finally gave in and said I could go to Winter Conference. We just barely made the entry deadline. I made enough money. There wasn't enough left to fly, so I'll be taking the bus. Mom doesn't want to drive. She said the roads will be too bad in December. I'll leave about 9:00 p.m. on Sunday night and arrive at the Salt Lake terminal at about 6:00 a.m. on Monday. That should be plenty of time before we board for Park City at 9:00 a.m.
Are you going on the bus, or is your aunt driving you up? I hope you can take the bus so we can sit together.
Robin was so excited her hands trembled. She could not wait for her aunt to come home to share the good news. They hadn't discussed how

she was going to get there yet. The cost included the bus ride in the event's tuition, but Michael offered to drive.

Michael spent more time at their house. At least three nights a week, he drove up from Springville for dinner. Robin had never seen her aunt so happy.

Their first actual date was a concert in Salt Lake. Margaret loved the symphony. Robin was sure Michael did not care for it, but went anyway.

The second date was a college football game, which she was sure her aunt knew nothing about. They had enjoyed a game once while sitting on the couch. Margaret talked the whole way through, asking questions about what a penalty was and why the players wore such tight pants. Michael did not seem to mind. He knew everything there was to know about football, bragging about having been a quarterback in high school and winning a state championship.

Having someone to cook for now seldom resulted in leftovers to share with the neighbors. Some of them complained—especially Mrs. Jones.

Michael was the reason Robin could go to Park City. He spent plenty of time admiring her artwork. Margaret hung on his arm the whole time, of course. She even allowed him to look at some of her drawing journals. His interest appeared genuine, and he encouraged her to pursue her passion with everything she had.

More than once, Michael expressed his regret for not completing college and playing football rather than voluntarily joining the military. It seemed like the right thing to do at the time, since the conflict in Vietnam could not have been predicted.

Robin rose from her desk and entered the living room. Grandmother was not there. She peeked inside her bedroom to find her sound asleep. Robin worried about her grandmother these days. Mrs. Jones had told her when she got home from school that Grandmother spent most days napping. It was harder and harder to even get out of bed.

It was six o'clock. Margaret was generally home by this hour. The week's menu hung by a magnet. Following the instructions, Robin turned the oven on and set it to 350 degrees. She pulled a glass dish covered with aluminum foil out of the fridge. Her aunt's passion for cooking was rubbing off, and she helped in the kitchen often. Next time she went off to college, she'd be better prepared to cook meals rather than buy nothing but TV dinners.

Once the oven had reached the right temperature, Robin carefully laid the glass pan inside and pushed it closed. Then she set the table for three,

ANGEL IN FLIGHT

hoping Grandmother would join them. Robin even thought of placing a fourth, in case Michael showed up.

A car door slammed, and Robin hobbled to the window. It was dark outside, and all she saw were headlights. It looked like Michael's truck, but she couldn't be sure. A little snow had fallen the day before and turned to ice. Robin put on her coat and waited under the porch light. Her watch said it was seven o'clock.

A dark figure descended from the driver's side and stepped around in front of the headlights, illuminating errant snowflakes.

"Michael? Is that you?" Robin called out, hand over her brow.

"Yes! Be right there!"

Robin strained to see who was with him. It was her aunt, hunched over and wrapped in a blanket. She wanted to run to them, but thought better of it. The ice was making it difficult for them to navigate the sidewalk.

Fear gripped Robin. "What happened?"

"Your aunt had a minor mishap with the car," Michael said calmly when they reached the dim light of the porch.

Margaret appeared dazed and huddled close to him as they gingerly ascended the steps and entered the house.

"Are you alright, Aunty?" Robin had never seen her so upset.

Helping Margaret off with her coat, Michael hung it on the rack next to the door.

"I'm fine. I hit a little patch of ice."

"And the car?"

Michael laughed. "Nothing a little Bondo and a new bumper can't fix. She slid into a ditch. My buddy and I pulled her out and towed it into his shop. It'll be as good as new in a week or two."

Robin wrapped her arms around Margaret. "I'm so glad you are not hurt. I was starting to worry."

"I don't know how I'm going to go to work. The bus is too far."

"Maybe a neighbor can take you. Does anyone else go that way?" Robin suggested.

Michael poked his head into the kitchen. "Mm. Something smells good."

Robin took down another plate from the cupboard and set it on the table. The timer sounded, and everyone sat to eat. Grandmother was noticeably absent. Margaret questioned Robin with her eyes.

"She's been asleep since I got home. I checked on her several times."

"We'll save a plate for her," Margaret declared.

Margaret reached to serve everyone, but Robin took the spoon from her hand.

"Let's see if I know how," Robin suggested.

"Since when did you get all grown up?" she asked deliriously.

If she had not been in an accident, Robin would have guessed she was drunk.

Michael laughed. "Since she was about four."

Robin sidled up between the two and placed food on their plates. She even buttered Michael's roll and put jam on it the way he liked it, then poured him some milk.

"I could get used to this."

Robin prepared her own and sat. Their mouths spent the time chewing rather than talking.

When she got up to fetch the apple pie she'd put in the oven to warm, she said, "Jeremy wrote to me." She escaped into the kitchen before giving the others a chance to reply and returned with dessert.

Michael never referred to him by his first name. "What did Mr. Kess have to say?"

Robin's eyes darted between the two. Unsure how they might react, so she blurted, "He's coming up on the bus and wants me to ride with him."

Margaret scowled. "His parents are letting him ride alone on the bus? All the way from St. George?"

The complete story was, Jeremy could do about anything he wanted. He only had to pay for it himself. He had ridden his bicycle over 600 miles to art school last summer, camping and carrying all his clothes with him along the way. Robin had just missed meeting his sister and her husband from Salt Lake when they came to pick him up.

"Yes. He is riding all night and will be at the station around seven. Can we at least be there so you can meet him?" Robin flashed a pleading smile at Michael. "Then, if you want, you can drive us both up there."

Michael took a bite of his pie. "You made this?" he asked Robin.

She shook her head.

Margaret pretended to be mad at Robin. "I did. Last night. I was saving it for tomorrow night when you were coming over."

"Oops. My finger was on the wrong day," Robin said, covering her mouth.

"I think the two of you might have more fun riding the bus. You don't need us old folks meddling in your business. Besides, there's only room for three. Your aunt would have to ride in the back." Michael laughed when Margaret slapped him on the shoulder.

ANGEL IN FLIGHT

Margaret rubbed her face and neck. She winced when she turned her head. "I don't know how I'm going to make it in tomorrow."

Robin squinted. "I think you should go to the doctor instead. You look like you are in a lot of pain."

She knew all about that and saw the signs. All that time spent in casts and on the operating table made her an expert.

"I'll be fine. I'll take a couple aspirin."

"I can take you," Michael offered.

"To the doctor?"

"To work. Or both? You can call in sick, and Monty will give me the day off. I can go in on Saturday to make up for it."

"That's your football day," Margaret reminded him, petting his arm like he was a puppy.

"They've got a TV in the shop. There's a couch in there too. You can lie down while I work on trucks and watch the game together."

Margaret scrunched her face, then plugged her nose. "Stinks in there. How about I have dinner waiting for you when you come home."

Robin liked the sound of, 'when you come *home*.' He hadn't asked her to marry him yet, but they were acting like a couple. She wanted to blurt out, 'When are you going to propose?' but guessed it was only a matter of time. They had known each other long enough. Twelve, almost thirteen years, to be exact. It was time.

Michael stood and tenderly massaged Margaret's shoulders and neck. Her eyes drifted shut as she melted into his enormous hands.

Robin figured that was her cue to disappear and began clearing the table. The last thing she heard as she finished the dishes was Margaret offering to make up a bed for Michael on the couch. He was staying over! Now they were indeed a family.

"I'll go check on Grandma," Robin said while Margaret pulled blankets and a pillow from the hall closet. Then she whispered, "I can't believe you are letting him stay."

"His home is too far only to come back in the morning. The roads are icy, and I don't want him to wind up in a ditch like me."

Robin knew he could handle it. His truck had four-wheel drive and big tires. If he could drive up the side of a mountain with six feet of snow to rescue a little girl, he could drive home on a sanded highway. She narrowed her gaze. "There better not be any hanky-panky going on."

Margaret held her mouth to restrain laughter. "Where did you learn that?"

Shrugging, Robin disappeared into Grandmother's bedroom doorway. She held a hand in front of her nose to be sure she was still breathing. A nightlight next to the bed illuminated her silver hair. She looked so peaceful lying there.

Helene's head rested on her clasped hands, making her cheeks plump. Robin's hand lightly caressed her face, which made her stir.

"What time is it, dear?" she asked, opening her unseeing eyes.

"Pretty late." Robin glanced at the clock on the dresser and wondered why there was one in her room. She could not see it. Maybe the ticking sound was soothing to her. "Nine o'clock. Are you hungry? I saved you a plate."

"I guess I could eat a bite."

Robin helped her sit up and placed two pillows behind her. "I'll be right back."

"Why don't I come in there, so you don't trouble yourself."

"I don't mind."

Robin thought it was probably better Grandmother did not discover that a man would be sharing the same roof tonight. In fact, no man had ever stayed overnight in this house.

It felt strange. No, she'd never felt unsafe. They had good neighbors, and everyone watched out for each other. Boy, was there going to be plenty of gossip when the entire neighborhood sees that truck still parked in the driveway in the morning.

Robin patted her grandmother on the knee and left for the kitchen.

Margaret had already made up the couch.

"Where's Michael?"

"He keeps an extra set of clothes, toothbrush, and first aid kit in his truck. He'll be right back."

"Isn't that convenient?" Robin giggled and winked at her aunt.

"It sure is," Margaret gushed. "Thank you for helping with Mother. I hope she doesn't decide to wake up in the middle of the night and sit in her chair. She'll be in for a big surprise."

The two women giggled while Robin walked away with the plate and some silver.

26 — Still Life

Being the first one on the school bus granted Robin the pick of seats. She chose the front to avoid the humiliation of limping past the other students. That also meant waking up early. Weekends were her favorite; she could sleep in until at least seven, possibly eight.

When Robin turned on the light in the hallway, she could make out a figure standing in a nightgown stooped over the couch in the living room.

Oh, no! Grandmother poked at Michael with her cane. He held up his arms in defense, shielding his face.

"Who is that? I can hear breathing."

"Michael Smith. You know him." Robin guided the cane toward the floor and away from their guest.

Grandmother grunted and fell into her La-Z-Boy. The chair rocked back and forth, nearly hitting the window. "I'm sorry. Took me by surprise."

"I didn't mean to startle you, Mrs. Wood," Michael said, sitting up and wrapping a blanket around his bare upper body.

"Don't worry, she can't see you," Robin whispered.

Michael's pants draped over the arm of the couch. He glanced up at Robin, then back at his pants. His dilemma made her laugh.

"You take the bathroom first. I'll go pack my sack lunch." She peeked out of the kitchen doorway just as he hightailed it, with a blanket wrapped around his waist and pants in tow.

Robin brought a cup of tea and set it on the table next to her grandmother, and guided her hand.

"Why is he here?"

"Aunty had car trouble, and Michael was kind enough to bring her home," Robin told her so she wouldn't worry. "The roads are terrible, so he is going to take her to work."

Grandmother's face softened. "I wondered why I didn't hear her car door."

Hoping her logic had worked, she scrambled to dress and ready herself. Maybe it was not good to have one more resident taking up space in the house. She needed into that bathroom soon, or she would not have enough time to do her hair and put on her makeup.

Today was exciting. The art teacher finished the history lessons and promised actual drawing in class. Robin inventoried and sharpened her pencils. The drawing pad was new. She hoped it was the right size. This teacher failed to provide a supplies list and syllabus. All Mr. Page had instructed was to be ready to draw.

"Can I get you something to drink? Coffee? Milk? Juice?" Robin called through the bathroom door, hoping to draw Michael out.

"Coffee. Black would be great."

Robin tried to remember how to make coffee. She got out the percolator, filled it with water, and set it on the stove. Next, she rummaged through the cupboard and found an old can of ground beans. The instructions on the can were unclear.

"Grandmother. How much do I put in?" Robin asked, standing beside her.

"Does he like it strong or weak?"

"Strong," Michael said from the hallway. "Here. I'll help you."

Michael's hair was wet, face clean-shaven. Robin wondered how he'd done that so fast. He set a rucksack next to the front door and led Robin back into the kitchen.

Picking up the can, he asked, "How old is this?"

Robin shrugged. "Probably the last time Aunty made coffee for you."

"She bought this just for me? Five years ago?"

Patting his arm, Robin said, "Yes. She always prepared your favorite meal when you came over. We cleaned the house and yard for a day when she knew you were coming. You like pot roast and potatoes, apple pie, hot butter and honey on freshly baked bread, and your coffee black."

Michael frowned as he sniffed the can of grounds, then spooned them into the basket. "We'll make do for today." He opened the cupboard and pulled out two cups. "So, she's always, you know, liked me?"

Robin laughed and slugged him in the shoulder. He winced, pretending to be hurt. "You had no clue, did you? She was always as excited to see you as I was."

ANGEL IN FLIGHT

Margaret cleared her throat, standing in the doorway, makeup on, hair curled, and dressed for work. "Shouldn't you be getting ready? The bus comes in five minutes."

"Oh, crap!" Robin hustled the best she could to the bathroom. Margaret followed. She drew Robin's hair back and tied it with a rubber band to cover the scar. Robin lacked time to put on makeup, but brushed her teeth.

"Why did you tell Michael that?" Margaret hissed.

"Because." Robin spat and rinsed her brush. "You were too shy to tell him how you feel. And he's too dense to figure it out." She smiled at her aunt and pushed her out of the bathroom. "I need two minutes."

"The bus is here!" Robin heard her aunt yell from the other room. She shook her head and buttoned her pants. Great!

Robin wanted to go to school today. They were finally going to draw something! Not to show off, she simply sought inspiration, the way painting motivated her last summer.

She liked her English teacher and loved to read. Math was her least favorite class. History was boring, unless they talked about the Korean War. Now, after hearing some of Michael's stories, she desired to know more about Vietnam. She had kept her hand down when the teacher invited any student's parent who had served to address the class.

"You can't drive me. How am I going to school?" Robin asked her aunt after putting on her coat and picking up her things.

"I'll chauffeur both of you," Michael said, sipping from a steaming cup and making a bitter face. "I thought that swill they served in the army was bad." He poured the cup's contents down the sink. "They'll make a fresh pot at the shop."

Margaret threw the can in the trash. "I guess it's not like tea that keeps a while. I'll buy a fresh can when I go to the store." She added coffee to her growing shopping list.

He wrapped his arms around her and whispered, "We'll go together since your car is in the shop. I'll buy whole beans and a grinder. Then, I'll make you the best cup you have ever tasted."

"I don't like coffee."

"Trust me. You'll like this. I learned in Italy. They know how to make a great cup."

She peeled away when she caught Robin grinning at them.

After arguing over who would sit in the middle, Michael picked Margaret up and set her in first. She scooted over behind the stick shift.

He repeated the action, placing Robin next to the door, and shut it. "We're dropping Robin off first."

The more Margaret pressed against Robin so her shoulder wouldn't touch Michael's, the more Robin pushed back. Margaret glared at her. When Michael figured out what was going on, he placed a hand on Margaret's thigh.

"I need you closer, so I can shift. Your knee is in the way."

Margaret moved.

He winked at Robin.

When the truck pulled in front of the high school, Michael opened the door and tried helping Robin down. She pushed him back.

"I can do this," she said, looking around at all the other students who were waiting outside, plumes of vapor rising from their breath. She felt their inquisitive eyes as she slid off the seat and down to the icy pavement. Michael broke her fall. She glared at him. "I said I could do it myself."

She heard a few snickers from some boys closest to them.

"I'm going to need a shorter truck," Michael joked. He held open his arms for a hug, but she put her hands in her coat pocket and backed away. When she saw his sad face, she held hers out, too. They embraced.

"Have a good day, sweetheart," he said, loud enough for everyone to hear.

"I will. Thanks for taking care of Aunty."

Robin turned back just as she entered the front door to the school. Michael was still standing there, waving. She waved back. Something possessed her to even blow him a kiss. That drew a few inquisitive looks from a group of her female peers.

"Who's he?" one asked. "Your dad?" The questions blossomed more from admiration than mockery, given the tone of her voice. The girls continued to stare as Michael drove away. "And is that your mom beside him?"

Robin had never smiled so brightly.

The first-period bell rang, and everyone scattered, leaving her standing alone in the hall. Floating to her first class was the best way to describe how Robin moved. This class had no assigned seating. Scanning the room, she found the only open desk was front and center. The schoolbooks felt as heavy as a box of rocks, and she let them fall on her desk with a thud. She could never walk fast enough to deposit them in her locker. Her box of pencils slipped off and clattered to the floor. A few students laughed. Déjà vu!

ANGEL IN FLIGHT

To Robin's horror, Perry came to her rescue and picked it up. The sincerity and grace with which he responded left her, and everyone else, silent. A grateful smile replaced her displeasure at seeing him. An entire week had passed, and just now, she discovered he was also in her first-period class.

"Sorry, I missed the bus," Robin whispered to the teacher, Ms. Obrist, whose threatening expression remained unchanged.

It was everything Robin could do not to open her drawing pad and doodle during history class. Sitting in the front row under the teacher's vigilant eye didn't afford her that indulgence today. Instead, she let her eyes wander around the room at the maps and pictures of historical events hanging from the wall.

The print of an incomplete painting of President George Washington captured her interest. Why was it unfinished? What artist would do that? And why is it so famous? One of Robin's quirks was if she started something, she finished it, even if she did not like it.

"Miss Wood?"

Startled back to the present, Robin responded, "Yes. Ms. Obrist?"

"What is it about that painting that holds your interest more than my lecture?" Ms. Obrist again stood over Robin and joined her in admiration of the unfinished work.

"It's not done."

The students behind her laughed. Robin glanced over at Perry. He frowned at whoever it was.

"That's what would be called a *study*. An artist works out the details of a painting before creating the final product."

What a waste of time. As an illustrator, Robin was taught, time was money. Sure, she could do some quick sketches and present them to the client. The client would pick one, then she would finish the project in one session.

One of the visiting professional illustrators had said sometimes the client gets picky and will make several changes, but that only meant the price went up. Robin guessed a study was a more *fine art* thing.

"How come you don't hang the completed work?"

Ms. Obrist appeared stumped by that question. "I suppose sometimes the study receives more attention and is more valuable than the copies that come after. It's the original. Do you know who painted it?"

Robin shrugged.

"Gilbert Stuart. He went on to paint a hundred more finished portraits based on that study. Guess how much he charged for each one."

Again, Robin shrugged and shook her head.

A boy sitting a few rows back exclaimed, "A million dollars!" Laughter followed.

Ms. Obrist turned and glowered at the boy. "One *hundred* dollars. Per copy. Each one was done by hand, taking weeks if not months to complete."

That was not very much money for that long. Now if she were paid a hundred dollars for an illustration she could complete in an afternoon, that would be different. Perhaps an art career was a poor choice.

"Of course, a hundred dollars was a lot of money back in the 1700s," Ms. Obrist continued. "Now those paintings are priceless. Poor Mr. Stuart enjoyed little of their value. His benefactors did, and their families and heirs. Artists rarely receive the recognition they deserve until after they are dead."

Murmuring filled the classroom. Recognition for her paintings was not what Robin pursued. Money? Yes. To support herself. She wanted a career in art, as it was her passion. What drove her forward was the hope that someday those angels would revisit her, but under less dire circumstances, she hoped. Closing her eyes, she tried to picture them. A sort of melancholy gripped her. The images in her memory had faded.

"Now, Miss Wood, would you agree history is rather interesting?"

That elicited a nod and more attention to her lecture. Robin's eyes drifted to Perry a few times. His eyes darted back to the teacher every time she caught him staring at her.

Becoming self-conscious, she wondered if her scar was showing. She patted the back of her head. The ponytail felt like it was secure. What was he looking at?

Art was the only other class she and Perry shared. To avoid him, she arrived early one day and late the next. It was no use; he was always there, next to her. No one had ever purposely wanted to sit by her in all her school years, except Perry. Olive would have, but she lived in a different school district.

The art teacher had arranged the chairs in a wide circular pattern. A table stood in the middle displaying a bowl of fruit, a dinner bell, a feather, and a dried bone. Mr. Page teetered on a ladder, hanging a lamp from the ceiling over the still life.

Robin picked a desk farthest from the door and set down her books.

Mr. Page tugged on the electrical cord draped over the hanging fluorescent lights.

"Would you be so kind as to plug that in?"

ANGEL IN FLIGHT

She stooped to pick up the plug but could not quite reach it. Securing herself to the back of a chair, she kneeled on one knee and reached out. It still eluded her. Lowering herself to her bottom, she slid over the cold tiled floor and plugged it in. The lamp illuminated Mr. Page's alarmed expression.

"I'm sorry. I—"

"I managed."

Robin slid back to a chair. When she reached to pull herself up, someone's legs got in the way. She looked up. It was Perry, with a hand extended. Reluctantly, she took it.

Thank goodness no one else was in the room yet. Perry did not let go of her hand immediately. Man, was he tall! At least six feet. Almost as tall as Michael. Perry had real whiskers that were a lot darker than Jeremy's. He was definitely stronger. The dark, brooding sense about him disturbed Robin.

They had shared several classes since the ninth grade. With the last name Worthington, the two were often paired together. Last year, he was relentless, always offering to walk her to class, open doors, and help her with homework as long as no one was watching. But, if someone had made fun of her, he was the first to shy away. Or if she dropped something in class, he acted like she wasn't even there. Why now? Had he matured somehow?

Robin rolled her eyes when she found Perry's books next to hers. All the other desks were still empty. He stood behind her, hands on the back of her chair like a gentleman would hold a chair for a lady. Robin laughed.

"Um, they're stuck to the desk; you don't need to scoot the chair in for me." To ease his hurt feelings, she sat, then handed him her books. "You can put these underneath for me, if you want."

He placed them in the rack, then did the same with his.

Mr. Page placed a sheet of paper and pencil on each desk as he walked around the inner circle. "Have you done much drawing before?"

"A little." Modesty was Robin's best trait. She wanted to tell him she'd spent the summer at art school, but figured it would come out soon enough. "Do you like to draw, Mr. Page? Can we see some of your work?"

He chuckled. "Of course. I had a couple of showings back in the sixties."

Perry jumped in eagerly. "Yes. We'd like to see them."

"You are very kind, Mr. Worthington. I'll bring in a few next week."

Perry smiled at Robin. "You should see Robin's. She's really good."

"Is that so?" Mr. Page said with a look of surprise. "I guess I'll have that opportunity today." He straightened the objects on the table in the center.

Trembling with shock or desire to backhand Perry, Robin retraced her memory of when Perry might have seen her work. Never had they shared an art class. The only thing he could access was the drawing journal she carried with her everywhere. When would he have seen that? She snapped around to face him.

"How? When did you look at my drawings? I've never shown them to you."

Fidgeting, Perry's face drained of color; his gaze dropped to the floor. For a moment, Robin thought he might pass out.

"You snooped in my book?" she asked indignantly.

He did not deny it, so it must have been true.

"Stay out of my stuff!" she snarled.

Students had filed in and occupied the surrounding seats. Otherwise, she would have moved desks.

Perry winced. "But your work *is* outstanding," he managed a whisper.

The fierce glare melted when she noted the sincerity and admiration in his expression.

The bell rang. The last of the students scampered in and took their seats.

Instructing everyone on the importance of light and shadow, he said, "Leave the white paper untouched and draw different shades of gray all the way to black with the pencil. That creates the illusion of depth." He had the class first make a gray-scale at the top of the page. "If you aren't sure what shade the shadow is, hold up your paper and squint. Move the paper until the point on the object matches."

Robin learned something new. Quickly drawing the scale, she tried it. The device worked. The drawing formed on the page, stroke by stroke. Several times, Robin caught Perry trying to look. She blocked his view with her hand.

His drawing was excellent, and he was not shy about letting her see. Now she saw him from a different perspective, awestruck by his skill.

Mouth open wide, Robin said, "You are amazing!"

"High praise, coming from you."

The bell rang.

Mr. Page patted the corner of his desk. "Please put your name at the top and place your drawings up here."

Each student filed past and did as instructed.

ANGEL IN FLIGHT

Perry handed Robin the books he gathered from under the chair. Each gestured for the other to go first. She let out a roar of frustration and led the way.

At the desk, Robin waited for Perry to put his drawing down first. He just shook his head.

"I want to see it."

Robin held the drawing tighter to her chest. "Why?"

"Because."

"Okay, kids. I would like to go home, and you two are going to miss the bus." Mr. Page took each of the drawings and placed them under the stack. He gave Perry a sidelong glance. Robin took it as a warning or encouragement. It was less obvious than what Professor Anderson had given Jeremy, but close.

Perry paced Robin down the hall. Stopped at her locker, she hoped he would walk on by. He did not. She slammed the door harder than she meant to after retrieving all the books she needed for the weekend.

"May I walk you to the bus?"

"Isn't your locker the other way?" Maybe that would get rid of him.

He held up a stack of books. "I've already got what I need."

Shuffling toward the doors, she kept her eyes focused straight ahead. Students stared at the two of them walking together.

No! They were not a couple! She wanted to ditch him in the next hallway, but a rush of excited and angry students leaving late from a classroom blocked her path.

"I noticed you missed the bus this morning."

Of course, he would notice. "We had a guest stay over, and he hogged the bathroom."

"Was that who dropped you off?"

His was more than a casual interest in her. He *was* secretly watching her. Stalking her. Why was he making his move now, after all these years?

"Who is he?"

Even though they rode the same bus, he lived far enough away to avoid being a victim of her aunt's gossip factory. Surely Perry would have guessed Michael was her dad, or at least a stepfather.

"A friend of the family."

Silence followed them down the hall and through the front door of the high school. The buses lined up along the curb marked in red. She searched for bus number 12. Holding her books tight to her chest, Robin pulled herself up the steps by the steel rod just inside the folding bus doors.

Two kids had already taken her favorite seat at the front, and she had to walk past three more to find an empty one. Oh, what she wouldn't have given for a single seat next to another passenger, any passenger, she didn't care. But there were none. She sat on the edge and placed her books on the bench nearest the window.

"May I sit with you?"

Robin glared at Perry. "You know I have a boyfriend," she blurted.

Perry shrugged. "I know."

How did he know? She never talked about him. Not to anyone.

"I saw the picture he drew of you."

Robin looked down at her books and back up at Perry. Other students tried to pass. She moved over, giving him barely enough room to sit on the edge. Her shoulder pressed against his beefy arms as he leaned over, giving the others room. Robin picked up her books and moved against the window. He scooted closer.

"How did you deduce he was my boyfriend from that, Sherlock?" Robin snapped.

"The envelope. No one writes like that unless he is trying to impress someone."

That was true. Jeremy liked grand gestures. He was not much for flowers or other traditional romantic gifts, but he drew great flourishes in his drawings and his words. That still was not enough to be interpreted as *boyfriend*. In class, she had told Mr. Page that he was just a *friend*.

Now he was creeping her out. "Why do you know so much about me?"

Perry opened his mouth, but no sound came out. He glanced around as if worried someone was listening. "My mom works with your aunt. At the store," he whispered.

Great! Aunty and her big mouth! Robin spent her whole life trying to remain anonymous, undone with just a few words at the water fountain or lunchroom at work.

"Sometimes she picks my mom up, and they ride together. I know all about you going to art school and about the guy you met up there."

Robin buried her face in her hands and slumped in the seat. The bus stopped, and Perry rose.

"I'd like you to share with me more of your drawings sometime," he said a little louder. "Have a good weekend."

Opening her fingers wide enough, she tracked Perry the short distance to the door. He stopped, looked back at her, and smiled. Her eyes followed him down the stairs to the sidewalk. He picked up the pace to keep even with her as the bus drove off. She glanced back just in time to him waving goodbye.

Now she understood Jeremy's temptation of having a local and a long-distance girlfriend. She instantly felt guilty for even thinking of Perry that way. Her mind conjured many categories to compare and contrast the two. Being the last one to exit the bus afforded her plenty of time to tread in the deep waters of her dilemma.

Grandmother was alert and rocking in her chair when Robin stepped in. She set her books down on the credenza near the door.

"Have you heard from Aunty? I didn't see Michael's truck."

"No. Why?"

"Oh. Just wondering. Has Mrs. Jones been here today?"

"Yes. That kind woman read to me and brought me lunch."

"Grandma?" Robin's voice faltered as she sat next to her on the sofa.

"What's troubling you, dear?"

Grandmother's uncanny sense of a person's location and mood astounded her every time. Even before she lost her sight, she seemed to always know how to read Robin's thoughts.

"A boy at school won't leave me alone. We've almost always sat together because of our names, but he does it on purpose now. He knows about Jeremy, but—"

Grandmother stopped rocking. "Many a time, your grandfather fought with other boys in the schoolyard. I always thought he was a bully. Then I noticed a pattern. He used to bloody those who asked me to dance or held my books when we walked home from school. Is it the young man, Perry?"

She couldn't see Robin's look of horror and surprise, but surely she felt it. "Uh-huh. How did you know?"

"Yes, I know all about the Worthingtons. Margaret has spoken many times about inviting them over for dinner so the two of you could spend time together. She said he is always asking about you."

Why was Robin the last to hear about this? Was her whole life planned out? Jeremy lived too far away to fight for her. Should she tell him about Perry? She tried wiping the image of Jeremy and Greg fighting each other from her mind. Perry was as strong as Greg, but didn't seem like the bullying type. Ambivalence tugged at her insides. Now she wanted none of it.

"What should I do?"

As if measuring her response, Grandmother's eyes rocked back and forth behind her eyelids. "You are young. Plenty of time to choose. Your heart will tell you."

And her head! Yes, Robin was young. Her deepest fear was the longer she waited, the less likely someone would want her, given her condition. She did not want to be a spinster!

27 — Margaret in Waiting

The doctor prodded Margaret, having her sit this way and that. He examined her eyes, ears, and mouth. Tapping on her knee was the aggravating part. He wanted her to lift the hem of her dress, but she insisted he test her reflexes through her long skirt.

"I find nothing wrong, Miss Wood," he said, making a note in the folder splayed out on a counter next to the exam table. "I could order an x-ray, but I don't think it'll be necessary."

Relief washed over Margaret. She had seen enough doctors poke needles into Robin and contort her body into unnatural positions. Margaret's accident was just a bump in comparison. Her neck and head hurt a little, but the pain was tolerable.

"Great. I thought so, but my niece and boyfriend insisted I come."

Boyfriend slipped out of her mouth like she had been saying it for years. A few men came and went through high school, and the two years she attended college. One asked her on three dates, then disappeared when she insisted they wait until marriage to pursue a physical relationship. It devastated Margaret. The conclusion she came to was all men are selfish animals and thought of only one thing. Michael was different, though.

She shook hands firmly with the doctor and warmly thanked the nurse as she exited the exam room.

Margaret found Michael surrounded by children with their mothers in the waiting room, reading a story with high-pitched character voices. The depth of his voice returned while orating the part of the villain.

Remembering the many times he entertained Robin by reading to her, she marveled at his range. It melted any of her stress and made her forget about her pain.

The story enthralled the children. Not wanting to interrupt, she observed from a distance. He snapped the book shut at the end. One child begged him to read it again. Then he noticed Margaret and bid them farewell. The mothers also appeared unhappy when he left.

He approached Margaret and smiled lovingly. "You're going to live?"

Margaret nodded as he drew her into his arms. He helped her on with her coat.

The children waved through the clinic window as Michael lifted her to the seat of his pickup truck. He waved back.

When the truck lumbered down the slushy streets of Bountiful, Utah, in third gear, Margaret asked, "I know this might seem a little forward of me to ask. Why have you never married?"

She felt his arm tense, then relax. Maybe it was too soon. His face changed expression a dozen times. Perhaps a life review of his past relationships was playing out in his mind.

"I didn't want to drag a family all over the world, moving all the time."

That was a sensible answer, but it was not the truth. There was anguish in those eyes and that brow. The change in Michael's tone also betrayed him. Margaret employed the skill she had learned from her mother to read people by their actions and words. Those talents came in handy at work, too.

"You have had a girlfriend before?" Margaret could not believe she let that question escape.

Michael nodded, but remained silent.

She squeezed his arm tighter and laid her head on his shoulder. "You are so good with children. I'm surprised you haven't started a family by now."

Taking a deep breath and shifting gears when they reached the highway, he said, "Yes, I love kids. They are innocent. If they are mean to each other, it's because they experience it at home. Children are the same all over the world. They crave attention, love to play, and have active imaginations."

That didn't answer her question. Why didn't *he* want any of *his* own?

"Perhaps I should ask you the same question," Michael said.

Now she regretted pursuit of this line of inquiry.

Without hesitation, Margaret offered, "Father was on a ship that sunk in the war. Mother was so distraught. I left college and came home to take care of her. Gary had graduated from high school and was going off to start his military career. Mother begged him not to go, but he went anyway. My mother was already caring for my grandmother and couldn't work much. Gary sent home as much of his paycheck as he could. I went to work at the store in the lady's department. Not much chance to meet many single men in there."

That made Michael laugh so hard the steering wheel slipped in his hand, and they almost ran off the road.

"Watch out!" Margaret nudged the wheel back over and glared at him.

When he gained his composure, Michael said, "You felt like it was your place to take care of them. Very selfless."

"I don't know about that. I wanted a family and a career. But this is my life. My mother and Robin are my family."

Margaret let her head fall back on his shoulder. She wanted to include Michael in her family more than anything. How long could this relationship last with her being so much older than him?

"Robin had certainly been a challenge for you."

Yes, she had. Margaret remembered the days and nights spent in waiting rooms, changing bandages, sheets, and bedpans. She could still hear Robin screaming in pain until she cried herself to sleep.

"She was worth it. Such a beautiful girl and so talented."

"You've never dated?"

Margaret allowed her mind to look back on company Christmas parties and summer picnics. One eligible bachelor from the appliances department had requested her phone number and invited her to church. If she counted sitting on the front pew singing hymns and listening to a sermon as a date, then yes, she had dated. When he found out about Robin, he never called again.

And the boy at college who tried unbuttoning her blouse after buying her fried chicken? She was not sure which made her angrier, the grease stain on silk or how forward he was.

"One of Robin's doctors invited me out for a drink after his shift."

Surprised, Michael asked, "Did you go?"

"No. He was older than my father and divorced three times." Margaret placed a hand on the wheel in case he let go again. "You still didn't answer my question."

"I was engaged once," Michael finally answered. "To a German girl."

"And the other?"

"How——?" he gasped.

The other was obviously the one who broke his heart. He tried blinking away the tears. Margaret waited for the answer.

"I met her in a hospital."

A nurse? A doctor? Did he spend a lot of time in hospitals while in the military? "Why were you there? Were you injured?"

He shook his head. The truck turned down the street to Margaret's house. Michael took it out of gear but left the engine running after they pulled into the driveway.

"I fell in love with her voice on the telephone first. Then when I saw her come through the door, she was elegant and strong. Taking the news that her brother and his family all died would crush any woman. Not her. She remained steady and took charge."

His gaze landed gently on Margaret. It was then she realized he was talking about her.

28 — Diamond Christmas

Days passed, and the excitement for Winter Conference was agonizing. A giant pink heart framed the date on the calendar, marking when Robin would see Jeremy next. Only seven days to go.

Perry turned up the heat, sitting by Robin on the bus every day after school and mornings when Michael hadn't hogged the bathroom. If no space was empty next to her, the passenger would move with a word and the touch to the shoulder—no one messed with Perry.

Tracking her down at lunch, he said, "No one should eat alone." They talked little except about art and the history class they shared.

Word got around that the two of them were dating. Robin did her best to hide from him, but it was no use. Everywhere she went, there was Perry. When confronted, Robin said things like, 'we're just friends,' 'our mothers work together,' or 'we've known each other since junior high.'

One day, Robin finally gave in to Perry's requests. She brought some of her angel drawings to school. He studied them intensely, then handed them back with a quiet, "They're nice."

What? He didn't ask why she liked to draw angels? They're nice? That's it? She guessed her aunt had already told him or his mother her complete history, and that was why they had nothing to talk about. Asking him questions would imply that she liked him and was interested.

On the last day before winter break, Perry waited until they were on the bus to give her a wrapped gift.

"But I didn't get you anything," she said apologetically.

Perry shrugged. "It's not much."

"You want me to open it now?"

He shrugged. "Sure."

Robin tore into the package, since the next stop was his. A knitted stocking cap emerged. "A hat?"

"For when you go to Park City. It'll be cold up there. My mom didn't have enough time to knit matching mittens. She'll work on those while you are gone. I paid for the yarn and tried knitting it myself, but—"

Robin did not like to wear a stocking cap. Taking it off left the back of her head exposed. If she wore one, it stayed on until she got home. She made an exception and put it on.

"How do I look?"

"Great."

She then opened her art folder, pulled out the drawing he had studied the longest, and handed it to him.

"Merry Christmas."

He examined it some more. "Thank you. It's beautiful." Tucking it in his binder, he stood as the bus came to a stop. Glumly, he said, "I'll see you in a couple weeks. Merry Christmas, Happy New Year, and all of that stuff."

Shoulders slumped, Perry stomped through the packed snow to his house. She waved as the bus lurched forward, but he never looked up. Something told her this might be the last time he'd sit by her because, when she got home, she and her aunt were going to have a talk. The gossip with Mrs. Worthington had to end!

Robin set the table for four on Christmas eve. A meal of ham, turkey, yams, stuffing, creamed corn, green bean casserole, and her famous rolls made from scratch adorned the table. The house smelled like Christmas. The candles were lit. The scent of the pine tree standing where Grandmother's chair normally sat wafted through the living room.

Helene's La-Z-Boy moved to her bedroom now that the couch was Michael's bunk three or four nights a week. The bathroom scheduling challenge ended with the beginning of winter break.

Robin loved having him there. Michael made them laugh and told stories of his time working at the base out in the desert. She was most fascinated with the one about the things he had seen in the night sky.

When she heard the engine of Michael's truck pulling into the driveway, Robin bounded for the front door.

"Don't forget your coat!" Margaret called from the kitchen.

The beanie Perry had given her hardly left her head. Robin threw on her coat and *ran,* or rather, hopped through the snow like a rabbit. She practically tackled Michael as he slid out of the truck, arms loaded with presents.

"Are you staying overnight?"

"Someone has to let Santa in since you don't have a fireplace," he said, handing her half of the lighter presents to carry.

Once they got inside and laid the gifts under the tree, Robin shook one of the pretty boxes marked with her name. "May I open it?"

Margaret cautioned, "It might be fragile. Put it down. You'll have to wait until the morning."

Michael greeted Grandmother warmly when she appeared in the hallway. He helped her sit at the table. "You look very nice tonight, Mrs. Wood."

"Thank you. It's a tradition to wear this dress my mother sewed for me fifty years ago." Patting his hand once seated, she leaned into Michael and said, "You may call me Helene."

"I'm sure it looked just as nice on you then, Helene."

Robin noticed a little pinking of her grandmother's cheeks. Michael sure knew how to charm her.

Margaret pulled out the chair at the head of the table.

He shook his head. "Not tonight, my queen. It is yours."

She giggled, then sat.

Robin brought in the last of the plates and bowls of food, with Michael's help, and set them down.

The conversation started out casually. Margaret told of her day at work and her ride into town with Mrs. Worthington. She glanced over at Robin and said, "Dear. We mustn't wear a hat at the dinner table."

Robin was about to protest when Michael said, "I think she looks adorable in it."

She shot him a grateful smile.

Margaret scowled at Robin, evidently still angry at her lecture about meddling in her affairs. "Mrs. Worthington's son, Perry, gave it to her for Christmas. Susan knitted it. She is so talented. Wasn't that sweet? And he's such a nice young man."

The fake smile masking Robin's blazing indignation left the door wide open for extolling the virtues of Perry Worthington. She did not wear it because of him. It kept her head warm and covered her scar. Plus, agreeing with Michael, it looked cute on her, and she wondered why she hadn't discovered them sooner. It saved her a lot of time in the bathroom fixing her hair. In fact, she wanted five of them—one for each day of the week.

Michael's face turned sullen with every detail about the Worthingtons. He pretended to be interested when Margaret spoke of their house's enormous size, how much money Mr. Worthington made as a lawyer, and the exotic vacations they took.

Finally, he interrupted and asked Robin, "Are you excited to see Jeremy on Monday?"

The boiling in Robin's head reduced to a simmer. In a monotonous voice, she said, "Yes. He leaves on Sunday night. Will you be able to take me to the bus station on Monday morning?"

"Of course."

Just then, a horn sounded outside. Margaret frowned and approached the Christmas tree. She parted the curtains. "Who on earth would be visiting this late on Christmas Eve?"

Michael placed a coat around Margaret's shoulders and opened the front door. Gently, he nudged her to go outside.

The blast of cold air felt good on Robin's face, still burning from her fury over the discussion of Perry.

A man got out of a brand new four-door sedan, engine still running and headlights on. He stepped aside while Michael coaxed Margaret to sit behind the wheel.

Robin could hardly believe her eyes. Michael gave her a new car for Christmas! He shook hands with the man, who then stomped across the lawn to a truck waiting at the curb. She could hear elated screams coming from outside.

Margaret got back out of the vehicle and threw her arms around Michael.

Robin had caught the two of them stealing a quick kiss here and there, but never had she witness them lock lips so passionately. Her mouth dropped open in amazement. This was going to be the best Christmas ever!

After Michael turned off the engine and closed the door, they returned to the house; Margaret never let go of his arm.

"Honey, did you see what Michael brought me?"

"Yes. What kind is it?"

"A Buick, just like the one I…" She gazed past Robin at Grandmother. "… the one that broke down. But this year's model. It's got a stereo and everything." Margaret turned to Michael and kissed him again. "You are such a sweet, sweet man. Thank you."

"My pleasure. I'm sad I won't be taking you to work anymore."

"Well, you are in luck. I'm not driving that thing until the snow melts. So, you have at least another three months."

ANGEL IN FLIGHT

Michael laughed and hung up her coat. "We better not let that food grow cold."

When the meal was over, everyone gathered in the living room around the Christmas tree. Robin slid off the couch onto the floor and picked up each present, shaking it to guess what was inside.

"Do we have to wait?" she pleaded.

"Our family had a tradition of opening one on Christmas Eve," Michael offered, looking for Margaret's approval.

She reluctantly consented.

"Can I open this one?" Robin asked impatiently, holding up the heaviest one Michael had brought for her.

"Sure."

The box contained lots of little bottles of liquid paint. Next was a smaller box with what looked like a fountain pen and a little cup stuck to the side. The end threaded like a screw into something.

"What is it?"

"You don't know?"

Robin shook her head.

"It's an airbrush. The compressor and hose are in one of the other boxes."

Airbrush? Robin had heard about them at art school, how some illustrators used them to make wonderful book and album covers.

"I wouldn't know how to use it."

"I'll teach you. Simple. Plug that end into the compressor hose and turn it on. Put paint in that little cup and push the button." He sat down on the floor and demonstrated how to move the lever and press the trigger, weaving his hand from side to side. "We use it all the time to do paint jobs on cars. We can hire you to design murals. People pay big money for that stuff."

"Cool!" Robin took the brush from Michael and parroted his movements. She felt giddy with anticipation.

"I got you something," Margaret said, tapping him on the arm. "Honey, see that green and red one?" She pointed at a large box toward the back wall.

Robin set down the brush and scooted around the tree. She handed it to Michael.

Shaking it, Michael asked, "What is it?"

"A giraffe. What do you think?" Margaret said humorously.

"Tear it open, like this." Robin helped him rip the wrapping paper off.

Curiously, Michael asked, "You don't save the paper?"

"No. Why would I do that?"

"My mother always tried to use the paper at least twice. We had to use great care opening presents."

Robin frowned. "That takes too long."

Michael laughed as he finished peeling away the paper, wadding it up, and throwing it at Robin. "Had you going, didn't I?" He opened the box and held out an extra-large wool sweater that buttoned down the front. He held it against himself. "Perfect. Now all I need is a pipe and a pouch of tobacco. And a red leather smoking chair, right there where the Christmas tree sits now."

Margaret playfully slapped the side of his head. "There won't be any of that nasty stuff in my house."

Grandmother cleared her throat. "Your father smoked a pipe nearly every day of his life. *Half and Half.* I can still smell it. Oh, how I miss that man." Tears formed in the corners of those cloudy eyes. "So, young man, you can smoke that pipe anytime you want around me when Margaret's off to work."

"Mother! Don't encourage him."

Helene grinned.

"Grandma, it's your turn. Do you want a big red box or a little green package with a white bow?" Robin hefted both as if weighing each one.

Margaret pointed at the smaller of the two and mouthed the words, 'that one.'

Robin placed it in her grandmother's hands and helped guide her fingers.

"I think I know what it is—my favorite fragrance. I thought I could smell it. Chanel No. 5. Thank you." She held it under her nose and drew in deeply.

"You are welcome, Mother."

"I guess you're next," Michael said, turning over onto his knees, facing Margaret.

"I already got mine. Did you see that shiny blue Buick out there in my driveway?"

Robin searched through the stacks of gifts and pulled out two. She held them both up. "The white one or the pink one?"

Michael reached into his pocket and pulled out a small box. "How about a black one?" He opened it and held it in front of Margaret.

The boxes fell from Robin's hands and landed with a thud. She grabbed her face with both hands. Not believing her eyes, she crawled closer, grasping her grandmother's hand.

ANGEL IN FLIGHT

Helene broke the silence. "What's happening, dear?"

Margaret sat frozen. Her hands didn't quite reach the gift Michael was offering. Time stopped.

"Michael is proposing."

The widest grin she'd ever seen formed on Grandmother's face.

The Christmas lights sparkled in Margaret's eyes as she glanced between the ring and Michael. Robin wondered if she was ever going to breathe.

"Miss Margaret Wood?"

"Yes?"

"Will you be my wife?"

Margaret squeezed huge tears from her eyes. She drew his head toward hers, their foreheads pressed together. Stifled sobs escaped her lips as they softly formed the word, 'yes.'

SHELLY PULSE

29 — Adoption

This was the first Christmas morning that Robin slept past seven. Michael made her go to bed before midnight, threatening that Santa would pass her by. Of course, she knew the real reason. She pretended to need to use the bathroom twice and caught the two of them making out on the sofa. After that, she lay awake and played out all the scenarios of how their lives were going to change.

The excitement had proved too much for Grandmother, and she went to bed well before everyone else. Robin struggled to read her true feelings about the engagement. All she had repeated was, 'Well, well, well. Isn't that just something?' Robin was now eager to hear what she had to say when the other two weren't around.

Robin rubbed her eyes and scratched her birdnest-for-hair as she staggered down the hallway, still dressed in her pajamas.

Michael was up, a fresh pot of coffee percolating on the stove. "Good morning, merry sunshine. What makes you wake so soon?"

That was more cheer than she was used to hearing that early. Robin had listened to that little poem before, but she could not remember where. "How does that end?"

Michael let the last word trail out, sounding like a cow. "You chased away the little stars and put away the moon."

She giggled. "I remember now."

"I used to say that to you when you woke up from the anesthesia."

No wonder she couldn't quite remember; she was unconscious.

"Aunty up yet?"

Michael blew into the steaming cup with a sly smile. "Not yet. Thought I would let her sleep in."

"How late were you guys up?" Robin asked as she poured herself a glass of orange juice and peeked out at the couch. The blankets lay neatly folded and stacked at one end.

"Two, I think. And don't you go putting any ideas in that pretty little head of yours. She went her way, and I stayed in here. We're waiting until we marry. As should you."

Robin wrinkled up her nose. Yuck! She tried shaking that image out of her head.

Opening presents did not have the same draw as in past years. It would be hard to top what happened last night. She strode into the living room and looked outside. Then a huge smile formed on her face. She nearly spilled her glass of juice.

"It snowed!" she shrieked. "It snowed again, Michael. Come look!"

There on the front lawn was a fresh blanket of the pure, fluffy white stuff. The new car had at least six inches covering it.

"I saw."

He joined her at the window. A fresh set of footsteps led out to his truck.

"I forgot a couple more presents in the back and had to bring them in before they got too soggy." Michael tapped with his toe three boxes that had once been shiny and bright, now wrinkled, and dye running.

This was all too much. Robin never got more than a few presents from her aunt and grandmother. They were almost always art journals or clothes.

Having Michael around as a quasi-dad would be worth sacrificing her time in the bathroom. They would need a bigger house. Of course, if she went off to college, she would be leaving in a couple of years. They would have to tolerate each other. Then it occurred to her. He would sleep in the master bedroom and would share her bathroom. She slapped her forehead.

"I challenge you to a snowball fight," Robin said, poking Michael in the chest. She set her glass in the sink and headed for her bedroom to change clothes.

"Then you better open this." Michael handed her one of the wet boxes.

Setting it on the kitchen table, she did. A new pair of snow boots emerged from under the tissue paper. The surprised look made Michael smile. She wrapped her arms around his neck and squeezed.

"Thank you."

"They just slip on. No more lacing. And they match your hat."

ANGEL IN FLIGHT

Robin changed into jeans and a sweater. The boots were a little big, so she put on two pairs of socks. Beanie on top, she stomped back down the hall, drifting from side to side.

"These are great!"

Coats and gloves on, she and Michael trudged through the deep snow out to the middle of the backyard. The sun was coming up over the mountain and made all the little crystals shine. It was magical. She picked up a handful of snow and tried to pack it into a ball. It just fell apart. She tried it again and threw what she could at Michael. It mostly showered her.

That made him laugh. He threw some back, making a cloud of fine angel powder in the air.

Oh, how it sparkled. It reminded her of the whirling beings that hovered over her on the mountain. This time, though, it was Michael's face she saw. He was her angel!

At that moment, she stretched out her arms, closed her eyes, and tossed her head back. She let herself fall backward into the snow. Thick enough to soften her fall, the snow caught her with a satisfying thud.

"What did you do that for? You could have hurt yourself doing that," he warned.

Robin wriggled her arms. She pushed out with her legs to scoop the snow back, forming a snow angel.

Not to be outdone, Michael stood beside her, arms outstretched.

"Are there any rocks on the lawn?"

"I don't think so."

He let go.

"Ow!" he said when he hit. "Not as deep as I thought."

"You okay?" Robin laughed hysterically.

"Nothing a chiropractor can't fix."

Together, they scraped their arms and legs until they dug nearly to the grass. Exhausted, Robin turned toward Michael, who was gazing straight up into the sky.

"You really love her, don't you?"

"Yes."

"Why did you wait so long?"

The silence mixed with the quiet of Christmas morning.

"I was scared and didn't want to uproot you from your home. I just couldn't see it working out. Plus, I wasn't sure your aunt would say yes, her being older than me."

Propping her head on her hand, Robin said, half-scolding, "She would have said yes."

Michael turned over and did the same. "You think so?"

"Of course. That woman went crazy every time she talked to you or when you were coming over." A long pause followed. "And I did too," Robin snickered. "I guess you two finally figured it out. Me, not so lucky."

"What do you mean?"

"Perry or Jeremy? Grandmother says my heart will not betray me. The problem is, since the accident, I feel my heartbeat in my head." She explained that whole thing. "Aunty thinks I'm too young to decide. I don't want to wait and end up—" Robin caught herself.

"Too old to start a family of our own, like your aunt and me?"

"There's still time, isn't there?" Robin sat up and threw snow at Michael. "If you get married on New Years', I could have a little cousin by next Christmas."

"You worked it all out, didn't you?" Michael shoveled with his big hands a bunch of snow and dumped it on her head. "How about a little brother instead?"

Robin wiped away the powder and puzzled. "Brother?"

"What if, say, your aunt and I adopted you?"

She choked on that word. "Adopted? At sixteen? Can you do that?"

Ruining the perfect outline of his snow angel, Michael crawled over. His knees touched her extended foot. "You are still a minor. I'm pretty sure we can."

Robin's cheeks felt red-hot. The blood pounded hard in her head. This moment was unreal. "Why would you do that?"

"The second I saw your little face buried in that snow, I fell in love with you. I knew that if I had a little girl, I'd want her to be just like you."

Robin rolled over and fell onto his lap. She grabbed his collar and sobbed, not believing her ears.

Michael held her until she wiped away the melted snow that had mixed with her tears.

Still buried in his grasp, she walked beside him to the back door, unable to see the path. "I got you." He scooped her up into his arms and carried her up the steps, his neck drenched from her tears.

Margaret opened the door and let them in. "What's wrong? Is she hurt?"

Robin shook her head as she bawled. Through her snuffs, she said, "Michael wants to adopt me?" He set her down and held on while she steadied herself.

Margaret's eyes locked on Michael's. "You would do that?"

"Yes. If that would be okay with you."

ANGEL IN FLIGHT

For once, Margaret remained speechless.

Looking up into her aunt's eyes, Robin said, "I can help take care of my little baby brother or sister."

The look of surprise and ambivalence on Margaret's face told Robin that the two had not discussed all that baby business yet.

As if on cue, Margaret said, "We'll have to see about that."

SHELLY PULSE

30 — The Bus

Monday finally came. It was the beginning of the four-day Winter Conference. Robin set her alarm for 4:30 a.m. Even though her hair would be covered by her new hat, it had to be perfect. Deciding which of the three new colorful outfits she got for Christmas was her greatest challenge. The rainbow-colored one was her favorite, but she decided to pack that one away for a special night with Jeremy. She settled on the blue one. Jeremy commented once about how wearing blue enhanced her eyes.

A new red and white full-body ski suit also went into the suitcase. Not exactly her favorite color. 'Why red?' Robin had questioned Michael. 'So they can find you if you get lost in the snow,' he had replied. She had to admit that was very funny.

The instruction packet announced they would not be doing any work, but encouraged the attendees to bring a drawing pad to take notes. Lectures would begin at 8:00 a.m. with plenty of snow and tourist activities in the afternoon and evenings.

Michael loaded her suitcase into the back of his truck. If that motor didn't wake up the neighborhood, Robin was not sure what would. The windows shook when he started the engine and revved it full-blast around 6:30.

Poor Margaret appeared exhausted. The late nights and early mornings planning a wedding, cooking for her fiancé, taking care of Grandmother, and answering the door when all the nosy neighbors came calling had taken their toll on her. Plus, she still had to put in a full shift at the store all week. Love was a lot of work.

"Why don't you drive us in my car?" Margaret stared longingly at her new Buick that sat undriven.

"Not until the roads clear up. Safer in my four-wheel drive." He patted the seat. "Hop in." He pinched Margaret's thigh after lifting her up.

"Hey. Watch it!" Margaret growled, then followed with a playful smile.

Leaving out the pinching part, Michael helped Robin in and pushed her legs around. "Buckle up. Don't want you bouncing all over the cab. There are some crazy drivers out there who don't know how to drive in this stuff." He winked at Margaret.

She glared back. "I've been driving in snow my whole life. I didn't realize how bald the tires were."

The bus station was about a half-hour from the house on a typical day. Michael made it there in twenty-five minutes, sliding around corners and spinning his wheels as he went. That made Robin laugh like she was on a carnival ride. Her aunt scolded him countless times to slow down.

"I promised Robin to get her there by seven when Jeremy's bus arrives."

He kept his promise. They pulled into the parking lot right at 7:03 a.m. Robin scampered through the snow, looking for the St. George terminal. The space was still empty, leaving her anxious.

The air was crisp, and the sky turned the clouds shades of red, pink, and orange. She understood why Jeremy wanted to paint a sunrise. They were stunning. Perhaps one day, she would try her hand at it.

Closing her eyes, Robin let the warmth bathe her nose and cheeks. "This is going to be a great day," she murmured.

With baggage in hand, Michael and Margaret finally caught up to Robin and stood on either side of her.

"I hope he makes it," Robin proclaimed loudly over the roar of the other buses' engines.

"I'll go check." Michael set down the suitcase and disappeared inside the doors to the station.

Robin's gaze met Margaret's. "Are you still happy with Michael?"

"Yes. I can still hardly believe it. Are you?"

"Oh, yes. More than ever. I'll be sad leaving you."

Vapor from the cool air punctuated every one of Margaret's words. "I'll be fine. You are going to have a fantastic time. Remember, this is also about your career. Learn as much as you can."

Usually, Robin bristled at her lectures. This time, Margaret was right. The number one reason for going to the conference was meeting big-named illustrators, examining their work, and making connections that would later land her dream job. She also wanted more than ever for Jeremy to hold her in his arms. Couldn't she do both?

A bus entered the lot from the street. Excitement boiled to overflowing when it turned into the empty lane. Robin shielded her eyes from the bright headlights and stepped back. Her Jeremy was on that bus and would walk down the steps at any moment.

Patience ran dry. Every passenger who got off the bus was *not* the one Robin was waiting for.

A hand laid on her shoulder from behind.

"Honey?" said Michael's voice.

Without turning around, Robin snapped, angry when the last person stepped down. "What?"

"Look up there." Pointing past her toward the top of the bus, Michael asked, "What does that say?"

"Reno?" Robin covered her mouth. "Not St. George. They parked in the wrong spot." She turned around to find a young man standing next to Michael.

"Look who I found," Michael said, patting him on the back. "His bus was reassigned."

He had the biggest smile. "You came?"

Robin recognized the voice, but not the mouth that uttered the words. "I did." She glanced down at his feet. Gone were his stilt shoes. Looking back up into his eyes, she gasped, "I would not have known it was you. You've grown."

He nodded. "About four inches since summer." Jeremy held out his arms.

Falling into his embrace, Robin's head fit under his chin. She pulled back and studied his face, just to be sure. His chin jutted out, and his jawline was pronounced. The eyebrows were not as blond, and his skin was clearer. Sure, he had a few blemishes, but most of his acne had vanished. So much had changed. She ran her fingers through his short hair, down along the edge of his chin, then laid her hand on his cheek. "What happened to all your hair? And you have whiskers. Real ones."

Jeremy laughed. "That too." He pulled her hand into his. "Sorry. I haven't shaved since yesterday. It's pretty rough."

Michael cleared his throat. "Why don't we go inside. Warmer and the air, cleaner." He picked up Robin's suitcase and marched toward the station, Margaret trailing.

Arm tucked inside Jeremy's, she couldn't take her eyes off him. "How was your trip?"

Leading the way, he kept his eyes on the ground, so they wouldn't trip in the frozen footprints. "Long. Didn't sleep much."

Jeremy seemed nervous when Michael interrogated him after everyone sat on the benches inside, facing each other. Deferring to Robin for guidance, she just shrugged.

"Robin tells me you like to run and ride bikes." Michael sat forward as if interested in not only what he said, but how he said it.

"Yes. Longer distances. Mile. Two-mile. Cross-country."

"What are your plans for college? Any aspirations for the military?"

"Um."

Margaret placed a delicate hand on Michael's clasped and clenched fists.

"Dear. They are seventeen. I think we can let them explore the possibilities after high school."

"Now is when they need to—"

Margaret stopped the grilling with a kiss.

Jeremy's arm crept slowly around Robin. "Probably art school. Utah State is offering me a scholarship. The Air Force also gave me one back in the ninth grade for a science fair project."

Robin sat forward and frowned. "Ninth grade? Science fair? You never told me about that. What was it about?" Of course, how could he? She had done most of the talking all summer.

"The Transpiration of Geraniums and Coleuses with the Effect of Wind and Light." The words rolled off his tongue like he had said them a thousand times.

Letting out a guttural laugh, Robin tugged on his coat sleeve. "You are such a dork!"

"You should have seen my big goggle glasses and puka shell necklace. I was a stylin' dork."

That even made Michael loosen up and laugh a little.

"What is it *you* want to do?" Margaret asked.

Jeremy looked into Robin's eyes, studying her face as if seeing it for the first time. "Air Force sounds appealing. I'd love to fly. My dad wants me to go into the family business selling shoes. He thinks a college education is a waste of time. For now, I like art, and I like Robin." His eyes joined Robin's just as their lips did briefly.

Robin felt and looked the same. She hadn't changed. But Jeremy? He barely resembled that skinny little blond boy from last summer. His hair was short and straight. He had a maturity about him Robin wasn't sure she liked. The carefree, relaxed, funny Jeremy she knew had vanished. Perhaps he was so stiff from meeting her parents and would relax when they were alone. Her *parents*? That's right!

ANGEL IN FLIGHT

"Hey, Mr. Kess," Robin started. "Aunty and Michael have news." She lifted Margaret's left hand.

Modeling the simple gold band and small round diamond, Jeremy took Margaret's hand in his.

Robin laid her head on Jeremy's shoulder and squeezed his arm. "He proposed on Christmas Eve. Isn't that romantic?"

Ignoring that question, Jeremy studied the setting. "Good clarity and color, with a brilliant cut. Very nice."

"You sound like an expert," Michael said.

"I worked in a jewelry store for two weeks. The guy promised to make me a master jeweler."

One more thing Robin didn't know about Jeremy. From now on, she would let him do the talking.

Sitting up a little straighter, Michael acted like he was conducting a job interview. "Why did you quit?"

"I showed up for work one day after school, and cops had surrounded the place. The guy made off with a million and a half in diamonds and was hiding in Mexico. Left his wife and seven children."

Everyone remained quiet until Robin said, "Who's the storyteller now?" She slapped his leg with the back of her hand. "How did you go from shoes to diamonds?"

Feigning injury, he asked, "You don't believe me?"

"No," she teased.

Margaret added her humor. "He'll never be unemployed. Shoes and diamonds will always be in demand."

Michael laughed the loudest.

Jeremy let go of Margaret's hand. "It's beautiful. Congratulations. When is the wedding?"

A hesitant glance at Michael said they hadn't discussed the date yet. "Perhaps in the spring or a traditional June wedding," she said, more like a question.

Robin blurted, "They are going to get married this weekend after the conference. They need to hurry and make me a little brother."

Margaret shouted, "Robin Wood! You hold your tongue, young lady. That's not—"

A turn of her face with Michael's firm hand and a kiss on her lips halted the rebuke.

Jeremy covered his eyes with both palms. Was he laughing or embarrassed?

"I'll be her Maid of Honor. You'll come to the wedding, right?"

He peered out through his fingers. "Do you think we should board our bus now?"

"Nice way to change the subject, Mr. Kess." Robin reached up and kissed him on the cheek, which turned even rosier.

Showing her watch, Margaret said, "You've got an hour. Hungry?"

Jeremy nodded vigorously.

"What young man isn't?" Michael quipped. He produced a brown paper grocery sack and handed it to Robin. "Margaret packed you snacks for the road."

"That was very kind. Thank you." Jeremy peeked inside.

Robin slapped his hand away. "I'll do the serving."

"Left-over Christmas turkey or ham sandwich? But you can't drink the root beer. That's mine." She handed him a can of lemon-lime soda.

"Turkey." He ate voraciously. "I haven't eaten since last night."

Robin's finger crossed his chomping lips. "Don't talk with your mouth full."

"Like the way you did at—"

She covered his mouth and glared.

"Sorry." He finished the sandwich in three more bites and peered inside the bag again.

"The rest is for the trip. The next meal is dinner."

Spying a candy vending machine, Jeremy reached into his pocket and pulled out a handful of change. "Be right back."

"You two have enough money?" Michael produced three twenty-dollar bills and handed them to Jeremy. Robin snatched the cash from Michael's hand, leaving Jeremy hanging.

"I'll take care of that." She put it in her purse while Jeremy beelined for the machine.

Since leaving the military, Michael had let his hair grow long. A neatly trimmed beard showed speckles of gray. Not seeming to mind, Margaret ran her fingers through his bangs, revealing the face Robin knew best.

"That was very generous." She kissed him. "You didn't have to do that."

"Don't want them running out."

Michael picked up Robin's suitcase while Jeremy lugged his own. The two women lagged a little behind as they made their way to the bus marked 'Special.'

"Isn't he cute?" Robin squeaked a whisper to her aunt.

"Yes. Very handsome."

There was worry in her voice. "He's changed so much."

ANGEL IN FLIGHT

"Are you concerned that he has moved on?"

Robin's stomach flip-flopped. She hoped not. His behavior toward her said he was all hers. "If he grows much taller, he might."

The two men strode down the icy walk and into the parking lot. She guessed Michael was giving him a lecture, as Jeremy was doing all the listening and agreeing. Other passengers already crowded around the door to the bus.

Stopping at the curb, Robin turned to her aunt. "Thank you for letting me go. I promise I'll pay attention to the lectures."

Margaret drew her in close, smashing the sack of food between them. "I love you, child. I always have. You are growing up, and I'll need to deal with that."

Love? She used the word love! Hearing that made the tears gush. Sure, she had heard it a few times before, but it had a particular tenderness and honesty this time. Gone was the tone of resentment Robin always sensed. Something had changed, and Robin was not sure it was Michael's doing.

"I love you, too." Robin did not bother to wipe away the tears. She hoped Jeremy and the other students wouldn't see her bawling. "I'll miss you."

"You'll do fine, dear. You're only gone for three days this time. It'll fly by, and you'll be home before you know it." Margaret pulled a fresh handkerchief from her coat pocket and blotted Robin's cheeks.

After handing their suitcases to the bus driver, Jeremy took the food sack from Robin, and they waved their goodbyes.

Robin lingered a moment and allowed Michael to wrap his arms around her. It didn't matter the other students were watching. Now Margaret used the handkerchief for her own eyes. Robin had never seen her aunt cry like that before, except when Michael proposed, of course. She always stowed away her emotions like luggage, and now she was finally opening them up.

"I get the window seat," Robin demanded when Jeremy plopped down.

"I sat in the aisle all night long."

She set the sack down and folded her arms, blocking the aisle. The passengers all glared at Jeremy. When the pressure was too great, he relented.

"Thank you."

After one last wave to all the family and friends, the flock of students, teachers, and other attendees settled in. The bus pushed back and headed out of the parking lot. Jeremy put his arm around Robin. She wiped away the moisture that was forming on the window with the sleeve of her new sweater.

"What did Michael have to say to you?" Robin asked.

Jeremy shrugged.

"I mean it. What did he say?"

"Advice."

"Like?"

"Something about not waiting too long to let the ones you love know how you feel… like he did, I guess."

He stared at her.

She waited for him to follow Michael's advice. All he did was study her face, then finally kissed her.

"Seems strange to see you so bundled up. And, I like the hat." He tugged a little on the pompom. "It looks good on you. I like how your hair peeks out and frames your face. So adorable." He stole another quick kiss. "I need to draw you like this."

Strange, indeed. Robin's boyfriend liked the hat that another boy gave her for Christmas, but she would leave that part out. "Look. It even matches my new boots."

Jeremy leaned away and eyed her up and down. "There is something different about you, too. Have you grown?"

She slapped him. "Are you saying I look fat?" It was probably true. After starving all summer, then helping in the kitchen when she returned, she had gained more than a few pounds. All Robin's clothes fit a bit too tight. Her aunt returned many of them for the next petite size bigger after Christmas. She was happy, and that's all that mattered.

He winced and rubbed his shoulder. "No. I wasn't saying that. I guess I better quit while I still have an arm."

The bus engine roared as it turned onto the highway leading up the canyon to Park City. Wiping the window again, she found piles of snow on the side of the road as tall as the bus. She buried her face in Jeremy's chest.

"I can't watch."

Jeremy squeezed her tighter when the tail-end of the bus slipped to one side. Her body quaked uncontrollably.

"Shh. Want to trade sides?"

Hearing others' voices comment loudly on how close the bus was to the edge of the road, Robin screamed into Jeremy's jacket, "This was a bad idea." The images of the plane crash flooded her mind. A loud thud vibrated through the seat.

ANGEL IN FLIGHT

Jeremy held her tighter still. "I understand. Shh. You will be okay." He muffled her soft bleats with his fingertip.

The bus came to an abrupt stop, slamming them into the back of the next seat. Robin raised her head and peeked over.

The driver exited. She could hear more bumps and rumbles. Jeremy reached past her and wiped the window, and together they peered outside.

Acting like he'd never observed snow before, Jeremy asked, "Isn't that the most beautiful thing you've ever seen?"

Unfolding before her eyes, a wintery landscape of the entire Salt Lake Valley spread as far as she could see. Robin looked down and saw the sheer cliff with only a guardrail between the bus and certain death. She trembled.

"Keep your eyes up here," Jeremy said. He tapped on the window, pointing at the snow-capped mountains on the other side of the valley. "That's Nevada over there. Do you know what Nevada means?"

Thinking him a master at diverting her away from fear, Robin shook her head.

"It comes from the word for snow in Spanish."

Those mountains now became her favorite, given she loved snow so much. After almost dying in it, she shouldn't. Robin dreamed of living on a covered mountain for the rest of her life with angels always surrounding her.

She sat up straighter. "I want to live there. On top of the tallest one."

"It would be cold."

"I don't care. I love it."

Jeremy pulled back the cowl of her sweater and kissed her neck, making her shudder. "I prefer warm places."

They were from two different worlds. Jeremy lived in the desert. She lived in Bountiful, with plenty of farms and fruit orchards, and snow could pile up within hours. He was from a reasonably large family, enjoying a comfortable life with his real mom, dad, and siblings. Oh, what she wouldn't give to have that!

Just as Robin closed her eyes and laid her head back to enjoy his caresses, Tina popped her head over the seats. "Hey, you two love birds!"

Startled, Robin sat up, adjusted her hat, and tucked her hair back in. She hugged Tina. "Why are you on this bus? I thought you lived near Park City."

"My family's down in Salt Lake for the holidays. Plus, I wanted to hang out with you guys. I was so excited when I saw you both on the roster." Then Tina ruffled Jeremy's bangs. "And look at you. Mr. GQ. All grown up. Wow! What did they put in the water down there?"

"Nuclear waste from the Nevada test sites," Jeremy said, making ghoulish gestures with shrugged shoulders and gnarled hands.

"And you, Robin? You weren't sure if your mom could afford it."

"Um, my *uncle* helped me with the tuition this time." Robin couldn't remember the story she'd told Tina about her family.

Coming to her rescue, Jeremy said, "Yep. Good ole Uncle Mike. He even gave us spending money. Is Tom coming?"

Great way to redirect the conversation! Impressive, Mr. Kess. Before long, Robin wouldn't need to make up stories or evade questions. Soon she'd have someone to call Mom and Dad like everyone else.

"Yes." Tina's eyes rolled back as she hugged and kissed the air. "I can't wait to hold him in my arms."

"I thought you were dating someone else," Robin reminded her.

"Not dating. My parents keep trying to set me up. I told them about Tom. They don't like it but, you know me. I usually get my way."

Jeremy jumped in. "And Tom? Is he on the bus?" He scanned the other passengers.

Mockingly, she said, "His mommy and daddy drove him up there in the big Suburban that they use to transport dead bodies. It gets the best traction."

"Have you met his parents?" Robin asked.

"Yes, I spent two weekends at the mortuary. I got to touch a corpse. It was so creepy. We even made out on the embalming table. His parents are *cool*, too. *Laid back*. I guess you must be in that line of work."

Jeremy covered his face and groaned.

"That mortuary is a mansion. Tom has the whole upper floor to himself. His own private bathroom and living room. He's got two TVs, one in his bedroom. I had to stay in the guest bedroom downstairs, so they could keep an eye on me. With that place being dead quiet and creaky floors, I didn't dare creep up to his room."

"That must have been fun. I would have never known," Robin said with a hint of jealousy. "I wish someone would have driven me to St. George to see Jeremy at least once."

He looked away.

"Hey, lover boy," Julie said, slapping Jeremy on the shoulder from behind. Jeremy stood and gave Julie a hug, then sat back down. Then, Julie practically fell in his lap, giving Robin a hug. "Hello, my little elfin girl. How are you? I missed you guys." She pinched Robin's cheek, drawing a distressed look from her.

Tina helped pull Julie off them.

"We missed you too," Jeremy said for the both of them. "Adrian coming?"

Julie wrinkled her brow and threw her head back. "Adrian, who?"

The bus driver leaped up the stairs and announced, "Everyone, please return to your seats. Sorry about the scare back there. A chain came off. It should be a steady ride from here."

"Where are you sitting?" Robin asked.

Julie nodded toward the back. She and Tina scattered to their seats.

Robin kept her eyes closed the rest of the way, tucked snugly in Jeremy's embrace. Occasionally, she came up for air and kissed him passionately. It differed from the first time. Yes, he was still a good kisser, but the desire in his eyes was more intense, wanting, much like the way Michael gazed at her aunt. This was a good thing, wasn't it?

SHELLY PULSE

31 — Winter Conference

The bus entered a lane leading to a three-story building made of stone with a steeply pitched roof. An inviting, warm glow showed through the lobby windows and several shops offering food and winter clothing surrounding the chalet. The circular plaza by the entrance was large enough to accommodate buses and vans.

Professors Anderson and Matthews welcomed each passenger as they descended the stairs.

Robin shook hands with Dr. Anderson.

"So glad you could come. Both of you." He greeted Jeremy with a side hug and measured his height with his other hand. "My, how you have grown."

Although the professor instructed them for eight hours a day for two months, Jeremy appeared uncomfortable letting him into his space. After a slap on the back, Jeremy hid behind Robin.

Professor Matthews approached. He was never one to make eye contact, let alone shake hands or hug. "Hello," he said with a half-smile, then moved on.

A heavy sigh preceded Jeremy's, "Thank goodness."

Backing into his arms, Robin asked, "What is with you?"

"Just don't like people touching me, except you, of course." He squeezed her.

That renewed her hope that she was exclusively his. Spying her suitcase as the driver unloaded all the luggage onto freshly shoveled cobblestone, Robin broke free and shuffled her boots through the crowd. Jeremy followed. She tried lifting it.

"Let me." Jeremy's face turned bright red when he hefted her case. "What do you keep in this thing, an elephant?"

How could it be that heavy? Michael had no problem lifting it into the back of his truck this morning. When he let go of his breath, he also released a teasing chuckle.

"I would have believed that last summer. Not now." Robin squeezed his tensing upper arm.

Once his suitcase was offloaded, Jeremy followed her through the hotel entrance to the registration counter.

"Checking in with the art group," he said.

Jeremy's voice had dropped an octave. It sounded so deep, so mature, so adult. Bewildered by how much he had changed, she wondered if she could be enough for him. Her mood turned suddenly gloomy.

"Name?" The woman behind the counter peered over her glasses.

"Jeremy Kess."

The clerk scanned a sheet attached to a clipboard. "Oh yes. You are in Group A. Suite 210." She checked something off the list and handed him a key. "And you, miss?"

"Robin Wood."

A question entered her mind. Would she change her name to Smith if Michael followed through on his offer to adopt her?

"Oh yes, Group E." The desk clerk let the key dangle over the counter's edge, but Robin didn't immediately take it. "Miss?"

"Yes. Sorry," she said, coming back to the present. "Which room?"

"You are in Suite 214."

Jeremy asked, "How close is that to 210?"

A smile grew on the woman's face as she glanced between the two of them. "Just down the hall. Lights out by midnight. Everyone has to be in their own room." She winked.

Midnight? Plenty of time. Better than last summer. Plus, who would be monitoring?

Other female students were already claiming their spot and had the door propped open to suite 214 when Jeremy walked in and set her suitcase on the floor. Tina bounded up.

"Isn't this great! I saved you a bed next to mine."

"Thanks," Robin said. "And Julie?"

Tina displayed her saddest face. "She's in 215 but trying to switch with someone." She twirled like a ballerina. "Just look at this place. Something out of a fairy tale."

Robin followed her gaze. She had to admit, it was magnificent. Original watercolor and acrylic paintings under glass frames of winter ski events lined the walls. She recognized some of the famous artists' names.

ANGEL IN FLIGHT

Chandeliers hung from a vaulted ceiling. Since she'd spent a good part of her childhood staring at old, ornate hospital high plaster ceilings, she was somewhat of an expert. Most people didn't notice.

Moving closer to the window, Robin tippy-toed to peek outside. Now *that* was the view she *wanted* to see. A ski lift scooped people up and hauled them to the top of the mountain. At seven thousand feet elevation, Park City sat above the clouds. She had to shield her eyes from the sun's glare. That's what she had forgotten—her sunglasses.

Jeremy produced a pair from his jacket pocket and put them on. With that clean-cut appearance, he could have passed for an FBI agent or pilot. A warm memory diffused in her mind of her dad wearing those while flying.

"I guess I know where some of those sixty bucks are going," Jeremy said. "Here. Try these."

Robin put on his sunglasses. It made everything look sharp and more colorful. "These are great. Where did you buy them?"

"K-mart. Two dollars. Not going to spend ten bucks when I'm just going to scratch or lose them. They look better on you. Keep them."

She handed them back. "How about we get some that are a little more girly?"

Tina laughed. "I know what you mean. Now, let's unpack you." She shoved Jeremy. "Go! We girls need to change clothes. Orientation starts in half an hour."

Dejected, Jeremy grabbed his suitcase and left.

"Don't you want to go find Tom first?" Robin asked Tina, hoping for a moment of privacy in their shared room.

"Nah. I'll see him soon enough."

Tina's cavalier posture toward Tom surprised Robin. How long ago had she seen him? Why did she not care about him as much as she did Jeremy? Tina did say her father had someone else in mind for her. Perhaps she had her *Perry* and a distant boyfriend. Love certainly was complicated.

The two girls unpacked their suitcases and admired each other's new Christmas outfits. Tina changed clothes, right down to her bra and panties, in front of Robin. The flat chest, narrow hips, and broad shoulders took her by surprise. If not for lack of beard or deep voice, she would have guessed Tina was a man.

Much like her aunt Margaret, Robin had developed larger breasts earlier than most, but kept them well hidden. Because of her disability, Robin never had to dress down for PE in school, missing out on the locker room and shower experience. Since nobody had ever gotten undressed in front of her before, she had no one else but herself and the lingerie section of Margaret's Sears catalog to compare.

Tina's smooth, unblemished skin appeared tanned but had no lines. Robin had always assumed it was from laying out in the sun. Now she guessed it was because of her Native American heritage. She had no scars, except a rather large one right below the knee cap.

"How did you get that?" Robin immediately regretted asking when she realized Tina might ask about hers.

"Fell off a horse when I was little. Got a nasty one right here too." Tina bowed her head and pulled back her black hair.

A sizable gash appeared from under all that thick mane. Sharing a similar injury made them even better friends, but Robin wasn't ready to show hers.

Tina patted her knee. "I was in a cast for three months."

Three months? Robin was in and out of casts for three years! But, she figured, it still had to be just as painful for Tina. How had she not noticed that before at the lake? "Aren't you afraid of what guys think of it?"

"Tom digs it. He says it makes me look tough. And he says he likes *strong chicks.*"

"Has he seen the one on your head?"

"Yep." Tina pulled on a tighter sweater that followed what little curve she did have. Her head popped out, and she shook her bobbed hair. "Aren't you going to change?"

"No. This will work."

"Suit yourself."

The two girls walked out of the suite and joined Julie and Jeremy waiting at the end of the hall. Tom emerged from 211. Tina grabbed his face and aggressively pushed him against the wall, locking her lips on his.

"Missed ya," Tina said, smacking her gum.

Tom flipped her around and returned with the same move.

"When you guys are finished. We have ten minutes until the lecture starts," Julie said, flipping her hair back.

Julie had not changed a bit since summer. In fact, Robin even caught her eyes wandering over to Jeremy, sizing him up. Robin tucked her arm in his, drawing a bit of a scowl from Julie. Knowing what Jeremy thought of blondes, she watched his response to Julie's body-check. He must not have noticed, as his eyes remained on Robin. That made her happy.

The others headed for the stairwell. "Coming?" Tina asked, tugging on Tom's hand like a child's pull-toy.

"Nah. We'll take the elevator," Jeremy said. "Meet you in the lobby."

ANGEL IN FLIGHT

Robin flashed him a grateful smile when the elevator doors closed. He winked back.

She kind of wished Jeremy would pin her against the wall like Tina did Tom, but figured they didn't have enough time before the doors opened. How far could he lift her off her feet this time?

The gang was back, minus Adrian. Together, they walked in the direction the other students were moving. There were a few fresh faces. She wondered who else had been invited besides the summer class.

They found their seats at the back of an auditorium, which Robin guessed doubled as a movie theater. She was right. The curtains opened to reveal a large white screen. A podium sat to one side, with chairs lined perpendicular to the edge of the stage.

Professor Anderson shook hands with several of the students, then bounded up the stairs. The pudgy Professor Matthews, with his short legs, struggled up the steps.

Another gentleman, casually dressed for winter, made his way toward the front. Professor Anderson rushed down the steps again to greet him.

Robin recognized the man when she made out his profile. It was Henry Foster! Now she wished they'd sat closer. Her heart raced.

"Be right back." She stumbled over Jeremy's legs and made her way to the outer aisle. Henry was about to ascend the stairs when she weaved through the obstacle of students and stopped him.

"Mr. Foster. You may not remember me, but I met you last summer."

His eyes lit up. "Of course, I do. You draw the most beautiful angels. You even inspired me to try a few of my own." They shook hands warmly.

"I wanted to thank you for taking the time to come. I admire your work completely and hope to be half as good as you someday."

He chuckled. "Well, then, I'm very flattered. You don't have far to your goal, as I recall."

Professor Anderson pulled Henry away and guided him up the stairs. Once the staff and guest speakers were seated, Dr. Anderson stepped to the podium and invited everyone to sit.

A hush fell over the auditorium when Robin finally made it back to her place next to Jeremy. "I got to talk to him," she whispered enthusiastically.

"Who?" Jeremy asked, rubbing his knees after she banged into them.

"Henry!"

"Shh," came a rebuke from an adult in the next row.

Jeremy obviously had not been paying attention. He had been too busy talking to Tina. Men! One-track minds.

"Thank you all for coming. Glad most of you made it safely. We are missing staff and a few members of the art community who were delayed by the holiday storm."

It now made sense why adults outnumbered younger students by almost double. They were probably college students and working artists. She liked the direction this was taking her.

"Our first guest, some of you know, is Mr. Henry Foster from San Francisco, California. He has had a distinguished career as an illustrator, with his work published in such names as Sports Illustrated and Reader's Digest. His work has also been featured on countless book and album covers. Please help me welcome, Mr. Henry Foster!"

The applause was deafening. Robin sat forward and joined in with a whistle.

The woman in front of her glared back.

She whispered, "Sorry. He's my favorite."

Mr. Foster approached the microphone. "It is a real honor to be invited to your conference this week. As I look out over this group, I'm a little hesitant to call you kids. My dear friend, Don, has shown me some of your latest work. I would put it up against any professional working in the industry today. I applaud you, Don, for your excellent service to these young artists."

Mr. Foster applauded Dr. Anderson, and the audience followed cheerfully.

"I've been asked to show you some of my illustrations and to give you a brief history of how I came to become a commercial artist." He waved his hand toward someone at the back of the auditorium.

Everyone turned around to see. A beam of light streamed out of a little window as the overhead lights lowered to dark.

"Go ahead and show slide number one, please," he said directly into the microphone.

Jeremy whispered to Robin, "Do you know how to ski?"

"No. Shh."

"Neither do I. I've only been tubing before. Are you going to take lessons?"

Robin sat forward, trying to listen to every word of the lecture. The slides moved too fast. She held a finger to her lips. "Be quiet. We'll talk after."

Someone closer to the stage called out, "Slow down!"

ANGEL IN FLIGHT

The images stopped altogether. The audience grew restless, and many turned to investigate what was happening. It appeared someone in the control booth struggled to correct a malfunction.

Robin sat back. "I've only tried the bunny hill, holding on to a rope. I don't want to break anything."

Jeremy asked out loud, "What's a bunny hill?"

Three people in front of them now turned. In unison, they shushed Jeremy.

He raised his hands in defense. "Sorry."

A picture reappeared on the screen, and the audience grew quiet again.

"First, I draw the basic figure on the canvas or board, depending on the texture I want. I don't use graphite; that repels water and bleeds through the acrylic. I primarily use Prismacolor. They blend nicely with the paint."

The lecture continued. Robin hung on every word.

"Is it twelve o'clock yet? I can't reach my watch."

Everyone within ten feet shushed him.

Robin pushed the button on the watch on the wrist draped over her shoulder. It lit up and displayed 10:45 a.m.

He groaned.

The people directly in front of Robin stood and faced Jeremy. "How many times do you have to be told?" They moved seats, all the while giving Jeremy the stink-eye.

"This is so boring. No naked girls. All he paints are golfers and football players."

Tom and Tina's laughter shrunk to restrained whimpers.

Robin glared at them. "Knock it off, you guys. We'll get kicked out."

"Yeah, be quiet." Tom slapped Jeremy on the back of the head. "Some of us are trying to listen."

Perhaps Robin was wrong about his level of maturity. She threatened to move if he didn't quiet down.

Mr. Foster motioned for the projectionist to move to the next slide. "Here is one I did for Sports Illustrated. As you can see, it depicts a famous scene from a golf tournament when Jack Nicklaus won the…"

"I'll take lessons if you will." Jeremy interrupted Robin's concentration.

Robin whispered, "Or we can stay in the lodge and make out."

Jeremy brightened and sat up straighter.

"But only if you be quiet!" she hissed.

"Oh yes. We can take out our acrylic paints, illustration board, colored pencils, and paint for Sports Illustrated. It can be of some famous skier jumping over a mogul or spraying powder down some black diamond." Jeremy stopped when Robin shot him missiles of fire from her eyes.

When there was a lull in the lecture, she asked, "I thought you knew nothing about skiing?"

"I said I don't ski. I didn't say I don't know anything about it."

Robin jabbed him in the ribs. The light came up in the auditorium while the room filled with applause. Robin stood, whistled, and clapped louder than anyone else in the room.

The professor joined Mr. Foster at the podium.

Jeremy consulted his watch now that his arm was free.

"It's only 11:15," he yelled over the din. "I paid three hundred bucks and rode a bus all night long for this? And now it's over?"

"Yes! We get out early," Tom exclaimed. "The rest of the day is skiing for all the university staff, courtesy of the high school art students. What a racket."

Professor Anderson spoke into the mic. "Thank you, Mr. Foster. I hope each of our students and faculty can conceptualize the bright future ahead for this program."

Mr. Foster grabbed the mic, causing feedback that made everyone cover their ears. He glanced out over the audience. "Now I see about forty new competitors. I'm not sure it was a good idea to give away all my secrets." The room filled with laughter.

Robin opened her packet and pulled out the list of activities the attendees could choose from. At the top was a guided tour of some art galleries in town. Another was an ice sculpting event. "We could go build an ice statue if you want," Robin offered to the group.

Tina said, "Nah. We're going skiing. Catch you guys tonight." She and Tom disappeared into the crowd exiting the theater.

Julie's eyes flitted between the two couples. "I think I'll take my chances on the slopes. Find my next hunk of a man." She ran after the other two.

"So? What are we going to do?" Robin waited for Jeremy to decide.

"I guess we can always visit the art galleries and make snowmen any time we want. It's not every day we can take ski lessons. Just like skating, isn't it?"

Dread surged through Robin's whole body. No, it was nothing like skating. There were no bars to grab—only a rope on the bunny hill. She was bigger than the last time she tried. The only good thing was if she tumbled, the snow would break her fall. Then again, it was hard-packed by so many other skiers since there had been no fresh snow in two days. It wouldn't be that fluffy stuff she landed in when she was four.

SHELLY PULSE

32 — Bunny Hill

The ski boots made Robin feel stable, yet brought back nightmare memories of the casts and braces she used to wear. She could buckle one of them, but Jeremy helped her with the other. After being fitted for skis and poles, they joined the other six students and one adult, who had opted for lessons. Aunt Margaret would kill her if she knew she was learning to ski.

Robin doubted her decision the moment she clicked her skis on following the professional's step-by-step instruction. She steadied herself with the poles.

Jeremy's cheeks and nose turned rosy. His rapid, shallow breath came out in puffs of mist; his legs were like rubber. No, Robin couldn't see the terror in his eyes through the sunglasses, but she knew it was there. She let the pole dangle from the strap when she placed a hand on his arm to steady him.

Her words were comforting. "You are doing great."

He nodded nervously, but she could tell he wasn't buying it.

"We should have chosen ice sculpting," he said, his jaw quivering.

To diffuse his fear, she said, "I think it was *you* who said we'll never have this chance again." His grimace said she made the anxiety worse.

Despite his floundering, Jeremy looked adorable in the powder blue and yellow matching pants and jacket. His hat had a big red stripe. It did not have a pompom like hers, but it came to a point, making him look a little dorky. He needed to pull it down. Now was not the time to tell him.

The instructor lectured on how to stop, turn, and fall. "If you fall, it will most likely be on a slope. It is downhill skiing, which means mountains," he said, pointing up the bunny hill.

That drew a few nervous laughs from the students.

"Turn your body, so it is lying up the hill. Bring your poles together and push yourself up." He demonstrated by purposely falling over, then righting himself. He made it look too easy.

Robin gripped the handles. They would have been useful during the many times she'd fallen. She considered carrying a set with her from now on. Her aunt had encouraged her often to use a cane, but she refused. They were for the elderly. But ski poles? They would be cool. Then again, maybe not. People wouldn't appreciate the holes in their floors.

Next, the instructor covered etiquette. Robin found it humorous that ski slopes had 'rules of the road' like driving a car, except a ski run was always a one-way street. After answering a few questions, the teacher led them over to a rope that snaked through an elaborate pulley system up the hill.

Jeremy grabbed hold of the line right behind Robin. "I get it now. All the beginners spend most of their time on the ground. They look like rabbits trying to stand up."

He was right. Many had fallen and were grappling with their poles to stand. She vowed not to be one of those.

Robin turned back to find Jeremy straining with knees bent and stance widening as they went forward. "You need to point the tips back toward each other, or you'll be the rabbit."

"Me? Nah. I'll be ready for those expert runs by one o'clock. You just wait."

Soon, Jeremy's skis were so far apart he was nearly doing the splits. He let go of the rope and fell backward. The instructor expertly circled back and helped him up. He wedged his way alongside Jeremy as he grasped the rope again.

Robin waited for Jeremy at the top of the hill. When he and the instructor finally arrived, she said, "What took you so long?"

He couldn't answer.

"You need to relax."

The quiver in his voice came from a trembling jaw. "This is harder than I thought. I'm not sure I want to do this." He pushed his bent sunglasses up on his nose.

"Too late. You are here. We want to be there." Robin swept the end of her ski pole across the horizon then drew circles in the air toward the bottom of the very shallow slope. "Lots of room. Go slow. You can do it."

Together they pushed off. Robin kept the points of her skis almost touching. It was like magic. She glided along slowly at first, then picked up speed by letting the tips move apart. Then she practiced slowing by bringing them back together.

The feeling was exhilarating. Never had she experienced this level of freedom, of movement. For the first time, she was like everyone else and could go without the limitation of her disability.

"Whoa!" Jeremy screamed as he flew past Robin.

Horror washed over her when she witnessed Jeremy crash right into another skier, sending them both tumbling down the hill, skis detached and sliding in all directions.

"What is your problem, man?" the other skier shouted. He pushed himself up and brushed off the snow.

Jeremy lay prostrate, writhing in agony and holding onto his knee. Robin came to a stop right beside him.

The ski instructor halted with a flourish, powder spraying everywhere. "Wow. You took a pretty hard fall." He disconnected his skis and dropped his poles. Kneeling beside Jeremy, he asked, "How's your leg? Can you extend it for me?"

"I don't know. It really hurts."

The gritted teeth told her his pain was genuine. A crowd gathered. Two skiers with big red crosses on their coats slid in and made their way through.

"Give him some room. You can all go back to practicing. We have this covered," one of them ordered.

The onlookers dispersed.

The medic said, "You need to go to the first aid station."

Robin slid the rest of the way to the bottom, following the instructor who carried Jeremy's gear. She disconnected from her skis. Jeremy limped toward her with the medic's help. No wonder the first aid station was so close to the bunny hill. If there was going to be an injury, it would be here.

Dr. Amanda Myer greeted Robin as she took hold of the injured Jeremy Kess and thanked the medic. "Let's put him over here." The doctor slapped a table upholstered in green Naugahyde.

Once Jeremy was seated, the two women helped him lie down, supporting his legs and swinging them up on the table. Robin removed Jeremy's glasses and hat. She knew that pained expression on his face all too well.

Kissing his sweaty forehead, Robin said, "You're going to be alright." She lost count of how many times her aunt had said those words.

Tears squeezed out the corners of his eyes as he winced.

"You've been tearing them up out there, I see," Dr. Myer said, with a high-pitched song in her voice Robin found delightful. How did such a childlike sound come out of a woman so stout?

Through heaves of pain as she lifted his leg, Jeremy said, "Once I got moving, I couldn't stop or steer."

"First time?"

Robin answered for him. "First time for both of us. We're here for an art conference. The emphasis is more on skiing this time than art."

Dr. Myer glanced at Robin's legs. "I noticed you limping. Do I need to take a look at you too?"

"Prior injury. I'm fine."

"Good." The doctor tugged on Jeremy's pants. "I think I'm going to need these off."

Jeremy's eyes grew wide and darted between Robin and the doctor.

Robin teased, "Didn't your mother teach you to always put on a clean pair of underwear? Just in case?"

Horrified, Jeremy replied, "It wouldn't matter how clean my underwear is if I were unconscious."

Both women laughed.

"I'll leave so you can have your privacy." Robin faced the door. "I'll wait outside."

"I want you here," Jeremy beckoned.

Dr. Myer asked, "Aren't you two a couple?" She unsnapped Jeremy's ski trousers.

Robin was about to answer, but waited for him to respond. She wanted to know the answer to that as well.

Jeremy's staccato speech revealed his growing delirium. "We met. Last summer. Two months."

Robin threw her arms up in the air. "And now, the first day back together, what does he do? He breaks his leg."

"It's not broken," the doctor assured her. The two helped Jeremy take off his parka and pants, leaving him in a sweater and underwear.

Robin had seen plenty of boys in swim trunks or athletic shorts, but never in their undies. The pictures in the catalog were usually white—Jeremy's, a dark blue. The muscular definition of his thighs and calves didn't match her recollection of his skinny legs from last summer.

His knee was a fiery ball of swollen red tissue. Dr. Myer again lifted and bent it gently.

ANGEL IN FLIGHT

"Hyper-extended and sprained, but definitely not broken. Let's wrap this up and get you some ice packs. I suggest you stay off the skis for a couple of days."

"Black diamonds by one, huh?" Robin badgered Jeremy.

He cupped his face. "I hope it'll be healed in time for track season."

"You run track?"

Jeremy nodded. "Mile and two-mile."

"Excellent. What's your best time?"

"Four forty-two."

Dr. Myer raised an eyebrow. "Not bad. I used to throw discus and shot put. Played some softball. I tried to run. My legs were too short. But skiing? Now *that*, I can do, all day long. You just need to take some more lessons, and you will glide down those black diamonds in no time."

Robin doubted that. Being a desert dweller, Jeremy needed his feet firmly on the ground. Knowing him, at least to the extent that she did, he would try to master anything given enough motivation.

"Have your sports doctor at home follow up on this knee. Meanwhile, take a couple of these now to shrink the swelling." She pulled out a bottle from a drawer and handed it to Robin. "Two before bed. They'll help with the pain and make him sleep."

Jeremy sat up. Robin expertly fed his feet into his pant legs one at a time. Whenever anyone used that old cliché, 'He puts his pants on the same as everyone else,' she could honestly say that she didn't. It was a chore, and now Jeremy would know what it was like, at least for a few days.

"You two go rest," the doctor ordered as she left the room to help another injured skier.

Jeremy eyed the ski boots. "Do I have to put those back on?"

Robin shook her head. "Let me go get our stuff out of the lockers. I'll return the boots and skis and be right back for you."

SHELLY PULSE

33 — The Healed Angel

Opening the door to suite 214, Robin found they had the place to themselves. Suitcases and clothes of other students were strewn about the floor and furniture haphazardly. She tossed their belonging from the couch to the side, making room for Jeremy to lie down.

"They think their mothers will come to clean up after them," she muttered as she spun Jeremy around and had him sit. Robin took the crutches she had rented for him with part of the $60 and leaned them against a pillar. "Where's your key?" she asked, palm up.

"What for?"

"I'm going to find you something more comfortable to wear. Did you bring any sweats?"

"Warm-up suit."

After an agonizing minute of searching his pockets, he handed her his room key.

It didn't take long for Robin to figure out which bedroom was his. His suitcase remained packed. She lugged it over to his bed and snapped it open. There on top was a neatly wrapped box with silver ribbon and a bow.

Snooping through other people's stuff wasn't something she did, but Robin couldn't help herself this time. Pulling back the curly ribbon, she read the card, 'Merry Christmas, From: Jeremy, To: Robin.' She shook it. It didn't rattle. Holding it to her ear, she tried again. Nothing. It was heavy. She guessed it was another drawing journal and rolled her eyes, setting it aside.

Sorting through Jeremy's suitcase, she found that all his underwear was different shades of blue and one pair of red, but no white. She thought that red one would look hot on him, that and maybe a red Santa hat. Shaking that image from her mind, she pulled out a light blue jogging suit and matching pants. A theme was developing here. He liked the color blue as much as she did.

Digging deeper, Robin found a shaving kit and unzipped it. There was the requisite toothbrush, paste, floss, an electric shaver, and a bottle of acne cream. She put it all back and zipped it up.

At the bottom of the pile of clothes, Robin discovered a drawing journal. She hesitated. To her, they were sacred and were for her eyes only. She'd be mortified if someone else leafed through her pages without permission. Twice, she opened it, then slammed it shut again. Had anyone ever read hers? Perry admitted he'd thumbed through a few drawings, but that was her travel drawing pad. What she kept inside her desk was different. It had her innermost thoughts and secret feelings. Was Jeremy's filled with the same?

The agonizing moment passed, and she decided not to open it. She would ask permission first. Robin slammed the suitcase closed, then tucked the gift, journal, shave kit, and warm-up suit under her arm and scampered back to her suite.

"What took you so long?" Jeremy stood in the kitchenette, drinking a glass of water.

"You are not supposed to be up," Robin scolded.

"I was thirsty. What do you have there?" He set the empty glass in the sink and held out his hands to relieve Robin of her burden.

"Your clothes."

"What else?"

"I want you to shave before you kiss me."

Jeremy smiled coyly. "Presuming I'm going to do that."

"You better."

"What's that shiny thing?"

"A present."

"Why?"

"Because it's for me."

"And you know this how?"

Robin flopped the clothes on the table with his drawing journal on top.

She pulled back the ribbon and opened the card taped to the package. "See? To Robin. That's me. I am Robin."

Jeremy pulled out a chair and sat down hard. "Ow."

"May I open it now?"

"I was going to wait until tonight, but if these drugs kick in, I might not make it that long."

"So that's a yes?"

He nodded.

Robin tore into the wrapping. She struggled to remove the ribbon off. Inside was a brown cardboard box with a shipping sticker addressed to Jeremy, sent from a publishing company.

A smile formed on his lips as she tried hard to open the securely sealed flap.

He held out his hand. "Let me try." He worked his fingers under and loosened it for her, then handed it back.

Out dropped a large illustrated book into her lap. Robin picked it up and turned it over. She couldn't believe her eyes. It was a compilation of Henry Foster's work. The blood rushed in her head. The beat in her ears was deafening. No tears, just admiration, as she thumbed quickly through the pages.

"How did you know?"

Jeremy chuckled. "Your aunt."

Wait. How would she have known? She hadn't mentioned it to Margaret. Robin traced back the possibilities, then it hit her. Perry must have mentioned it to his mother, who passed it on to her aunt. It's a wonder the message got through.

"When did my aunt tell you?"

"Once when I called."

"When did you call?"

"About a month ago."

"Why didn't you tell me?"

"Your aunt is a nice lady. Easy to talk to. She sure loves you."

Now the beat in her head turned to pounding rage. "How come no one told me you called? What did you talk about?"

"She asked me a thousand questions. Then she told me all about your childhood, what you were like growing up. She even mailed me more pictures of you. Said they were duplicates. I offered to pay my dad back the five dollars for the long-distance phone call." Jeremy laughed.

Robin closed her eyes. This was turning into a nightmare. Did she tell him about Perry? "Did she say how she knew who my favorite artist was?"

"No. You must have told her. It's what she said you wanted more than anything."

Relief showered down on Robin. She opened her eyes and examined the pages of the book more closely. "I so badly want to learn to paint like him."

"He's pretty good. I've discovered a painter named Sargent and another, Waterhouse. Those two are my favorites. Someday."

Robin put the book down and laid a hand on Jeremy's journal. "May I?"

Jeremy fidgeted in his chair. "Are you sure you want to?"

"What am I going to find, a bunch of nude drawings?"

Him not answering told her she had hit the mark.

"Maybe some." He shrugged. "You can skip past those." Jeremy pushed himself up to his feet and hobbled to the couch.

Robin followed with book, journal, and warm-up suit in hand. "We should get you changed." She set the books down and pulled off his ski pants. This time, she got a better look at his legs. Even with the bandage, she admired every muscle from his underwear to his toes. Then she helped him put on his jogging pants.

"I'm a little warm. Can you help me with the sweater?" Jeremy held up his arms while she pulled. The t-shirt underneath clung to it.

My, how his chest had developed. No longer did he have the pecs and abs of a young boy. He was a man in every sense of the word. Last summer, he had no chest hair. Now a little tuft was growing in the middle, and his skin appeared less tanned. He pulled the t-shirt out of the sweater and put it back on.

"Have you been working out?" Robin asked, a little on the lustful tone scale. She wanted so badly to reach out and touch his chest.

"A little. I run a lot. My best friend plays football, so I spot for him all the time. He has weights in his basement." Jeremy grinned at Robin. "Why?"

"You… never mind." Robin shoved him over onto his back. "You need to lie down." She lovingly helped him raise his legs. A pillow went under his head and another under his injured knee. "It is a little warm in here." She pulled off her sweater and flung it over the back of the couch.

Jeremy's eyes fixed on Robin's, making her nervous. "Have you ever wondered what it would be like to do nothing all day but paint? Wouldn't it be nice to make enough money from art but without the pressure of deadlines?"

Now Robin was wondering if the drugs had kicked in. For her, pressure and deadlines motivated her to finish her homework. She saw the business of commercial art being no different. But why would he be talking about art when they were stripping off sweaters?

"Are you thinking you don't want to illustrate anymore?"

ANGEL IN FLIGHT

He laid his head back. "I do. It's just, I'm not sure I want to draw stuff other people want. I want to create what *I* want—what appeals to me. Of course, it would be nice if other people bought it."

"In other words, a fine artist."

"I guess you can call it that. I want to take my time." His eyes drooped.

Robin sat on the floor in front of him. He turned over and placed his hand on her shoulder, and kissed her cheek. Two minutes later, he was out.

Great! She waited all this time to be alone with him, and he falls asleep. Her eyes landed on the drawing journal lying on the coffee table. She picked it up and opened the cover.

The first page was a dedication to his favorite author, *J. R. R. Tolkien*, followed by an ink sketch of him. He had filled the following pages with some nudes, alien beings, horses, dogs, and pictures of girls Robin guessed were friends and girlfriends, past and present. He had even tried his hand at poetry. Some of them made her laugh at how poorly they rhymed.

A paperclip protruded about halfway. Robin discovered a face she recognized staring back—a color photo of her when she was about ten or eleven. Aunty must have sent it to him. Underneath the picture, Jeremy had rendered her likeness in colored pencil. A few more images of her and the accompanying drawings appeared on pages that followed. Some were in graphite; one was in ink. The rest of the book was blank.

What could she read into that? No other girls had captured his interest since then, but her? Did he keep another journal at home about all his other conquests? She filed that thought away and focused on the positive.

Here he was, lying next to her, the man she couldn't stop thinking about day and night. Yes, asleep, but they were together. She put the book down and studied his face.

Jeremy had a serene expression. He breathed deeply. She let her ear fall on his chest and listened to the sound of his heartbeat. It didn't match the quick pace of the one she heard in her head. His was deep and slow, about one for every two of hers. He stirred and laid flat. She ducked to avoid getting hit by his thin but muscular arms. His t-shirt hiked up a little, and she poked his belly. It was flat and taut.

Robin's hand rested on his stomach that rose and fell with each breath. It lacked the ripples of those bodybuilders she'd seen a few times on TV or in magazines. She rolled over onto one knee and gently kissed his lips. When he reached up to scratch his nose, she pulled away.

Suddenly, the door to the suite opened. Two students busted through, laughing and pushing each other.

One stopped and gestured toward Jeremy. "What is he doing here?"

Robin shushed them. "He hurt his leg skiing."

"Oh, yeah. We heard about that," the other thundered.

That woke Jeremy. He sat up.

"Just have to change. We won't be long," said the first girl.

"We met some hot ski bums, and they are taking us to eat," said the second. They disappeared into the bedroom.

Robin guessed that what they were wearing when they came back out would lead to a little more than just sharing a good meal.

"Aren't you going to be a little cold in that?" Robin asked.

"Joe will keep me warm by the fire at the lodge." They laughed and left, slamming the door. Robin could hear them all the way to the elevator.

Sleepily, Jeremy said, "I'm sorry. I should go back to my room."

Robin ran a finger up his stubbly chin and laid it on his lips. Then kissed them. She pulled one of the big pillows off the back of the couch and wedged her body beside him.

Snuggling into his chest and shoulder, she was careful not to bump his injured leg. It was then she noticed she, too, was wearing only a t-shirt. She had never worn anything but long sleeves outside of her house, ever!

Clasping her hand, he lifted her arm. It was the first time she had let anyone see the scar on the underside. The sunlight from the south-facing window lit it up. He traced the scar's curves and bumps from her wrist all the way to her upper arm with the tip of his finger. Then he drew her arm close to his lips. Closing his eyes, he kissed the deepest wound. That continued for as far as he could reach.

The beating of her heart slowed. This act was so natural and spontaneous. Jeremy didn't ask questions and seemed unaffected by her scar when he opened his eyes.

Wetting his lips, Jeremy said, "I think we should document the events of this day." His free hand stroked the back of her uncovered head.

Robin replied with a sense of urgency, "I want to draw you crashing in the snow." She reached for her purse and Jeremy's drawing diary. Turning to the next blank page, she sketched.

Jeremy remarked as he laid back, tucking his hands up under his head, "How ironic and poetic is that?"

Robin thought it curious how his elbows sticking out looked like wings. "Now *you* know what it's like."

"I didn't lie there for eight hours. My rescuer was there in seconds."

"No. But you saw an angel."

Jeremy squinted as if trying to recall having witnessed a visitation.

"Me! Silly."

He groaned. "Yes. That's true."

Robin showed Jeremy the sketch.

"Incredible how fast you can do that. A little exaggerated with the broken leg, don't you think?"

That made Robin laugh. She closed the book and set it on the table. Lying back next to him and pinning him down, she kissed him.

"Not fair. I can't defend myself."

"Too bad. I'm in control here."

She held her lips on his longer this time. When she had to breathe, she sat up and pulled off her t-shirt, leaving just her camisole and bra underneath. Jeremy appeared puzzled, then a little scared.

"What are you doing?"

"I want you to see something."

Now it was his turn to sit all the way up, letting his bandaged legs flop over the edge of the couch.

"What?"

"You'll see. Ready?"

She lifted the hem of the gold satin camisole up to reveal a massive scar on the side of her ribs and hip.

Jeremy's face grew somber. He reached out and touched the rough texture of the flesh. Spreading his fingers, he measured the shape. "It's almost as big as my hand."

Robin twisted to reveal more on the other side. She removed her camisole completely. Jeremy's eyes lit up, and his expression changed to delight. His hand stopped short of exploring farther.

"I wanted you to know what you are getting yourself into. What you'd have to live with every day if you stay with me. No surprises." The multitude of stitches appeared as centipedes crawling all over her body. "I'd understand if you don't."

His fingers continued to trace each of the lines all the way down to her hip. "I could never get tired of looking at you. This is what makes you, you. Unique. Certainly not boring."

"Don't you find them grotesque? Hideous?"

"Heaven's no."

Robin peeled off the band securing her ponytail, and tossed it on the table. Sitting forward, she pulled him into a full embrace.

"Do you mean it?"

She buried her face in his neck, kissing it clear to his chin, then to his lips. Robin drew his hand up and placed it over the scar on the back of her head. His fingers gently stroked the tender flesh. Then he laid his hand flat against it as if it became one with her.

"It doesn't change a thing. You are my angel," he whispered between her kisses.

THE END

About the Author

Shelly Pulse's kindergarten teacher noted, 'She has a very active imagination.' which made reading the perfect escape for her. She spent most of her childhood addicted to reading mystery, romance, and historical novels. Summers were spent with her backside tanned and not her front so she could continue to lie in the sun and read, head down, lost in the world created in her mind by the authors. She hid in bookstores while her family shopped at the mall.

Today, she still loves to read and uses that imagination to write and entertain others. She writes general and women's fiction. Some of her works wander into adventure and thriller with elements of science fiction.

If you enjoyed this book or have a thoughtful comment to share, please leave a review on Amazon.

You can also follow Shelly and other HT authors on social media at: https://www.facebook.com/helioterramedia

Find out more about this and other authors and books published by HelioTerra Media, LLC at: https://helioterra.com

Write to us at shelly@helioterra.com

Author's Notes

This book is loosely based on a story my husband, Doug, recounts of when he was chosen to participate in an advanced art program in high school. He tells of a gifted fellow student he met depicted by the character, Robin, in this story.

Since the narrative involves some detailed knowledge of small aircraft operation and potential failures, we sought the expertise of a licensed pilot. Our late friend, Sean, just happened to have those credentials. He had been a military helicopter mechanic in the United States Army and a private pilot. Many of his words appear in Chapters 5 and 7. Without him, those scenes would have not had the emotional impact they now have.

In fact, much of Sean's personality is infused in the Gary Wood character. Drawing on the relationship with his wife and daughter, the flashback scenes were easy to write. Sean was taken from this world too soon and his spirit resides with us still.

Art and angels, in all their forms, still play a huge role in our household today.

Made in the USA
Middletown, DE
30 May 2022